DOCUMENT
OF THE LAST
NAZI

D1044610

DOCUMENT
OF THE LAST
NAZI

A NOVEL BY
MATTHEW EDEN

General
PAPERBACKS

First published in Canada by General Paperbacks

Cover design: Brant Cowie/Artplus

ISBN 0-7736-1169-X
Printed and bound in Canada

Tuesday
April 26, 1977

Chapter 1

Thin warm rain was falling, and drops hung on the strands of the rusted barbed-wire fence around the old prison on the Wilhelmstrasse. On the high wall an American infantryman, helmet polished for ceremonial duty, rifle slung on his shoulder, stood back from the rain that slanted in under the roof of the guard tower, watching the road out beyond the wire, slick and black in the rain, and the wet-shiny rooftops of the cars passing.

The rain had darkened the top of the red-brick prison wall and blackened the wide strip of bare earth, the death strip, between the wall and the barbed wire. Rain dripped from the strands of another wire fence, which surrounded the prison halfway between the wall and the outer wire. This inner fence was not barbed, and there was only the gentle rain dripping from the bare wires, but it carried four thousand volts of electricity, and day and night for the thirty years it had stood there no one had ever tried to cross it, to break into or out of Spandau Prison. Month by month, through all those years, the guard had changed: British troops, then French, then Russian, then American, and then British again, and on and on, while four prison directors and their staffs of jailers, all from the Four Powers, the main World War Two allies against Hitler's Germany, stayed permanently in the prison. All guarding the Nazi leaders sent there after the war crimes trials at Nuremberg: seven men at first, and now for many years only one.

The sentry paced to the other side of the tower and stood looking down into the prison yard. From his post on the side wall he could see one end of the garden that spread behind the red-brick buildings, and the leaves of the trees were dark green and shiny in the rain. All the flower beds and fruit bushes in that garden looked as though no one had touched them for years, and weeds and grass grew along the sandy paths.

The sentry was damned if he could understand why they had to keep doing this, guarding this place, with just one old man down in the cell block—old Rudolf Hess. The sentry had never even heard of him till a year ago, when the Army sent him to Berlin and he'd been stuck in this guard detail. This month was the second time he'd been at Spandau, and it bored the hell out of him. And, Christ, the old guy had been in here for thirty years. *Thirty years.* They locked him up nine years before I was even born, the sentry thought. Every time he came up here on the wall he thought about it, and it still didn't make any sense to him. The old guy had been deputy to Adolf Hitler and he must've been really something then, but he sure as hell didn't look like anything now, when he walked out there in the garden. Just an old man—white hair, walking a little bent over, most of the time with his hands behind his back. Any time the sentry saw him he wondered what he could be thinking after thirty years. If he was thinking anything. Everybody said he was crazy. And this was his birthday—eighty-three years old today, for Christ's sake. The sentry didn't think it was right to keep him here. It didn't make any damn sense.

Out on the Wilhelmstrasse a US Army ambulance turned away from the traffic and drove slowly down the short road to the prison. The sentry, walking back around the tower, saw it just before it went out of his sight below the top of the front wall. The guard in the tower on the front of the wall was watching it too.

Guards down in the courtyard dragged open the high green gates and the ambulance drove in over the wet cobblestones, its windshield-wipers ticking. It stopped outside the administration block, at the front of the prison, and the driver and the soldier with him jumped out and trotted up the long flight of stone steps, and inside.

From the other side of the prison yard a black four-door Mercedes drove around and stopped behind the ambulance. An Army driver climbed out and stood beside the car, his cap pulled low against the rain and his neck down in the collar of his waterproof. He stood watching the door at the top of the flight of steps.

It opened and four men walked down to the courtyard. They were in civilian clothes, but each one was an army colonel, the allied prison directors: American, Russian, British, and French. All of them looked tense.

8

The driver straightened to attention and saluted. He opened the rear door and the Russian, British, and French officers climbed in.

'I'll ride in front with you,' the American colonel said.

'Yes, sir.' The driver shut the door and opened the front door for him.

An armed guard had formed up on the cobblestones beside the gates, rain dripping off their polished helmets. As the black Mercedes pulled away from the administration block the green steel gates were opened again. The guard presented arms as the car drove slowly past, and the gates swung shut behind it as it gathered speed along the road out to the Wilhelmstrasse.

The troops were dismissed, and as they walked back into the guardhouse the door at the top of the stone steps opened again and the two men from the ambulance stepped carefully out, carrying the front end of a stretcher. Two prison guards, British and Russian, carried the other end. They had carried it through from the cell block, at the back of the great building. A doctor and an orderly walked on either side. On the stretcher was an old man, a plastic sheet draped across, pulled up to his chin, to keep the rain off his blankets. As he was carried carefully down the steps the doctor stayed beside him, watching his face. It was white, and his hair was white, but his eyebrows were black and very thick, the eyes set deep.

Gently they slid the stretcher into the back of the ambulance, and the doctor and orderly stepped up inside with it, the jailers behind them. As the doors closed the doctor unstrapped the mask from an oxygen tank at the side of the ambulance, to have it ready if they should need it on the way to the hospital. He hoped they wouldn't. He'd done what he could inside, in the cell, with the oxygen and injections. He hoped he'd been in time, but this was an old man—eighty-three years old today. The doctor hoped to God they could save him. If they couldn't, he had no idea what would happen. But there'd be hell to pay. He knew that.

Another Mercedes drove around from the side of the prison building and stopped near the gates, waiting for the ambulance. Four soldiers sat in it, all bareheaded and with civilian raincoats over their uniforms, to hide them. A sergeant was behind the wheel, a captain beside him, and two enlisted men in the back. The captain and sergeant had sidearms strapped under their raincoats, and all of them had automatic rifles in the car, out of sight on the floor. They had orders to be inconspicuous. They had to escort the ambulance out of the British sector and into the American, to the Army hospital, and it had to be done without anyone in Berlin suspecting that anything had happened to Rudolf Hess.

The captain was sitting half-turned, looking through the rear window at the ambulance, and as it began moving away from the front of the prison he murmured: 'All right, Sergeant.'

The Mercedes moved forward over the cobblestones, the ambulance behind. The gates opened and they drove out. They turned south on the Wilhelmstrasse and the sergeant moved the Mercedes smoothly and fast through the traffic.

The captain looked back and saw the ambulance keeping pace with them. He wished it could use its siren, so they could really move, but the orders were very firm: do nothing to attract attention.

'Look at this, sir,' the sergeant said.

The captain turned and looked at the road ahead. Coming up fast toward them in the northbound traffic was an American military police jeep. An Army truck was a length behind it. As the jeep passed, its roof and windows buttoned in place and gleaming with rain, the captain saw four MPs inside. Two more were in the cab of the truck, and as it passed he looked back and saw it was full of them, sitting along both sides under the canvas roof, the last two men crowded close against the tailgate, looking out at the rain.

'Think they're going to Spandau, sir?' the sergeant said.

Nodding, the captain turned and sat back in the seat. 'That's where they're going.' Those MPs were going to sew everything up very tight. And it would stay tight until they knew how this thing had happened to Rudolf Hess.

Chapter 2

When the buzzer rasped Strang was in the bathroom, drying off from the shower. He was expecting no one, and he always told people never to drop in without phoning first. Either someone down in the lobby had pushed the wrong button accidentally or they were pushing any button and hoping someone would let them in. He went on drying himself.

But the buzz came again, longer, and carefully he hung the towel on the rail and took his robe off the hanger, shrugging it on as he went down the hall to the foyer.

He pushed the button inside the front door and said into the speaker: 'Who is it?'

'Jack. Sorry, Phil, but it's urgent.'

'Come up.' He pushed the button to open the front door. What the hell could Tillman want? It wasn't more than an hour since they'd said goodnight at the Mission, and there'd been nothing urgent then.

He opened the door and stood waiting. Down the hall the elevator doors opened and Tillman stepped out. Strang could see something was wrong. Tillman was never able to hide it. He was fifty-two years old and many things made him anxious. Four or five years ago, before the Watergate mess and before Congress began investigating The Company, the CIA, Tillman had been a much different man, people said. Maybe he had, but Strang hadn't known him then. He liked Tillman, because of his dedication, but he thought he'd worry himself into a heart attack one day.

'Hope I'm not disturbing you.' Tillman walked in.

'No. I was getting ready to go out to dinner.' He led the way down the hall, toward the living room.

'Afraid you'll have to get a sandwich at the Mission.'

'What's up?'

'Big trouble out at Spandau. Either Hess tried to kill himself or someone tried it for him.'

11

Strang stopped at the entrance to the living room. 'Hess? Why the hell would anyone try to kill him?'

'I don't know anything about it yet. The Army's investigating. An MP lieutenant just came out to the house and told me. There's very tight security on it. That's why I came without calling you first. I didn't want to say anything on the phone.'

Strang thought the phones were probably secure but Tillman, of all people, wouldn't have wanted to take the chance. 'How did it happen?'

'Poison. That's all I know.'

'He must've tried to kill himself.' Hess had tried it two months ago, slashed himself in two or three places. But yesterday the Soviets had given him a reason to try it again. A few months ago his lawyer had made an appeal to Moscow for his release— only to Moscow because the west had been willing for years to free him—and Moscow had rejected it yesterday, the day before his birthday. It had been very big in the German papers this morning—not so much the rejection, which everyone had expected, but the timing, which no one had believed was coincidental. Moscow's birthday gift, the press called it. 'When was it?'

'Lunchtime. Christ knows why the Army kept it to themselves so long. Phil, d'you mind getting dressed? I'd like to get over to the Mission as fast as I can. I'd like you to come too.'

'I'll be two minutes.' In four strides he was across the room and into the bedroom. After all his years in Spandau, why was Hess trying so hard now to finish himself? You'd have thought he'd resigned himself to it long ago. And it shouldn't have shocked him that the appeal was denied. That had happened three or four times before. Moscow always rejected the appeals. But maybe yesterday had been one too many, coming with his birthday. Maybe it had been too much for him, the knowledge that the Soviets still had their teeth into him and would never let go.

Buttoning a light blue shirt, Strang called: 'How is he, Jack?'

'Don't know.' Tillman stood in the doorway. 'He's in the Army hospital. I don't imagine he's very good, not at his age.'

'No.' Strang had on tan corduroy trousers, flared. He snatched a yellow cravat from the closet and tucked it into his blue shirt. He almost never wore ties. He liked to dress casually, to feel free and loose. 'What d'you want me to do?'

12

'Look into it for me. The Army's ready to give all the help they can. They know there'll be serious diplomatic trouble for us here, if he dies. Christ knows what Moscow would do.'

'No. But if he dies, he dies, Jack. There isn't a damn thing we can do about that.' In February they'd patched him up fast, and there was no damage. But how many of those shocks could old Hess stand?

Tillman said nothing.

Strang took a dark brown suede jacket from the closet. 'Let's go.' As they walked out to the front door he pulled the jacket on, turning the cuffs back, and the cuffs of his shirt over them.

The rain had stopped and there was the smell of fresh-damp grass in front of the apartment building. Tillman's Mercury was parked in the crescent driveway. The building was a new tower in the Zehlendorf district, a couple of kilometres from the US Mission. Usually Strang walked to the office and back. He used his car only if there was some kind of emergency. City driving, sitting trapped in stalled traffic, was no pleasure. He felt much freer when he walked.

'D'you know Colonel Goodblood?' Tillman, looking right and left, drove carefully out into the street.

'No, but I know who he is.' Goodblood was the Provost Marshal for the American garrison in Berlin. In his two years here Strang had not met many of the people at the Mission, except the ones he worked with, in The Company. The only way to meet the others was at receptions and parties, and he went to very few of those. He spent most of his time with the locals, Berliners— agents he was running or people he was hoping to recruit, or West German security men.

'He's expecting you, anyway. I told the MP you'd be handling it for us.'

'What're you going to do now, Jack?'

'I'll get a message off to Langley and let them know about this.'

'Why not wait an hour or two, until we know more?'

Tillman turned on him. 'I don't *want* to wait any God damn hour or two!'

Strang stared at him, then slowly turned his head and stared out of the window.

It was quiet in the car, and Tillman concentrated very hard on his driving. Then he said: 'I'm sorry, Phil.'

'Don't worry about it. You're old enough to be my damn father and that gives you the right to yell.'

'I'm not that old.'

'The hell you're not.'

Tillman chuckled.

Strang was pleased to hear him. Tillman was a little less tense now. But that wouldn't last long if Hess died. It would be serious. Very serious. Tillman was right about that.

A lot depended on old Hess. An awful lot. Maybe war or peace in Europe. It was incredible but it was there. The military guard at Spandau was the last visible symbol of the World War Two alliance of the west and the Soviets against Nazi Germany, of the Four-Power treaty for control of Germany and Berlin at the end of the war. American, Soviet, British, and French occupation troops had had joint control of Berlin because of that agreement, which gave all of them free access to any part of the city. It hadn't lasted long. Three years after the war the Soviets had sealed off East Berlin—but they'd always insisted on their right to send their armed troops marching through the Brandenburg Gate and across West Berlin to Spandau, every four months, when it was their turn to guard the prison. For years, eleven years now, there'd been only old Rudolf Hess, there for life. The Soviets had always refused to release him, even in sixty-six, when Speer and Schirach finished their twenty years and the west wanted to let Hess go too, rather than leave him there alone. And whatever other reasons Moscow gave—that Hess had been Hitler's deputy and one of the toughest Nazis and all the rest—the real one was that they wanted him there so they could keep sending their troops into West Berlin, as a reminder that they still had treaty rights there. It was true that they hated Hess's insides, but the real reason was the political one. They'd even said once that after Hess was dead they wanted the Four-Power guard maintained at Spandau.

But what would Moscow do if he died now? The west had never insisted on their own rights in Berlin. They'd let the Soviets chip them away piece by piece—blockading, harassing, sealing off East Berlin with the Wall—and had never resisted. But what would happen if the Soviets insisted on guarding

14

an empty prison? Would that finally be too much for the west? And what if they said no, and tried to keep Soviet troops out? Would Moscow just move in and take West Berlin, as they'd always threatened every time there was a crisis? If they did, that would mean war. Washington had guaranteed the security of West Berlin too many times to back down. It would be impossible. If Moscow got away with West Berlin, West Germany would be next. Oh, it was serious, all right. Tillman had reason to worry. And it all hung on that old man, Rudolf Hess.

They were in the heavy evening traffic on Clayallee. Up ahead Strang saw lights in many windows of the Mission. A few people were working late tonight.

At the gate of the American compound they showed their identification to the guard, and Tillman drove in and parked beside the Mission. They walked in, across the lobby and into an elevator.

'I'll wait for you in my office,' Tillman said. 'Will you let me know how it goes with Goodblood?'

'As soon as I've finished with him.'

Tillman got off at the second floor, to go to the political section. The political section was the CIA cover in West Berlin, and officially Tillman was chief of the section; unofficially he was the CIA station chief.

Strang watched the doors shut behind him, and stood waiting for the third floor.

Chapter 3

Goodblood shook hands and smiled, but it was a tight smile.
He disapproved of Strang's yellow ascot and flared corduroys.
Strang had seen it when he walked in. His clothes threw a lot
of people off balance. They expected Brooks Brothers, the
three-piece pinstripe, and because of his casual look they often
relaxed and didn't take him completely seriously. They never
seemed to notice that his ascot was very precisely arranged and
his clothes carefully groomed. It was usually some time before
they realised there was nothing at all casual about him. It was
a useful advantage.

'Sit down, Mr Strang. I'll tell you what I can about this.'

Strang sat in a straightback wooden chair, watching Goodblood walk back around his desk, very upright. He saw he
wore built-up shoes. Even with the elevators, he was only
medium height, about a head shorter than Strang.

The desk was dark polished wood, and very bare: a wide
green blotter with a two-pen stand in front of it. Beside the
blotter was a closed manila folder. An American flag and a
unit flag stood behind Goodblood's high-backed swivel chair.

'What's Hess's condition now, Colonel?'

'They're still working on him at the hospital. I don't know
why he hasn't bought the farm yet, but he's holding on. Must
be a tough old bird. All those years on prison regime must've
given him the constitution of an ox.' Sitting very straight in his
chair, Goodblood rested his hands on the blotter, fists lightly
clenched.

'I hope so.'

Goodblood looked reassured that Strang understood the
gravity of it. 'I do too. Believe me.'

'Have you confirmed whether he tried suicide or someone
tried to kill him?'

'Not yet.' Goodblood eased his index finger in and rubbed
his right eye behind the round, steel-rimmed glasses he wore.

'But I've got plainclothesmen all over that damn prison. We'll find out what happened there if we have to fieldstrip it and everyone in it.'

'It happened at lunchtime, right?'

'That's right. Today being his birthday, they let him choose his menu for all his meals. He likes fruit, old Hess.' Goodblood sounded almost fond, speaking of Hess, and his face looked less hard, the mouth less tight. 'There are cherries and raspberries in the prison garden. They ripen in July—a month when the Russians have control there—and one of his complaints for years has been that their troops get out in the garden and strip off all the fruit before he can get any. They're like a plague of God damn locusts going through there.' He shook his head. 'So he likes fruit, and at lunch he wanted an apricot pie. They baked him one, and he had a good slice of it for dessert.'

Goodblood pulled the manila folder over from the side of his desk and opened it on the blotter. 'I've got a report here.' The ceiling light reflected from the tops of his glasses and he looked down to read. 'Two jailers on duty in the corridor near his cell—one American, one Russian—heard him groaning and ran in to check. They found him on his cot, holding his stomach, with his knees pulled up. He lost consciousness almost at once. They called the medical officer on duty, the American doctor, and he went there on the double. As soon as he got down to look at Hess he smelled the odour on his breath.'

'What was it, Colonel?'

'Cyanide. Has the smell of bitter almonds.'

'God.'

'Yes. The doctor injected him with sodium nitrite and sodium thiosulfate, and gave him some oxygen. Meantime, the American doctor, who's in charge there this month, called the Army hospital to be ready for him.'

'Was the cyanide in the pie?'

'In Hess's slice. He'd eaten more than half of it, but we've analysed what he left—and it's loaded with cyanide.'

'What about the rest of the pie?'

'Couple of people in the kitchen had eaten some of it, and they'd had no problem. We've analysed the rest and found nothing. It was just Hess's slice.'

17

'So he could've laced his own piece of pie.'

Goodblood closed the folder and slid it back to the side of the desk. 'He could have. I don't think I'd blame him.' Back straight, he sat staring at Strang through his steel-rimmed glasses, waiting for him to disagree.

'Because Moscow turned down the appeal, you mean?'

'Of course that's what I mean. This is an eighty-three-year-old man who's been locked up for thirty years, and those Russian bastards are still trying to break him down.' Goodblood was bitter. 'I don't imagine you ever read the German papers, but they . . .'

'I read them every day, Colonel.' He couldn't decide which was more incredible, that Goodblood could read German or that the arrogant bastard assumed he himself couldn't. 'I read what they said about Moscow this morning.'

For the first time Goodblood looked friendly. 'D'you speak it too?'

Strang nodded.

Goodblood smiled. 'I haven't come across any CIA men here for a while, but three or four years ago I had some dealings with a couple of them—and they couldn't speak more than twenty words of German between them. Christ knows how they operated here.'

'I've been here two years, and I was in Bonn for three—and I haven't met many Army officers who could speak it either.'

'You're right. I won't argue with you about that, Mr Strang. Too few of us get close enough to the locals to learn the language—wherever we go—and it's a bad mistake. I love the German language and the people—respect them. I've got tremendous respect for the Germans. They're tough and hardworking, and you can't keep them down. God, I've been here eight years and I don't ever want to leave.' Goodblood had become warm and enthusiastic. 'D'you have any objection if we go on with this in German?'

'None at all.' It was going to be a lot easier in German, he could see. He'd get a lot closer to Goodblood.

'Das ist wunderbar!' Goodblood waved a hand across the office, getting up from his desk. 'Let's sit over there and be more comfortable.'

Across the room, against the wall, was a brown leather

18

couch. Two brown leather armchairs were set in front of it, on either side of a coffee table.

Strang sat in one of the armchairs and Goodblood sat at the end of the couch, crossing his legs carefully, not to spoil the crease in his trousers. His uniform was very sharply pressed.

In German Strang said: 'Could Hess have got the cyanide to use on himself?'

'Yes, Mr Strang, he could.'

'Who was the last visitor he had?'

'No, no.' Goodblood shook his head. 'He wouldn't have got it from a visitor. He's only allowed one visit a month, a half-hour a month. And the visitor's not allowed to give him anything or have any physical contact with him, even to shake hands. A couple of the jailers stay in the visiting room to watch. He couldn't have got it that way.'

'You're telling me someone in the prison could've given it to him—one of the jailers?'

'It's possible. Security's tight out at Spandau. It always has been. The rest of us would like to make it a little easier but the Russians've never agreed. They insist we play hardball. So it's tight—but, yes, he could've got the cyanide. When Albert Speer was in there he had one of the staff smuggle out the manuscript of a whole damn book. Most of the jailers and the service staff—people in the kitchen, orderlies, cleaners, and so on—have been there for years. Most of them—not the Russian jailers but most of the others—have a lot of sympathy for old Hess. Hell, so do I. If he told one of them he wanted to finish himself off, I think he'd have some help. That's one of the things we're investigating now.'

'How many people are in Spandau—guards and staff?'

'There's the military guard, about forty men—ours this month; the four directors and about thirty jailers; and about twenty service personnel, from neutral nations—nations that were neutral during World War Two, that is—or who were displaced persons after the war. Say a hundred altogether. We're going to question them all—except the Russians. We've already had trouble with them.'

'How, Colonel?'

'They won't let us question their people. They've insisted on doing it themselves.'

'Oh, for God's sake.'

'Yes, they're sons of bitches.' Goodblood rubbed his eye. 'But we've gone along with them on this—with the stipulation that their director does the questioning himself. We won't allow any damn team of KGB inside Spandau. They're satisfied with that. We've been concentrating first on the civilian personnel. They all live outside the prison, and I didn't want any of them to be kept in there too long this evening. Technically I suppose we've got the right to keep them in there as long as it takes us to satisfy ourselves they know nothing about it, but I want to keep their goodwill. If one of them got mad at the way we were handling him, and told the press about it, that this had happened to Hess . . .' Goodblood shook his head.

'That can't be allowed to happen.' The press had got the story of the suicide attempt in February. Christ, if this story got out too, public opinion would be so damn strong—not just in Germany but through the west—that Washington would be pushed into doing something. Washington and the British and French. They'd have to put pressure on Moscow to let Hess go —even if he only had another day to live—and Moscow would never back down. It could easily get out of hand. 'Can those civilians be trusted to keep quiet?'

'I'm sure they can. They've worked most of their lives in Spandau. They're loyal people. If I'm doubtful about any of them, I'll have the Berlin police keep an eye on them outside the prison. But I don't think there's another way to handle this. We can't keep them inside till this case is solved.'

Strang didn't like it. Goodblood was right and there was no other way, but still he didn't like it. Until they knew how and why this had happened to Hess, he'd have felt more comfortable if everyone were kept in Spandau. He didn't like the feeling that someone or something might slip away.

'I'd like to have a look inside Spandau. Can that be arranged, Colonel?'

'Sorry. It's out of the question. The Russians wouldn't allow it. They put up a hell of an argument before I could get my investigating team in there. Didn't want us to go in unless a group of their people went in too. Finally we convinced them that this month we were in control and we'd damn well stay in control. They didn't like letting us move Hess to the hospital either, but that argument didn't last long. We pointed out that they'd be responsible if he died—and they folded. They don't want him dead. But they insisted on having accommodation for the four prison directors and some of the jailers near Hess's room at the hospital. They're all there, watching. No, we couldn't get you into Spandau.' Lightly, Goodblood ran a fingertip along the crease of his trousers, down the thigh to the knee. 'I tell you, Mr Strang, if old Hess had wanted to cause strain between us and Moscow he couldn't have found a better way to do it. And if he dies . . .' Shaking his head, he looked down at the polished toe of his shoe, turning it to catch the reflection of the light.

'Something about it bothers me,' Strang said.

Goodblood sat looking at him.

'If he had the cyanide, why didn't he just take it? Why put it in his damn apricot pie?'

'Who can answer that? Maybe he wanted to implicate us. Maybe he wanted to make it appear we'd done it—to kill him so we'd be able to shut down Spandau. Maybe he really did it to get us and the Russians into a tussle. Who can say? The possibility's there, Mr Strang. It's a hell of a thing to think about, that an old man who's been a prisoner for thirty years has got the power to put us into a fix like this. Maybe he decided it'd be a hell of a way to go.'

It was possible, Strang thought. 'But you're not assuming he did that? You're not just investigating to confirm he tried to kill himself?'

'No, no, of course not—but I don't see any motive for murder. D'you?'

'No.' Hess had come very close to dying—and might still— but if someone had tried to murder him, he couldn't imagine who or why.

Chapter 4

From the Mission he took a taxi to the Army hospital, and on the sidewalk outside, as the taxi turned into the driveway, he saw two Berlin policemen in the streetlight, walking casually and watching the road in front of the hospital. The taxi stopped at the main entrance and just in range of its headlight beams, parked near an emergency door, was a jeep with two MPS in it, talking to two others standing on the sidewalk. One of the MPS on the sidewalk turned and watched Strang as he got out of the cab.

In the lobby were four more MPS, two on one side, two on the other, and Strang felt them watching him as he walked to the reception counter. The security was tight. Hess was registered here as Schmidt, Goodblood had said, and a section of one floor had been sealed off for him.

'Good evening.' The receptionist smiled.

'Good evening. I have an appointment with Captain Edison.'

'Yes, sir. You're Mr . . .?' The receptionist watched his face. She had orders to be careful about strangers coming into the hospital, especially civilians.

'Strang.'

'Oh, yes, Mr Strang. Captain Edison said you were to go right up. I'll tell him you're coming.' She picked up a phone.

He took an elevator to the third floor. He had to see this man, this psychiatrist, but he'd always been sceptical about them. No one he knew who'd had any treatment from them—and that was almost everyone he knew—had finished better than they'd begun. Maybe they'd had a little more self-awareness at the end, but only enough to confuse them. What he disliked most about psychiatrists was their urge to control, to make everyone conform to their damn conception of normal. But this evening he had no choice. Only a psychiatrist could tell him what he wanted to know. For what it was worth, he had to have whatever Edison could tell him.

He walked down a corridor with numbered doors on either side. Halfway along was the number Goodblood had given him. He knocked.

'Come in!'

He opened the door as the shout came, and a man was moving around a metal desk in a small, square office. A big man, not quite as tall as himself but with big shoulders, and wavy blond hair and a thick moustache. About his own age or a couple of years younger, about thirty-two.

'Mr Strang.' Smiling, the man held out his hand. 'Captain Edison.'

'Captain. I hope I'm not keeping you late.'

'It's perfectly all right. I was leaving when Colonel Goodblood called, but he said you wanted to talk urgently about this. Old Hess has been a particular interest of mine for years. Glad to talk to you. Sit down.'

Strang sat in a thinly padded metal armchair, government issue. Edison's uniform jacket was on a hanger on a metal stand, with his tie draped over it, and he sat with the collar of his shirt open, cuffs rolled back.

'What is it you want to know about the old boy?' Edison sat back in his swivel chair, one knee against the edge of his desk, hands behind his head.

'Is it likely he tried to kill himself again?'

Edison smiled: white, even teeth below his moustache. 'I was afraid that'd be your first question.' He rocked back and forth. 'I don't think there's an easy answer. I frankly don't.'

'Good. I wouldn't have believed an easy answer.' It might be better than he'd expected. Edison seemed compatible. Maybe they could talk.

Smiling again, Edison came forward in his chair, resting his elbows on the desk. 'Before that attempt in February, I'd've said he'd never try to kill himself again. It's years since he did anything like that—and he tried it three times in the old days. I thought he'd settled down long ago. He's a very strange case, old Hess. Kind of a classic in psychiatry. I've never seen him but I'd give a year of my life for a few hours with him. I've read everything there is about him, all the psychiatric reports. He's been examined by squads of psychiatrists, the best in the world at the time—thirty years ago—and I've read all their

23

reports and I'm still not sure about the state of his mind. I wouldn't say positively, on the basis of all of it, whether he's slightly crazy or completely sane, and very damn clever, and has been fooling the world for years—including the psychiatrists. It doesn't help that at least a couple of the reports were'—he held a hand flat out and tilted it from side to side—'reshaped slightly, for political reasons.'

'They were?'

'Oh, sure. Does that surprise you? I thought the CIA arranged things like that every day.'

'If you don't tell me what you think of the CIA, I won't tell you what I think of psychiatrists.'

Edison laughed. 'Okay. But it's documented that during World War Two, after Hess flew to Britain, he was examined and found to be schizophrenic and insane—and Winston Churchill ordered the report rewritten because he didn't want to have to repatriate him on compassionate grounds. He wanted to keep him in England, to be tried after the war. Two or three years after the war, he was examined here, up in Spandau, by one of our people, who agreed with the British psychiatrist— and the Garrison Surgeon ordered him to rewrite his report too, because we didn't want to offend the Russians, who wanted Hess to be sane and wouldn't listen to any conflicting diagnosis. They didn't want anything to keep him from serving out his life sentence in Spandau—and they meant life. They really wanted to nail his hide. They wanted him executed at Nuremberg.'

*

Except for Switzerland and Vichy France, on May 10, 1941, in the second year of the war, Nazi Germany possessed all Europe from the Carpathians to the Pyrenees, from the northern tip of Norway to Greece, and was only six weeks away from driving all the power of the army's panzers and infantry and the Luftwaffe's bombers into Operation Barbarossa, the invasion of Russia. The war would be fought with a savagery that demonstrated Hitler's hatred of Communism. And Rudolf Hess's hatred of it was in every detail as deep as Hitler's.

On that May 10 Hess had been Hitler's deputy for eight

years, second in succession to the leadership of Germany after Hermann Göring. He was a member of Hitler's Secret Cabinet Council, and of the Council of Ministers for the Defence of the Reich, and he was an honorary ss Obergruppenführer, the equivalent of an army general. He commanded a huge personal staff, and his chief lieutenant was Martin Bormann. On the evening of that day Hess, a pilot since World War One, climbed into the cockpit of a Messerschmitt fighter and flew it to Scotland, parachuting near Glasgow, and that night he was a prisoner of the British, sitting in a bare room wearing a torn Luftwaffe uniform.

He told the British that Hitler knew nothing of his mission, but he had come to arrange a peace with them and he could tell them what Hitler's terms would be. Britain and Germany should become allies, he said, and with their combined forces they would attack and defeat Russia, the enemy of both of them.

Because Hitler wanted to discredit him and keep the British from gaining a propaganda advantage from his flight, German radio began broadcasting reports within days that Hess was insane. The British themselves were convinced of it. For the next four years, until the end of the war, he was kept under guard and, because he had begun behaving irrationally when he saw his mission had failed, and claimed he had completely lost his memory, he was for most of those years under observation by psychiatrists. Twice he attempted suicide.

In October, 1945, five months after the end of the war, Hess was flown from England to Nuremberg, in the American occupation zone of Germany, to stand trial for war crimes. He was held in Nuremberg jail with the other Nazi leaders who had been captured at the end of the war.

Twice before the trial began he was examined by panels of psychiatrists from the Four Powers, who found him hysterical and paranoid but fit to stand trial, though his amnesia would harm his defence. The Soviet prosecutor insisted he was sane and fit for trial; during the war the British had told Moscow why Hess made his flight, and all through the ten months of the trial the Soviets showed him no mercy.

The trial, before the International Military Tribunal, began on November 20, 1945, in the Palace of Justice. Hess, in an old tweed sports jacket, sat on the front bench of the defendants, next to Göring, and showed no sign that he recognised any of them. When the prosecution showed a film of Nazi concentration-camp atrocities, a few days after the trial opened, he looked puzzled and showed no emotion, though some of the other defendants broke down.

Next day he made a statement in the courtroom. He said his amnesia had been simulated, and he was ready to accept full responsibility for anything that had been done under his authority during the Nazi regime in Germany.

The trial went on for weeks and months, and by the end of February, 1946, Hess's memory apparently began to fade under prosecution questioning, but in the fall of that year, on October 1, the trial ended and he was found guilty of conspiracy and crimes against peace, and sentenced to life imprisonment.

The Soviet member of the tribunal dissented from the majority decision on sentence. He wanted death for Hess.

*

'The Russians were particularly tough on the old boy,' Edison said, 'but I'm sure we weren't much easier on him in those days. Nor were the British. The Russians would never admit he might be crazy because they wanted him tried and punished. The British, on the other hand, when they examined him during the war, must've been convinced he was crazy before they heard a word from him. What he'd done made no sense to them, flying over to them like that—and they'd been at war with the Germans for two years, and losing, so they probably thought every German was a little nuts anyway. That was part of the propaganda. In the circumstances, it'd be asking too much to expect an objective assessment of the state of a Nazi leader's mind, wouldn't it?'

'Probably.'

'I'm sure of it.' Edison propped a knee on the edge of his desk once again and rocked back in his chair. 'Though I don't doubt something happened to him when he'd been in England a few weeks and realised they weren't taking him seriously. I'm sure that affected him. God, can you imagine the power that

26

man had in Germany! He'd had a hand in planning all their military operations in Europe. Then he flew to England, convinced he'd be able to arrange an alliance that would change the shape of history—and found himself completely rejected by the British. Then disowned by Hitler.' He stroked his moustache. 'God, it was inevitable that the old boy would want to drop out. The amnesia, paranoia, all of it, just had to happen.'

'You think that's how it was?'

'I do. There's only one other thing I'm sure of—that I wouldn't accept any of the psychiatric reports on him as unbiased and clinical. I think all the psychiatrists who examined him, during the war and at Nuremberg, were influenced by the mood of the time. They couldn't be considered objective. They were human.'

'D'you think he's crazy now?'

'He's been locked up for thirty years. I'd be surprised if he weren't a little unstable. I know I would be. Whether he's crazy or not, I don't know. I'm sure no one does.'

'Could he have tried to kill himself again today?'

'That's the question, isn't it? That's still the big one.'

'Yes.'

Gently Edison lowered his chair and leaned forward with his hands on his desk, thinking.

'The attempt in February was his fourth,' Strang said. 'God knows he's tried.'

'Yes, but two of those were in England during the war, and it's more than just a possibility that his depression at the time was the cause. The same rejection that I suspect brought on his amnesia and the other irrational behaviour could've caused him to attempt suicide. He was a fantastically proud man. Still is, from all I've heard. The third time was at Spandau in the late fifties—and it wasn't considered a very serious attempt. A lot of people thought he did it for attention. I suspect that's what he was looking for in February too.'

'Why?'

'I think he might've been trying to get some sympathetic publicity while his lawyer was making that appeal.'

'You think he's that sharp?'

Edison nodded.

27

'It must've depressed the hell out of him yesterday, when Moscow rejected the appeal,' Strang said.

'Not necessarily.'

'Why d'you say that, Captain?'

'I'm not sure he wants to come out. Maybe he did once, but I'm not sure he does now.'

'But you think he slashed his wrists to help the appeal. I'd say that shows interest.'

Edison shook his head. 'I said I thought he was probably looking for sympathetic publicity. I doubt he cared much about the appeal, except for the attention that came from it in the press.'

'Are you serious?'

'I wouldn't joke with the CIA. I think he's content in Spandau. Ten or twelve years ago, when the last two of the others were released, he might've wanted to go too, but he's been there alone for a long time now. He's got that great pile of a place, built for six hundred prisoners, all to himself. He's guarded by troops of the most powerful nations in the world, and gets a great deal of attention in that prison. He's aware of his political significance in Spandau. All that could be very satisfying to the old man's ego. And he's got a powerful ego; there's never been a question about that. These public appeals for his release that come along from time to time must be very satisfying too, but I don't think he gives a damn about them.'

'Captain Edison, if you're right, d'you realise what it means?'

'No. What?'

'It means he had no reason to commit suicide today. That means someone tried to kill him. I don't know why anyone would do that, but if that's what happened it's a dangerous complication. A hell of a serious problem.'

'My advice is that you don't assume it was a suicide attempt, Mr Strang. I think you might have a serious problem on your hands.'

Chapter 5

Late in the evening a black vw beetle with one man in it drove across the cobbled courtyard at Spandau and stopped at the locked gates. An Army sentry and one of the prison jailers, an Englishman, walked out from the guard hut.

'Evening, Walter,' the jailer said at the driver's open window.

'Good evening, Mr Sims.' The driver was a small, bald man, about fifty-five.

'They're letting you go home, are they?' Sims smiled.

'Yes.' The small man was not smiling. What had happened at the prison that afternoon and then the questioning by the investigators had upset him, Sims thought.

'It's a late night for you.'

'It doesn't matter, Mr Sims. There's no one waiting for me. I was happy to tell what I could to the detectives. This was a terrible thing that happened.'

'You're right. Did they give you a pass?'

'Yes. Here.' Nervously the driver felt beside him on the seat, and his hand missed the folded slip of paper there. He looked down, found it, and held it out.

'No, bring it inside, Walter. The sergeant's got to have a look at it.' Sims nodded to the door of the guard hut, where an MP sergeant stood watching.

The driver climbed out of the Volkswagen and followed Sims across the cobblestones as the MP sergeant turned inside the guard hut, waiting for them. The sentry stood by the car.

'This is Mr Lichti, Sergeant,' Sims said to the MP. 'An old friend of mine. We've spent a lot of time here. Isn't that right, Walter?'

'Yes. A very long time.'

The MP was unimpressed. 'Have you got a pass to leave the prison, Mr Lichti?'

'Yes. Here.' Lichti held it out.

The MP took it to an old wooden desk against the wall of

the hut, under a window, and examined it beside the desklamp. It was signed by the captain in command of the investigating unit. The sergeant saw the signature was authentic. He wrote Lichti's name in a register on the desk, wrote the time he was leaving, and signed the entry. 'That's okay, Mr Lichti.' On the desk was a clipboard holding other passes, and he dragged it across and clipped Lichti's pass with the others.

'I may go now?' Lichti said to Sims.

'Yes, come on, Walter.'

As they walked out to the Volkswagen the sentry moved to the gates, to open them. Lichti got in behind the wheel and Sims shut the door for him.

'You get a good night's sleep,' Sims said.

'Yes. Thank you. You too, Mr Sims.'

'I will. It's been a busy day.'

'Good night.'

'Night, old man.'

The Volkswagen drove out and Sims walked back into the guard hut. The MP sergeant was sitting on the edge of the desk, stretching.

'He's a nice little chap, old Walter,' Sims said.

The MP nodded. He was tired and bored.

'Christ, he's been here twenty-four years.' Sims sat on a wooden chair against the wall and stretched his legs. 'I've been here nineteen myself.'

'What is he—German?'

'No, Christ, no. No Germans work here. He's Swiss.'

'What does he do?'

'Assistant chef. Bloody good cook too.'

The MP took a packet of cigarettes from the desk. 'He'd be a good man to know.' He held out the cigarettes.

'No, thanks.' Sims shook his head. 'Yes, it's always useful to know a cook. That's what we always used to say in the British army.'

'That's what we say too.'

*

Lichti drove out along Spandauerdamm, heading southeast across the city. He lived alone in an apartment on the top floor of an old four-storey house in Kreuzberg, a working-class district in the American sector.

He drove around the Kreuzberg hill, across the Teltow canal, and turned into his street, off Lindenstrasse. He switched off the ignition and took out the keys, reaching for the door handle.

'*Guten abend,* Walter.'

Lichti jumped and his head snapped around to the open window. A tall man was bending down and smiling at him, one big hand on the window ledge.

'Good evening.' Lichti tried to smile. 'You made me jump.'

'You're late tonight.'

'Yes. There's an investigation and . . .'

'Yes. Come and tell us about it.' It was a very firm invitation, and the man nodded back along the street. A car was parked there, and in the streetlight there was the silhouette of a man behind the wheel.

'If you please, I'm tired. I want to . . .'

'Come and talk, Walter.' Now it was an order. The big man opened Lichti's door. 'Come.'

Lichti got out and walked with him, back along the sidewalk to the waiting car.

Wednesday
April 27, 1977

Chapter 6

In the morning the rainclouds that had been over Berlin for a
week had cleared, and there was bright sun. When Strang was
halfway to the Mission, walking through the quiet Zehlendorf
streets, he saw a silver-grey Audi coming towards him, beginning
to slow as it came closer. He tensed. Things could happen in
Berlin, and sometimes they did. Then the driver's face was
close enough to recognise, and he relaxed.

The Audi stopped at the kerb ahead of him, and he walked
to the open passenger window and bent down to it.

'It's early for you, Dieter,' he said.

'These days I have to go to bed early—so I get up earlier.'

Strang smiled, but the driver looked solemn. And he looked
tired. He was chewing gum, slowly, tiredly. His name was
Kluger and he was an officer of the West German Internal
Security Office, the *Bundesamt für Verfassungsschutz*, and he
and Strang often worked together. He was forty-three, and six
months ago he had married a woman of twenty-seven. She was
very active and Kluger had begun to worry about how long he
could keep up with her. Twice he had spoken to Strang about
it, lightly, but Strang had sensed the concern. Now for a month
he had not mentioned it, but always looked preoccupied.

'In a few months she won't let you out at all.'

Kluger twitched a smile on and off. There was no enthusiasm.
'Let me give you a ride.'

'I like to walk.'

'I mean this way.' Kluger nodded ahead, out toward the
Grünewald, the big wooded park beyond Zehlendorf, along the
shore of the Havel.

'I haven't got time for a ride in the park, Dieter.'

'You're busy. I know. That's why I want to go somewhere
private. I want to talk to you about it.'

Casually Strang said: 'About what?'

'The Hess thing.'

35

'What Hess thing?'

'The Hess thing at Spandau yesterday.' Now Kluger smiled.

Strang stood up from the window and looked back and forth along the sidewalk. There was no one either way. He opened the door and swung in.

'How much d'you know?' he said.

'I know Hess was poisoned.'

'Dieter, there's heavy security on this. We're trying hard to keep the lid on it. You know how much trouble there could be if this broke to the public.'

'It won't leak from us.'

'Who told you about it?'

Kluger chewed his gum, looking pleased.

'For Christ's sake, has she screwed you out of your mind! This is important. I think someone tried to kill Hess—and whoever told you about it could know something. If he's working for you, he could be working for someone else. Who is it?'

'No.' Quickly Kluger shook his head, and laid a hand on Strang's shoulder. 'The man's all right, Phil. I guarantee that. He's an informant, sure, because we like to know what's going on in there—mainly we want to know what those Soviet sons of bitches do when they're in control there. That's all. The man works for us, but not against you. You think I'm crazy? You think I wouldn't know if he were playing both sides? He's all right. Don't worry about it—but don't ask me again who he is.'

Strang sat looking at him. He didn't like the feeling that there was something out of his reach, that he couldn't control—but at least he could be sure that this informant of Kluger's was working only for him. If Kluger was sure of it, he could be too; Kluger was as cautious as he was himself.

'It might be lucky for you I know about it. Maybe I can help you.' Kluger looked across the street, at the big houses in the well-kept gardens. 'D'you want to come for that ride? I don't like sitting and talking on the damn street like this.'

'All right, let's go.'

Kluger drove fast, and he chewed his gum quickly as he drove. He was very Americanised. The chewing was a habit he had learned from American troops as a child in Regensburg at the end of the war. Then he had gone to the United States on a

Fulbright scholarship, to UCLA, and studied political science. Because of his fondness for Americans, the Internal Security Office had sent him to Berlin twelve years ago, to work with them there, their most sensitive point of contact with the Soviet Union in Europe.

As they drove further west through Zehlendorf they could see, beyond the rooftops, the sunlight on the tops of the pine trees in the Grünewald, and then they cleared the last of the houses, and there was the dark green spread of the trees. Kluger parked the car at the edge of the woods, and they walked in along the shore of the Schlachtensee, one of the long, narrow lakes among the trees.

'You really think someone tried to kill Hess?' Kluger said. 'You don't think he might've tried to kill himself again?'

'Murder's what I'm starting to concentrate on. I've got a dirty mind, you know.'

'I suppose I have too, because I agree with you.'

'D'you know anything, Dieter?'

'I know some people with a motive—and the means to do it, to hire someone.'

'Who?'

'How closely d'you watch the Nationalists?'

'I don't read all their speeches. They don't change much.' The National Party was very right-wing. Neo-Nazi. They even had an enforcement group that they called the security committee, which wore no uniforms but otherwise was the same as the Brownshirts that Hitler used to use against his opposition in the early days of the Nazis. The security committee brawled with anyone they considered left-wingers: student radicals, social democrats, unionists. In the last few years there'd been three or four big street fights, especially bad in Munich and Hamburg. Nothing heavier than fists and clubs, but bad scenes, riots. And in the last municipal elections in West Germany the Nationalists had taken an average fifteen per cent of the vote, twenty per cent in many of the smaller towns; they were much stronger than any right-wing party had been in Germany since the end of the war. Two things they spoke for most often in their speeches were German reunification and unrestricted rearmament for West Germany, including strategic nuclear weapons.

'Have you noticed it's a long time since they talked about Hess?'

'No.' That was something else the Nationalists used in their speeches from time to time: the injustice of keeping Hess locked up. Not that they gave a damn about injustices or even Hess; what they really wanted was that Moscow should lose the pretext for sending armed troops into West Berlin. They wanted to remove that Soviet presence.

'You don't watch them closely enough, Phil. They haven't mentioned Hess for about eight months.'

'What d'you think that means?'

'I started thinking about it last night, when I heard about what'd happened. I don't have any sympathy for Hess, but . . .'

'Oh, come on, Dieter, for Christ's sake!'

Kluger looked sharply at him. 'What the hell d'you mean?'

'I've been here five years and I've never heard a German with anything good to say about Hitler or anything that came out of that time. D'you know how uneasy that makes me?'

Kluger looked uncomfortable and said nothing, but he was chewing his gum very quickly, agitatedly.

A rabbit ran across the path ahead of them as they walked, and disappeared in the grass, in a clearing where sunlight shone bright through the trees.

Quietly, looking away at where the rabbit had gone, Kluger said: 'D'you want to hear what I've got to say or d'you want to talk about whether I'm some kind of crypto-Nazi or not?'

'I came to hear what you've got to say, but don't apologise for anything you feel about Hess. I've got some sympathy for him, and it wouldn't shock me if you had. Thirty years in jail is long enough.'

'Maybe. That's not what I want to talk about. I don't want to talk about it.'

Strang glanced at him and saw his jaws still working quickly on the gum. He wished he hadn't jumped on Kluger. But sometimes it was hard to keep quiet when one of them started making all those noises about rejecting the Hitler period. Kluger was a good man, though, and he shouldn't have embarrassed him.

'What about the Nationalists, Dieter?'

'As I was trying to say, I don't have any sympathy for Hess

38

—no particular sympathy—but I don't like the way the Nationalists make use of his situation. They've got the motive for wanting him out of Spandau. They stopped talking about him just about two months before his lawyer began working on the appeal for his release.'

'And you think that's significant?'

'Yes. It's years since the last appeal, and I don't think it's too much of a coincidence that they stopped talking about him and then this one started. They couldn't have made an appeal themselves—their motives would've been obvious. They needed a respectable front.'

'Who's his lawyer?' Strang said.

'A woman named Karin Hartmann.'

'Is she a Nationalist?'

'No. This is where it's tricky; there's no connection between her and the Nationalists. She's the farthest thing from a neo-Nazi.'

'And she's Hess's lawyer?'

'What does that mean? Does she have to be a neo-Nazi to be Hess's lawyer? You just told me you have some sympathy for him. If all the people who had sympathy for him were Nazis, there'd be a hell of a lot of Nazis in the world, my friend.' Kluger chewed his gum carefully. 'You're a strange bastard sometimes, Phil.'

'She's just a humanitarian. Is that what you're telling me?'

'I'm trying to. Her father certainly was. He was Dr Peter Hartmann, Hess's lawyer at the Nuremberg Trials. He died two years ago and she took over the practice.'

A couple came around a bend in the path, hand-in-hand, and Strang and Kluger walked on saying nothing until the sound of their footsteps had faded along the path.

'D'you think the Nationalists persuaded this woman to get to work on this appeal, Dieter?'

'They couldn't have approached her directly. I don't think she'd let a Nationalist into her office. But there's a connection. There must be. The timing was too convenient. I think they stopped talking about Hess because they didn't want to hurt his chances, to lose any of the support from respectable names that these appeals for his release always bring out. They're not stupid.'

39

'And when the appeal failed, you think they tried to kill Hess?'

'They've got the motive; that's what I said. And they've got the money to buy one of the people in Spandau. They could've done it. What the hell difference would it make to them whether Hess came out of there alive or dead, so long as Spandau was empty and the Soviets had no one to guard?'

It was interesting. Kluger might have something, Strang thought. He might. 'I'll talk to Fräulein Hartmann.'

They turned back along the path.

'How long d'you think you can keep the lid on this thing, Phil?'

'For ever, I hope.'

'Not if Hess dies.'

'I haven't thought that far ahead. It's bad enough now.'

'If he dies, it'll get worse. The story'll have to come out, and whether you say he committed suicide or was murdered, he'll be a martyr in Germany.'

'I don't want to think about that.'

'No, but keep it in mind.'

'I've got it. He'll be a martyr. The Nationalists'll get a lot of strength from his memory. You're right, Dieter.'

Chapter 7

Her office was in the centre of the city, off Bismarckstrasse, in an old stone building. There were few old buildings left in West Berlin—almost everything had been rebuilt on the cleared sites after the war—and when Strang had phoned her from the Mission she told him how easy it would be to find, among the modern steel and glass along the street. She had sounded fond of it.

The lobby had a high ceiling and a marble floor. Karin Hartmann's name was in a short list on an old glass-covered directory board on the wall.

At the side of the lobby a marble staircase curved up, and in the stairwell, in a shaft closed in by a steel-mesh grille, was an openwork elevator cage. Strang rode it to the fourth floor, and walked down a hallway with a terrazzo floor. All the office doors were painted black, the names on them in gilt Gothic lettering.

He walked into a small outer office. On the floor, in the sunlight shining through two windows, were tall potted plants. A grey-haired woman in heavy-rimmed glasses looked up from a typewriter.

'Guten morgen. I have an appointment with Fräulein Hartmann,' Strang said.

'Yes, sir. What name, please?' The woman was getting up. 'Strang.'

'Ah, yes. One moment, please, Mr Strang. Please be seated.'

'Thank you.' He looked at a smooth-worn leather couch against the wall behind him, beside the door, but did not sit down.

The secretary pulled open a door on the other side of the room, heavy-looking and covered with padded black leather, knocked on an inner wooden door, and opened it as she pulled the padded door shut behind her. It closed solidly and there was no sound behind it.

Against the wall, near the couch, were three shelves of law books in a glass-fronted case. Above them was a photograph in a narrow black frame. Strang went closer and looked at it. It was a picture of two men, standing smiling at each other. One was white-haired, and Strang did not know the face; the other was Willy Brandt. Behind them was the Schöneberger *rathaus*, the West Berlin city hall. Probably it had been taken sometime in the sixties, when Brandt was mayor of West Berlin, before he became Chancellor of West Germany. The white-haired man was probably the late Dr Hartmann, Karin Hartmann's father. The picture looked as though it had been there a long time.

'Mr Strang?' The secretary was holding the leather-padded door open. 'Miss Hartmann will see you now.'

He walked into a high-ceilinged office that was bright with sunlight. Five big windows were along one wall, and the sun had moved from one of them but was shining through the others. More tall potted plants were in a long row along the floor in front of the windows, the wide leaves looking smooth and waxy.

'Good morning, Mr Strang.' She was standing in front of a big mahogany desk. 'Karin Hartmann.'

She held out her hand and he took it. It was slim and smooth. 'It was good of you to see me so quickly, Miss Hartmann.' She was good-looking: high cheekbones and a straight nose, with dark blonde hair brushed straight down to just below the earlobes.

'You said it was important—but I'm afraid I won't have much time. Please sit down.'

They sat facing each other in front of the desk, in two chairs with wooden arms and black leather seats, and she crossed her legs, smoothing her skirt to the knee.

'I'm curious to know why someone from the American Mission would want to talk to me,' she said.

'It's about Rudolf Hess.' He was sure she'd suspected that, but she hadn't asked him when he phoned—just invited him over.

'What about him?'

'He's in our Army hospital. He was taken there yesterday.'

Her hands slid along her leg and, one on top of the other, gripped her knee. 'When?'

'After lunch.'

'But I haven't heard anything about it—nothing on the television. There was nothing in the paper this morning.'

'It's classified information. We're not making it public.'

'Why not? What's wrong with him? Is it serious?'

'Something happened at lunchtime. There was something in his food.' He was watching to see how she would take it.

'Do you mean poison?'

'Yes.'

'My God!' Quickly uncrossing her legs, she pressed her hands against the sides of her face, and the tips of her long, slim fingers reached up almost to her hairline.

She hadn't known a damn thing about it until this moment. He was sure of it.

'How bad is he?'

'The doctors say he's responding to treatment.'

Snatching her hands down, she shook her head quickly, impatiently. 'Responding to treatment! My God, what does that mean, Mr Strang?'

'It means he's not dead yet.'

'You sound as though it makes no difference to you, whether he dies or not.' Her lips were hard together and she looked very tense in the chair.

'I don't want to see him dead, Miss Hartmann.'

She turned and looked at the windows. Then she pushed herself up out of the chair, walked over there, and stood looking out. A watering can was on the floor at the end of the row of plants, and she picked it up and stood sprinkling water into the black earth in one of the pots that were out of the sunlight. Her head was down, watching the spray of water.

Strang sat listening to the patter of the water on the damp earth. From the back, with her head bent and shoulders down, she looked very depressed. He hadn't thought it would hit her so hard. He sat looking at her. She had damn good legs.

Carefully she stood the watering can beside one of the pots and walked back to her chair. 'Damn those Russians,' she said quietly. 'They're inhuman.' She sat down, shaking her head. 'Animals.'

'Because they rejected the appeal?'

'Of course. That's why Herr Hess did this.'

'You're assuming he tried to kill himself.'

She stared at him. 'Isn't that what happened?'

'We're not sure.'

'What else could it be?' As the alternative became clear, she leaned toward him. 'Do you suspect someone tried to murder him?'

'I think it's possible.'

She whispered: 'My God!' Slowly she sat back. 'Why would anyone want to murder him? It makes no sense. The Russians hate him, of course, but they wouldn't want to kill him, would they?'

'No. Certainly not the Soviets. They'd like him to live for ever—and stay in Spandau.'

'Who else would want to kill him?' She shook her head, looking around the room. 'I'm sorry. I can't believe this is true. I'm just beginning to realise what it is we're discussing.' Her knees were tight together, and she spread her hands flat on them, looking down at them. 'It's incredible. It's a shocking thing.'

'Yes, it is.'

'But who would want to kill him, Mr Strang?'

'That's what I'm looking for now—people with a motive.'

She said nothing.

'Miss Hartmann, why did you decide to make that appeal for his release?'

'Is that difficult to understand? He's eighty-three years old and he's been in that prison for thirty years—thirty years in July. And six years in Britain and Nuremberg before that. Isn't that long enough? That was my reason. Isn't that an understandable reason?'

'I suppose so.'

'What do you mean?' Frowning, head on one side as though she was trying to understand something obscure and unpleasant, she snapped: 'Why did you ask me about the appeal?'

'I wondered if anyone had come and asked you to make it.'

'Anyone? Who?'

'Any politicians. National Party people.'

44

'Nationalists? D'you think I'd have anything to do with those damn Nazis?' Still with her head on one side, her jaw hard-looking, she sat staring at him.

'Someone who represented them might've come to you.'

'No one did. It's a ridiculous suggestion.'

No, she wouldn't have given any time to the Nationalists, he could see. Christ, she was angry.

'Who are you, Mr Strang? What do you do at the Mission? Are you one of those CIA people we hear about?'

'Is that important?'

'You're beginning to ask me some offensive questions, and I'd like to know why.'

'I want to know who might've tried to kill Hess. I thought you'd be interested in that too.'

'I am, but . . .' Her phone rang and she leaned across the desk. 'Excuse me.' She grabbed it up. *'Ja?'* Suddenly more gentle: 'Oh, yes, ask him to wait, Greta. I'll only be a few minutes.' She laid the phone down, sitting back. 'Why did you ask me about the Nationalists?'

'One of the things they want is to remove that Soviet guard from Spandau. They talk about the injustice of keeping Hess there, but what they really want is to get rid of the Soviets. They have a reason for wanting Hess out.'

'But do you think they'd kill him? I can't believe that.'

'I can. If you think about it, it might grow on you too. D'you really think it'd mean anything to them whether he came out dead or alive?'

She sat staring at him, then her blonde hair flicked as she shook her head once, fast, trying to shake out the thoughts he had put there and, getting up, she said: 'I can't believe it. And I can't tell you how it makes me feel, that you think I could be associated with such a thing.' She walked to the window.

Strang watched her, feeling the great coolness and distance between them. He'd completely turned her off, trying to connect her with the Nationalists.

Slowly she walked back, but now sat behind her desk, very businesslike and detached.

'Have I made it quite clear to you, Mr Strang? I made the appeal for Herr Hess's release because I think it's inhuman to keep him in that filthy prison. That was my reason. I happen to care about people and it troubles me when they're treated badly. I don't expect you to understand.'

'I understand one thing: asking Moscow to release Hess is hopeless. I try not to waste time on hopeless causes and I'm suspicious of people who do. I always wonder if it's just something they use to pass the time—instead of playing bridge or risking falling in love.'

Her hands locked together on her desk, fingers tensing against one another and, cold-angry, she said: 'Don't condescend to me, Mr Strang.'

'Then don't judge me. That's another thing I'm suspicious of: people who judge me. They always sound too damn smug to be convincing.'

The phone rang and she snatched it, glaring at him. *'Ja? One moment.'* Jerking the phone out to him across the desk: 'For you.' She almost threw it into his hand as he reached out.

He wondered who it was. 'Yes?'

'Mr Strang?'

'Yes.'

'Colonel Goodblood. Something's come up that you should know about. How long will you be, where you are?'

'A few minutes.' At the most, he thought. He was finished here. Completely.

'Something's happened. Drop by my office when you can. I'll bring you up to date.'

'Will do, Colonel.'

He handed the phone to her. 'Thank you.'

Not looking at him, she snatched it from his hand and slammed it down. 'I'm afraid I have no more time for you, Mr Strang. You have no other questions?'

'No. Thanks for your help. You're very gracious.'

As though she had not heard him, she leaned back in her chair. 'I presume that, in spite of your secrecy, Herr Hess's wife and son have been told what's happened to him.'

'No.'

'I shall tell them.'

'I don't want you to do that.'

'I don't care what you want.'

'If you tell them, the story'll get out.'

'Yes, it will.' She looked satisfied.

46

'There'll be a hell of a lot of publicity, Miss Hartmann, and all the usual people will start screaming for us not to send him back to Spandau if he recovers.'

'That's right, Mr Strang.'

'It won't help. Public opinion has never made Moscow think twice about Hess, and it never will. You'll be disturbing his wife and son for nothing. Don't do it.'

She said nothing, but he could see he'd convinced her. More than anything, probably, she'd said it to provoke him. He turned away, to the door.

'Why don't you Americans just keep him out, now he's in your hospital?'

He swung back. 'For Christ's sake, we don't know if he's going to live or die! He's eighty-three years old and he's taken cyanide.'

'But he might live.' She was on her feet. 'Couldn't you keep him out—just fly him out of Berlin to where the Russians can't get him?'

'It's a possibility.' But he knew it wasn't. Washington would never bring on that kind of trouble with Moscow, not for Hess. He just wasn't worth it. 'It's an option—but we wouldn't have any options if this story got out and there were public pressure. Moscow would dig its heels in and insist we slap him back in Spandau at once, no matter how sick he was. It'd just mean trouble.'

'I understand that.' She nodded. 'I won't say anything.'

'I think it's best.' He opened the door. 'Goodbye.'

'Goodbye, Mr Strang.' She walked to the door and held it behind him.

A blond man was sitting on the couch in the outer office, and he stood up when Strang came out, smiling at Karin Hartmann, and walked across the room to her. As Strang opened the door into the hall he looked back and saw them with their arms around each other.

47

Chapter 8

Strang stepped out of the taxi at the entrance to the American compound and walked into the Mission. He went straight up to Goodblood's office.

'*Guten tag*, Herr Strang.' Smiling, Goodblood shook his hand.

'*Guten tag*, Herr Oberst.' He saw this was how it was going to be between him and Goodblood; they'd speak German always when they were alone. It gave Goodblood real pleasure and things were easy between them this way.

'Come.' Goodblood led the way to the comfortable leather chairs across the office, and as they sat he said: 'It looks as though we've identified the man who gave us the trouble at Spandau.'

'Who is he?'

'A man named Walter Lichti. He didn't report for work this morning.'

'What's his job?'

'Assistant chef.'

'God.'

'Yes.' Goodblood looked down at his crossed legs and ran a fingertip along the crease of his trousers. 'Yes, Lichti was in the right place to put that cyanide in old Hess's pie.'

'Have you done anything about it?'

'I had the Berlin police go and check his apartment. They went in and found nothing, no sign of him.'

'Had he packed a bag, Colonel?'

'No sign of that either. Everything seemed to be there: shaving gear, clothes looked as though they were all there. But they couldn't find his passport.'

'What is he?'

'Swiss.'

'And he lives alone?'

Goodblood nodded. 'Never been married, always lived alone.

48

He's worked at Spandau for twenty-four years and there's never been a sign of trouble from him. He's always been well-liked there, by all the staff.'

Well-liked by all the staff, Strang thought. Jesus Christ. 'Wasn't he questioned last night, Colonel?'

'Yes, he was. He satisfied my people that he hadn't been in the kitchen at the time Hess's lunch was prepared. Two other people corroborated that.'

'It looks as though he knew more than he told.' And, Christ, they'd let him slip away. Oh, God damn. 'We've got to find him.'

'We're certainly damn well trying.' Goodblood's eyes were hard behind the steel-rimmed glasses. 'He won't get far. We've distributed pictures of him to the police here and in West Germany.'

'You think he got out of the city?'

'It's possible. He's had time. We're looking to see if he flew out or went through any of the checkpoints but . . .'

'Including into East Berlin?'

'Including that.'

'I can't believe he was working for the Soviets. I'm still convinced they're not guilty of this one.'

'I agree—but I still want to confirm he didn't go into the east.'

Strang nodded slowly, preoccupied. Who the hell had paid Lichti to do it? That was what they had to find out.

'Are your people questioning the others at Spandau now, Colonel—to see what they know about anyone Lichti might've been talking to outside?'

'Yes, they're doing that. He seems to have been a quiet little son of a bitch. They all liked him, but no one knows much about him. He didn't talk much about himself.'

'What about people where he lived?'

'The Berlin police're making some inquiries there. I hope they can turn something up.'

'Someone must've seen him with someone. If they bribed him to poison Hess, I don't imagine they did it easily. A man like that, working there all those years, must've taken a hell of a lot of persuading to do something as desperate as this.'

49

'Must've taken money too—probably enough to keep him comfortable for the rest of his life.'

'If they let him live long enough to spend it, Colonel.' And long enough to be found and questioned. Would they let him live that long?

Thursday
April 28, 1977

Chapter 9

At one-eighteen in the morning the phone rang on the reception desk in the lobby of the United States consulate, and the security officer on duty there picked it up: 'Consulate-general of the United States.'

A man speaking English with a German accent said: 'Pay attention! This is a warning. If Rudolf Hess is sent back to Spandau, your building will be blown up. Do you understand what I say?'

The security officer could not believe what he had heard, and he sat holding the phone. This was crazy. What the hell was this about not sending Hess back to Spandau? When had Hess ever been *out* of Spandau? This was a crank call, had to be.

'Quick! Did you understand?'

'Yes.' The security officer began writing down the man's warning. 'Who is this calling?'

The line went dead.

The security officer wrote down the time of the call.

A minute later the phone rang in the lobby of the Mission, across the compound from the consulate, and the guard there took the same message.

A few seconds later, a kilometre away, the receptionist at the US Army hospital took the call. An MP had been standing talking to her and he saw her face tighten.

Feeling suddenly very cold, she asked the man to repeat what he had said, holding the phone off her ear, and signalling the MP to listen.

As the MP put his head close beside the receptionist's, the phone between them, he heard the man say: 'If Rudolf Hess is sent back to Spandau, your building will be blown up. You understand?'

The MP snapped: 'Who the hell are you?'

The man hung up.

At once the MP began dialling, to report the call.

'What did he mean?' the receptionist said. 'What was that about Rudolf Hess?'

Still dialling, the MP said: 'Damned if I know.' But he had been told all about the man upstairs, registered as Schmidt. All the MP detail had been told how important he was. As he finished dialling, he said: 'Mary, I'll have to ask you to step away a little. I can't let you hear this.'

Still thinking of the warning, still chilled from it, the receptionist moved away along the counter, and the MP turned his back on her, bending close to the phone and speaking quietly.

Half a dozen kilometres to the north, in the centre of the city, the phone had rung in the British consulate, on Uhlandstrasse, and the night man there was listening to the same warning.

Chapter 10

Strang had been in his office less than ten minutes when the call came from Goodblood.

'Can you drop in to see me?'

'Something new, Colonel?'

'New and bad.'

'I'll be right up.'

He took the stairs to the third floor, running up two at a time, and Goodblood was turning from the window when he went in.

'Some interesting things happened during the night,' Goodblood said, and told him of the phone threats.

'How about the French—did they get any calls?'

'No. And the British got just the one. I guess that was a token, because Spandau's in their sector. But they touched all the bases with us.'

'What're you going to do, Colonel?'

'Put stronger guards on the buildings, and I've asked the Berlin police to increase their patrols on the street.'

'What's Hess's condition?'

'Improving. The old man's pulling through.' Goodblood smiled his thin smile. 'Unbelievable. But he'll be in hospital for a while yet.'

'Nothing'll happen so long as he's in there.'

'That's right—if these damn threats are serious.'

'Who the hell could've made them, Colonel?'

'I wish I knew. It seems the same man made all the calls. Our people and the man at the British consulate all agree on the voice. But who he was and who he's working for . . .' Shaking his head, Goodblood lifted a hip on to the corner of his desk. 'I hope we can track it down.' He had to stretch one leg to get the toe of his elevator shoe on the floor, and the other foot swung very high. He looked uncomfortable, but he wanted to show he could do it, sit on the desk and have his foot touching the floor.

'Whoever he was, Colonel, he must be with the people who poisoned Hess.' Only the people who'd done that could know he was in the hospital. There was almost no chance that anyone else would; the security was so damn tight. Unless.

'I think it's safe to assume that.'

'Unless there's been a leak.'

'That's not likely, Mr Strang.' The suggestion that his grip on security was loose did not please Goodblood.

'There's one possibility.'

'What's that?'

'Hess's damn lawyer.' He had told Goodblood how she'd threatened to blow the story.

Slowly Goodblood slid off the desk, his back very straight. 'Could she be responsible for this?'

'She badly wants to have Hess out of Spandau.' Strang got up. 'Maybe badly enough for this. I'll find out.'

Chapter 11

He went straight to her office, not phoning first, wanting to get to her fast and without warning, to watch her when he questioned her.

The grey-haired secretary looked up when he walked in, unsure, recognising him but not remembering his name. '*Guten morgen.*'

Already halfway across the office, he said: 'I must see Fräulein Hartmann.'

'Yes, but . . .' The secretary was getting up, pushing her heavy-rimmed glasses back on her nose as they began to slip, grabbing for a sheet of paper that slipped off her desk.

Strang reached for the knob of the leather-padded outer door to Karin Hartmann's office.

'Please, sir!' The secretary came after him as he tugged the door open and pushed open the inner one.

Karin Hartmann looked up from her desk. 'What do you want?' She was very cold.

'To talk to you.' He was aware of the secretary standing in the doorway behind him.

'I have no time for you. I'm preparing to go to court.' She looked down at the papers on her desk.

'You could go to court as a defendant if you don't give me the right answers to some questions.'

Her head snapped up. 'What?' In a rush she pushed herself up and stood behind her desk. 'How *dare* you talk to me in that manner! You're not in America. You have no right here!'

In three quick strides he was against the front of her desk, leaning across with his face close to hers. 'You've got to answer some questions. Answer mine now or I'll have the police ask them. Which way d'you want it?'

They stood glaring at each other, only the desk keeping them apart. Then casually she looked away from him and said to the secretary: 'It's all right, Greta. Please leave us.'

57

Backing out, the secretary pulled the door shut.

Carefully Karin Hartmann sat. 'Now tell me why you've come rushing in here like a maniac.'

'Who've you told about Hess?'

'No one.'

He saw a flicker in her eyes and around her mouth. A slight flicker of something. She was lying and she wasn't good at it.

'Who did you talk to?'

'I said no one.' More certain this time, and her face was controlled.

He stood looking down across the desk at her, and couldn't be sure about her. He didn't have the feeling that she was trying to hide anything important. Something had tripped her just then—maybe she'd told the secretary about Hess, or a friend—something that had made it impossible for her to say no, just now, without it catching at her. She was angry as hell, and damn hostile, but he didn't have the feeling that she had a lot to hide. He didn't think she was hiding any bomb plot.

'I thought I convinced you yesterday that it'd be better for Hess if all this stayed secret.'

'You did. I told you I haven't spoken to anyone. Why have you come bursting in here to ask me this?' As she thought about it, a possibility came to her. 'Has something happened to Herr Hess?'

'He's fine. He's improving. But a man phoned our Mission early this morning and threatened to blow it up if he went back to Spandau.'

Her mouth opened. 'Oh, my God!'

'He phoned the hospital too, and the consulate—and the British consulate. Someone's planning to use a lot of bombs.'

'And you came here because of that?'

He was sure she knew nothing of it. Either that or she was a really experienced liar, which he didn't believe, or some kind of nut, and he hadn't seen any sign of that. No sign of anything but unwillingness to be pushed around—and he liked her for that.

'You're the only outsider who's been told about Hess—and a few hours after I told you, we got the bomb threats. A hell of a coincidence, Miss Hartmann.'

'And it's nothing more than that!' She shook her head, her

blonde hair switching about her face. 'God! Do you understand what you're accusing me of?'

'I'm not accusing you. I want to know if you told anyone. Anyone. You could've talked to someone who talked to someone who could've made those phone calls.'

'No. No, I haven't. My God, how can you suspect I'd know the kind of people who would set off bombs?'

He said nothing.

Very suddenly she turned her head away and sat looking at a potted plant in front of one of the windows. Impatiently she rubbed with a knuckle under the eye that she had turned from him, but he saw the deep movement of her throat as she swallowed. When she turned back her face was composed but her eyes were moist-looking.

'Will you please sit down, Mr Strang?'

'I'm leaving now.'

'No. I want to say something and I don't like you standing over me.'

He sat in front of the desk.

'So you will never question me about anything like this again. I want you to understand that my only interest is that that poor old man should come out of Spandau and live in peace with his family for whatever time he still has. When I went to that prison in January, to talk to him about the appeal, he looked so old and helpless . . .' She pressed her lips together. 'Whatever he might have taken part in or believed in once, I don't know and I don't care. That was years ago. Forty years and more. How long can the desire for revenge continue, if we're to consider ourselves sane human beings? He was tried at Nuremberg by a tribunal that included, of all things, a Russian, a representative of a regime that had been responsible for millions of deaths—and they found him guilty of so-called crimes that didn't exist as crimes at the time he did the things they charged him with. Was that justice? . . .'

It was everything Strang had heard before, from all the people who thought it was a crime to keep Hess locked up—but he'd never seen anyone look as moved as she did, saying it now.

'. . . And when he was sentenced to imprisonment for life, who believed it would mean that—literally life? No one but the

Russians, those unbelievable barbarians. Even some of the six who were sent to Spandau with him had their sentences remitted, because they were considered too sick to be kept there. But not Herr Hess. The Russians will never let him go. And what is his crime, after all? He was a dedicated anti-Communist, for one thing—and he flew to England to try to persuade the British to join in a war against Russia. For the Russians, those are his real crimes, no matter what else they say. So he stays in Spandau enjoying Russian justice. I believe that's inhuman and I believe people in the west should insist on his freedom. That's what I want. Is that impossible for you to understand? Don't you feel any sympathy for that?'

'Yes.'

Her head tilted slightly, as though he had pushed it over. 'I beg your pardon?'

'I agree with you. I think he should be freed. I think he should've been freed years ago.'

'I didn't sense this in you yesterday.'

'I've been told I'm not easy to sense. You should've asked me what I thought. I might've told you.'

'Yes. You're right.' Slowly she smiled. 'Perhaps I became a bit prejudiced when I guessed what you were, what your work was. I was wrong to do that. You don't dress like a CIA man, and now you don't sound like one.'

'How many other CIA men have you met?'

'None, so far as I know. You're right again—that was more prejudice of mine. You'll accuse me again of being smug.'

'No. You're learning, Miss Hartmann.'

She laughed. 'Will you please call me Karin? If we're going to be so frank, we should use first names.'

'Yes. There's one more thing, Karin. I don't think you should spend too much of your life trying to get Hess out. Moscow'll never move. They'll never let him go.' It was something he couldn't begin to imagine, how it would be if anyone tried to lock him up for the rest of his life. But he knew he wouldn't take it—and to hell with all the existentialist stuff about being physically locked up but still spiritually free, and always keeping a part of yourself that no one could get to. You could say all that but it still wouldn't be freedom. Not for him. If he'd been one of those people in Spandau, he'd have made a jump for the wall after the first day, and let the guards finish him. But he couldn't tell her how he felt about all that. He wasn't going to be as frank as that. 'A lot of people agree with you, Karin, and it doesn't help. They've all said the same things about Nuremberg—they said them at the time and they've been saying them for thirty years: it was victors' justice and the real crime for Hess and the others was that they were on the losing side. And don't ask me that question about how many Americans, British, Soviets, and French would've been sentenced for war crimes since Nuremberg if they'd had to stand trial. And how many Chinese, Arabs, Jews, black Africans, and white Africans. You're a lawyer and you shouldn't have to ask me if Nuremberg was justice. It was revenge, and that's human. I just wish they hadn't tried to rationalise it. It makes it so damn hard to forget.'

'I really did misjudge you.' She started, jerking her wrist up, and looked at her watch. 'I'm sorry. I must go. I do have to be in court.' Scooping papers into a briefcase, she got up. 'I'm not sure you've persuaded me not to go on working for Herr Hess's release, but perhaps we can meet again and talk. Is it possible?'

'Yes, I think we can do that.'

'May I know your first name now?'

'Philip.'

Chapter 12

On July 30, 1945, twelve weeks after the Third Reich surrendered to western and Soviet forces, military delegations of
the Four Powers met in Berlin for the first conference of the
Allied Control Council, the military government for Germany,
which was to co-ordinate the administrations of the four allied
occupation zones.

Because even then, so soon after the war, the Soviet Union's
intention was to keep western troops from the area under its
control, the Soviet delegation had insisted that the Control
Council headquarters should be in the American sector of
Berlin. So the first meeting was held in the bomb-damaged
building that was Berlin headquarters of the US Army.

At the beginning of July, when the first western troops passed
through the Soviet front in Germany, through Soviet-held terri-
tory to Berlin, they had driven their vehicles into a ruined city.
Bodies still floated in the canals beside the rubble-filled streets,
and in the lakes among the shell-shredded, bullet-ripped trees of
the Grünewald and the Tegeler Forest. Berlin men and women
were being fed eight hundred calories a day and, working to
repair offices that would be used by the military government,
they were dropping exhausted until American trucks drove in
with food to give them hot meals. Complete city blocks had
been piled into brick and stone by the fire of Red Army
artillery and tank cannon, mortars and rockets.

In the centre of the city, in the Schöneberg district, ninety-five
buildings in every hundred were damaged, almost half of them
blasted into debris that filled the streets. But in Schöneberg was
the great palace that had been the *Kammergericht*, the Appelate
Court, more than five hundred high-ceilinged rooms, and it still
stood, damaged by bombs, among the shell-holed, tank-tracked
earth that had been its gardens.

Through July and the first week of August, US Army
engineers and German labourers worked to repair the battle
damage to the old building, and to landscape its lawns, and by

August 10 it was ready for the second meeting of the Control Council, and was now its permanent headquarters.

To the southwest, in Dahlem, another area in the American sector, they had also repaired a big three-storey building of one hundred rooms. It had been the head office of a national insurance association and had been chosen as headquarters of the Kommandatura, the military body that would govern Berlin separately from the rest of Germany.

At desks and tables in all the rooms of those two buildings and hurrying back and forth through the long corridors were men and women in the uniforms of the Four Powers. In front of the Control Council headquarters and the Kommandatura flew the flags of the United States, the Soviet Union, Britain, and France. They flew side by side for only three years.

On March 20, 1948, unable to agree with the western allies on the future of Germany, the Soviet delegation under Marshal Vassily Sokolovsky walked out of the Control Council and never returned. The Control Council never met again.

On June 16 Major General Alexander Kotikov led the Soviet delegation out of the Kommandatura, but it continued, with the commandants of the three western garrisons meeting every month, through all the years since 1948, discreetly supervising the government of the West Berlin mayor and his cabinet.

Today there was an extraordinary meeting of the Kommandatura. The Soviet commander-in-chief in East Germany had sent a message asking for it, and asked the western commandants to receive an officer he would send as his delegate. It was unprecedented but the western allies had not objected. They had no doubt that the Soviets wanted to discuss Hess, and they wanted to know the Soviet mood.

They met around the table in the conference room: Major General Benson, the US commandant; Major General Henshaw, the British; General Bourdais, the French; and Major General Igonin, the Soviet delegate. In front of each of them was a microphone, and they wore earpieces for the simultaneous translation. On a wall hung the photographs of the three western commandants, and of Major General Kotikov, who had walked out twenty-nine years before.

Igonin began his attack at once.

'I am here to inform you of my government's strongest

63

objection to the removal of Prisoner Number Seven, the war criminal Hess, from Spandau.' When the seven Nazi leaders had been taken from Nuremberg to Spandau and given their prison numbers, Hess was number seven.

'He was very seriously ill, General.' Benson said. 'He still is.'

'My country's director at Spandau protested at his removal at the time and said he should be treated in the operating theatre in the prison.'

'Your prison director isn't a doctor—and years ago the operating theatre at Spandau was agreed by all our governments to be unfit for use.'

'My country's doctor was not even consulted before Hess was removed.'

'Your country's doctor was not there at the time, General—and I think you'll agree it would've been unwise to wait his convenience. We couldn't be sure, in the circumstances, that Hess would co-operate.' Benson, heavily deadpan, glanced over his microphone at the British commandant, across the table. He and Henshaw knew each other well, and had the same sense of humour.

The British general sat back in his chair, amused, but showing it only in his eyes, and stroked a fingertip down the left side of his face, feeling the slight ridge of a white line of scar tissue that ran from the corner of his lip, twisted across his cheek and under his left eye, to the hairline. It was from a bomb, six years ago in Northern Ireland, when he was commanding an infantry brigade.

Igonin noticed nothing. 'My information is that Number Seven's condition now is satisfactory, and . . .'

Mildly Benson leaned to his microphone. 'Excuse me, General. Whose condition?'

'Number Seven's.'

'I'm afraid I'll have to insist that you refer to him as Hess. The numerical designation isn't familiar to all of us'—Benson glanced around the table from Henshaw to Bourdais—'and it's important that we have no misunderstanding here. No misunderstanding that can be avoided, that is.'

Igonin's right fist gripped his microphone stand. In his uniform with the braided shoulder boards he looked very square and wide in his chair.

'The prisoner Hess's condition is now reported to be satisfactory,' he said heavily. 'It is therefore my government's wish that he be returned immediately to Spandau.'

'That's completely out of the question,' Benson said. 'Hess's condition is much improved—you're right about that—but he's eighty-three years old, he's suffered cyanide poisoning, and he's been in hospital only two days. It would be an unnecessary risk—and an unwise one, if you'll forgive me—to move him from our hospital, where he's being given the very best attention. I hope the other members agree. General Bourdais?'

The French general's face was tanned and hard-looking, and his white moustache and short white hair made his tan look very dark. He looked much too young to be white-haired.

Bourdais said: 'It would be an act of the greatest stupidity to send Hess back to Spandau before his recovery is complete.' All the time he spoke he was staring at Igonin as though he loathed him, and until today they had never met.

Benson looked at Henshaw. 'General?'

'Oh, I agree absolutely. It'd be unthinkable to send him back there till he's completely fit. Wouldn't consider agreeing to it.'

Igonin sat looking at the three of them.

'If he were to be moved back prematurely, and died in Spandau, there'd be a great deal of negative public opinion, as soon as the circumstances became known,' Benson said. 'None of our governments wants that.'

'My government is influenced by justice, General Benson, not public opinion. Justice demands that Hess be confined in Spandau Prison.'

'But if he's sent back too soon he could die there. Your government doesn't want that, General. That was pointed out to your director the day before yesterday, when he objected to Hess being moved. I'm told he understood the significance without much elaboration.'

'And you tell me that if Hess were moved now, he might die?'

'Of course he might, General.'

'I shall communicate your opinion to my superiors.'

'There's something else.' Benson was looking at the notes he had made before the conference, on a pad in front of him. 'If he were to go back before we've determined how this happened to him, assuming someone tried to kill him, another attempt could be made—and the next one might be successful.'

'Do you not believe that what happened was an attempt to commit suicide—an attempt at a coward's escape, as he has attempted countless times before?'

'Not countless times, General. Four times, I've been told. No, we're not convinced it was a suicide attempt. As a matter of fact, we're almost convinced now that it wasn't.'

Igonin leaned forward. 'Now? Does this mean something has happened to make you believe it was an attempt to murder him?'

'A civilian employee at Spandau has disappeared, General, and we . . .'

'When? Excuse me, General Benson. When did this happen?'

'The man failed to report for work yesterday morning.'

'Yesterday morning? Why were we not informed of this?'

'There's nothing to tell, General, except that the man, whose name is Lichti, has apparently disappeared.'

'Disappeared! What you mean to say is that this man Lichti was the one who tried to kill Hess and now he has escaped.' Igonin's neck seemed to have come down into his square-looking shoulders, his earlobes almost touching his shoulder boards, as he leaned over the table.

'I'm saying we want to question him and he's at the moment unavailable. We're looking for him. I don't doubt we'll find him.'

'On behalf of my superiors, I request most strongly that we be permitted to take part in this investigation.'

'Your director has already been allowed to take responsibility for questioning the Soviet Union's jailers.'

'I mean we must be permitted to take part in the total investigation, in all areas.'

Shaking his head, Benson leaned to his microphone, said: 'Impossible,' and sat back.

'We have a legal right to participate in any activity that is related to the administration of Spandau and the security of the prisoners. A right by international treaty.'

'I don't think the treaty allowed for the possibility of a murder investigation, General. In any event, the United States

66

is in control of Spandau this month, and I interpret that as giving me sole responsibility for the conduct of this investigation.'

Quickly and smoothly, Henshaw said into his microphone: 'Since Spandau is in the British sector, I should, of course, have to agree to the presence of any investigators other than those of the controlling power—that is, the United States—and that, of course, I should be most reluctant to do. Most reluctant.'

Igonin said nothing.

Bourdais said: 'I agree most strongly with General Benson and General Henshaw. I have faith in the ability of General Benson's men to carry out this investigation and conclude it successfully.' While he spoke he sat staring hard at Igonin. Five years ago, when he was stationed in Marseilles, there had been a demonstration of Communist workers, which had turned into a riot through the centre of the city. One of them had thrown a gasoline bomb that had exploded in flowing flame all over his wife's car. She had not even had time to reach for the door handle. In the next six months Bourdais' hair and moustache had turned from black to white, and his hatred of Communists was total. He knew it was not rational, but he was completely unable to control it, as he had never been able to reconcile himself to the loss of his wife. With it all in his mind as he stared across the table at the Soviet general, he said: 'The suggestion that investigators from your command should interfere in the progress of this case is irresponsible and cannot be seriously considered.'

As though he had not heard him, Igonin said to Benson: 'Must I report this to my superiors as your final decision on this matter, General?'

'Yes. Point out too, General, that this investigation is being carried out not only in West Berlin but in West Germany and other parts of Europe. That's where we're looking for Lichti. We assume that if he tried to kill Hess it was because someone paid him to do it. We haven't considered it a serious possibility that, if he's left West Berlin, he's gone into East Berlin—or East Germany, for that matter.' Heavily Benson said; 'If he had, the implication would be obvious. You understand?'

'Of course I understand, and of course the man has not gone to East Berlin or East Germany.'

'Then there's very little your people could do to be of assistance,' Benson said.

He sat waiting for Igonin's reply, but he knew damn well there was nothing Igonin could say. He looked down at the notepad in front of him. All through the meeting, while he listened to Igonin and the others, he had been drawing thick black lines, some straight and thrusting, some in pairs that were sweeping and pincer-shaped, all tipped with arrowheads, like the lines that showed the direction on battle maps. Benson was an airborne officer, and as a young second lieutenant in World War Two he had dropped with the 101st Airborne into Normandy, then had stood with them at Bastogne. He had fought again in Korea, and had served three tours in Vietnam. This assignment, commandant in Berlin, was for a diplomat more than a soldier, he considered, but so long as he had it he would carry it out with all he had. One thing: if the time ever came when he had to go to work as a soldier here, as a commander of fighting troops, it'd be a hell of an interesting place to be. He wouldn't last long, nor any of his command, but it'd be interesting. Not dull at all.

Chapter 13

As he trotted up the steps from the U-bahn station Strang looked at his watch and saw he was four minutes early for Kluger. He walked up into the sunlight on the sidewalk and stepped to the kerb, turning to watch the people who had come off the train behind him. Just to be sure. He wasn't expecting a problem, but it was instinct always to be sure everything looked clear, to take no chances.

Two middle-aged women came up the steps together and crossed the sidewalk to a bus stop. A couple came up, the woman holding the man's arm, and they walked away up the street. Then an old man climbed slowly up, and stood near the two women at the bus stop.

A bus stopped at the kerb, and the women let the old man climb aboard, then followed him. Strang watched the bus go, then looked down Seidelstrasse for the silver-grey Audi.

There were a lot of women in Berlin like the two on the bus. It seemed to him that about thirty per cent of the population were single women of fifty or over. All widows or women who'd lost their fiancés or whatever during the war. And nothing had ever changed for them.

When he saw the Audi coming up in the traffic he looked at his watch and smiled. On time. Kluger always was.

The Audi stopped at the kerb, and he got in and they were moving off as he shut the door.

'How are you, Dieter?'

'Oh.' Kluger nodded, chewing his gum. 'I'm all right, I guess.'

'You don't sound all right.'

Kluger said nothing and Strang saw there was something on his mind. He thought he knew what it was, and he could feel Kluger getting ready to speak. It didn't look easy for him.

'Phil, d'you mind if I talk to you about something personal for a moment?'

Yes, it was the damn newly-wed problem. How much worse could it get before it began to affect his work? Christ, it was doing that now. He hadn't asked Kluger to meet out here so they could talk about his marriage.

'Of course I don't mind.'

It was not easy for Kluger to begin.

'What is it, Dieter?'

'Look.' Kluger took one hand off the wheel, circling it from the wrist as though he was trying to bring words from his mouth. 'When you were married, did you have any problems with sex?'

Oh, Jesus. 'No.' No, that hadn't been a problem. 'Why?'

'I don't know.' Kluger chewed quickly, tensely. 'D'you mind if I ask you if you and your wife . . .? No, I can't ask that.'

'What?'

'Would you say it's normal to want to do it three or four times a night? Every night? Does that sound all right to you?'

'Sounds all right to me, Dieter.'

Kluger laughed, but it was very quick and nervous. 'You bastard. I'm serious about this.'

'All right. Are you saying Irene wants to do it three or four times a night, seven nights a week?'

'Right.'

'And you can't make it?'

Kluger glanced at him. 'I wouldn't say it's as black-and-white as that.'

'Then what's the problem?' They had to get some of this out of the way, because Kluger wouldn't be good for anything else till he was more relaxed.

'I'm usually too damn tired by the time she starts playing around.' Kluger turned on to the road that ran northeast to Lübars, the old village where they were going for lunch. 'Did you have that problem?'

'No.' If they were going to talk about Kluger's marriage, they'd have to do it without talking about his own, which had, anyway, been finished for seven years. 'But I was only twenty-five when I was married.' And twenty-seven when we separated. In and out, bang-bang.

70

'Christ, I'm not ninety. I'm forty-three. It's just that I'm ready to sleep by midnight. That's not new. I was like that when I was eighteen.'

'Have you tried telling Irene that things might work better if you played your games before dinner, so you could go to sleep at midnight?'

'I couldn't tell her that. She'd think I was making excuses.'

'She's going to think that, anyway, if you don't talk to her soon, Dieter.' Now he was sitting here giving advice about the importance of frank little talks with the wife. Communication. Pauline should hear him now. But they'd never had Kluger's problem. That would've been simple to talk about. What hadn't been simple was having someone expect you to open your whole life for them and wanting to move in so close, to know every thought and feeling, that you'd have had no private space left if you'd allowed it to happen. That had been impossible for someone as private and solitary as he was. But Pauline, when she'd understood clearly how he was, had never tried to change him. Just said, after beating her head against him for two years, that each of them was perfectly fine, but they didn't fit together, and though she couldn't imagine herself with anyone else after him, she thought she'd much rather be alone. And he'd never stopped admiring her for that.

'I think you're right, Phil. I should talk to Irene about it.'

'Will you?'

'Yes.' Nodding and chewing vigorously, Kluger smiled. 'Yes. I'll do it tonight.'

'Good luck.'

'Thanks.'

'I've got a woman problem too.'

Kluger looked cautiously at him, suspecting a joke. 'Who?'

'Karin Hartmann.'

'Oh? Have you had trouble with her?'

'No—but there was some trouble after I talked to her yesterday. Someone threatened to blow up the Mission and a few other places.' He told Kluger about the phone calls.

'Christ! D'you think she knows anything about that?'

'I don't think so.' He shook his head, looking out the side window. 'I don't think so.'

'You don't sound convinced.'

'I think I'm convinced, Dieter. I talked to her a couple of hours ago, and I'm inclined to believe she's all right.'

'I couldn't imagine she'd have anything to do with bombs, Phil. She's a hell of a fighter. She doesn't give up. That's her reputation. But I don't think she'd have anything to do with this.'

They turned off the main road, down the road to Lübars.

'But she could've told someone else about Hess—someone without her inhibition about bombs.'

'Did you ask her?'

'Of course I asked her and of course she said no—but I'm not sure.'

'You don't trust her, do you?'

'I've got no reason not to. As a matter of fact, I like her. But I could be wrong.'

'No. That's not possible.'

'Fuck you.'

Kluger laughed. 'Please! Not you too!'

Strang smiled. 'I want to know about her friends. Anyone she might've talked to innocently. There might be someone who's not as innocent as she is.'

'I'll check our data, first thing after lunch. If there's a suspicious-looking connection somewhere. I'll let you know.'

'Let me know anyway, will you? It's on my mind.'

Kluger nodded. 'I'll let you know, yes or no.'

They stopped at the end of the village street, across from an old red-roofed inn where they came sometimes for lunch.

Strang reached for the door handle.

'What about Lichti?' Kluger said. 'Is there anything new?'

'No.'

'I talked to the police just before I drove out to meet you. They've got nothing either. Certainly nothing to connect him with the Nationalists.'

'There doesn't have to be anything stronger than money.'

'He'll be found, Phil.'

'I hope so.' Strang opened the car door.

Chapter 14

It was the middle of the afternoon when they got back from lunch. Strang went to his apartment, to work there. He'd begun working at home as much as he could because Tillman, with the pressure of the Hess case, was becoming more and more nervous, and Strang did not like to see how it was affecting him.

When he had been there about twenty minutes, sitting thinking, the phone rang and it was Tillman.

'Christ, Phil, I was beginning to wonder where you were. Hess's lawyer's been calling, trying to get you for an hour and a half. She just called again.'

'What does she want?'

'She wouldn't say. She wants to talk to you.'

'Is she at her office?'

'Yes.'

'I'll call her now, Jack.'

He dialled her number, and when the secretary put him through and she came on the line he heard at once how nervous she was.

'Oh, Philip, I've been trying to reach you.'

'I just got a call from the Mission. What is it, Karin?'

'Something's happened here and I . . . Could we possibly meet?'

'I could be at your office in about twenty minutes.'

'My car's downstairs. May I come to where you are? I'd like to get out of here.' She was very rushed and excited.

'I'm at home.' He gave her the address.

'Thank you, Philip. In a few minutes.'

He put the phone down. Something had happened. What? What the hell had shaken her?

He walked out to the foyer and stood waiting for her, and when the buzzer sounded from downstairs he pushed his button and said into the speaker: 'Yes?'

'It's me, Philip.'

'Come up.' He pushed the button to open the front door, and stood at his door to wait for her.

She came out of the elevator, looking left and right for him, and came hurrying down the hall.

He took her by the elbow and led her inside. 'What is it?'

'Someone's broken into my office.'

'Come and sit down.'

He led her down the hall to the living room. It wasn't just a simple break in; he could see that. Something damn serious had happened.

She sat in an armchair and he pulled one for himself up in front of it.

'Tell me about it, Karin.'

'Someone broke in while I was at court, while my secretary was at lunch. She didn't know anything had happened. I didn't know until I got back and went into my office.'

'What did they take?'

'An envelope. It was in my safe. They opened it, the safe. I don't know why they did it.'

'What was in the envelope?'

'I don't know. It was sealed. It was something I was holding for Herr Hess.'

Oh, Christ. 'How did you get it?'

'My father left it. Herr Hess gave it to him in nineteen forty-six, at Nuremberg, when he thought he might be executed. It was to be opened after his death, and my father held it in safekeeping. He left instructions for me to hold it.' With both hands she smoothed her hair back from her temples. 'It's been in the safe for years. All those years.'

'Did Hess tell your father what was in it?'

'No. I don't think so. I'm sure he didn't. My father said he didn't. He would have told me, if he'd known.'

'And you have no idea?'

'No. None.'

'Did your secretary know you had this envelope?'

'Greta? No.'

'You're sure she'd never seen it? Never knew anything about it?'

'I'm quite sure. It's been in the safe for thirty years. My

father never spoke of it, even to me. I knew nothing of it until I read the instructions he left when he died. I looked at it then, but I'd never thought of it again until yesterday.'

'What d'you mean? What did you do with it yesterday?'

'After you'd told me about the poisoning, I looked at it. I didn't open it, but I looked at it. On the front of the envelope were Herr Hess's instructions, in his handwriting and signed by him. It just said: "In the event of my death, it is my wish that you ensure that the contents of this envelope receive the fullest public attention." I was tempted to open it. I spoke to a friend about it, and he advised me to do nothing until it was confirmed that Herr Hess was dead.'

Quietly he said: 'So you did tell someone about Hess.' He knew it. God damn, he knew he'd seen something in her face this morning.

'Yes.' She looked away, then back at him. 'I'm sorry, Philip. but I was very upset when you left yesterday. I was worried that Herr Hess would die. Yes, I spoke to a friend about what had happened to him. But it wasn't relevant to tell you about him. He couldn't possibly have known anything about those bomb threats.'

'Why not?'

She stared at him. She could not believe he was suspicious of her friend. 'Because I say so.' Her lips pressed tight together.

'That's not a good reason, Karin.'

Very patiently she said: 'He wasn't there when those phone calls were made. He left Berlin yesterday morning.'

'Where did he go?'

'Please!' She came forward in the chair, hands on her knees. 'There's no possible reason to involve him in this.'

'All right, but humour me. Where did he go?'

'To New York.'

'Is he American?'

'Yes.'

He smiled. 'Then I guess he must be all right.' He thought of the blond man who'd been waiting in her office yesterday, the one she'd put her arms around.

Softening, smiling, she sat back. 'Oh, yes, of course.'

'Would I know him?'

'I doubt it.'

75

'Does he live in New York?'

'Yes.'

'Some of my best friends live in New York.'

'God. You never give up.' She laughed. 'I don't think he'd be one of your friends, Philip. He's a lawyer who's very active in civil rights.'

'He could still be a friend. I've got no prejudice against lawyers—or civil rights.'

'His name's Joseph Ross.'

He shook his head. 'Never heard of him. Is he blond?'

She leaned forward. 'How did you know that?'

'He was waiting for you when I left yesterday.'

'Yes! That's right. That was Joe.'

'Is that when you told him about Hess's envelope?'

'Yes. We were going to the airport, and I wanted to have his advice before he left.'

'Did you show him the envelope?'

'Yes. He read the instructions and said I should wait.'

'He reads German?'

'Yes. And speaks it and writes it. Is that so strange? So do you.'

'But I work here.'

'He comes here often.' She looked content. 'He likes it here.'

'I don't think I want to know any more.'

She chuckled.

'Why was his advice important? Is he an expert on Hess?'

'I thought you didn't want to know any more about him.'

'Not about him and you. Just about him.'

'I see. Yes, Joe's very interested in Herr Hess. He helped me work on the appeal. That's why he was here, as a matter of fact. He's been here for two weeks. We've been waiting for the Russians' answer.'

'He must've been disappointed.'

'Yes. Very. He was very angry.'

'I can imagine.' He nodded, looking sympathetic with Ross's disappointment. 'Does he know other people here?'

'Oh, yes, of course.'

'Other people working on the Hess appeal?'

'Yes. One or two.'

'But you don't think he could've spoken to any of them—

and told them about Hess's poisoning, or even the envelope?'

Her mouth opened. 'Why? Why should he?'

'For the same reason you told him about it, Karin. People like to share secrets.'

'No. Joe wouldn't have done that. He's much too discreet. And he didn't see anyone. I went with him to the airport from my office. We didn't meet anyone else.'

He didn't want to keep pressing her about Ross, to make her withdraw and close up, but he had to have answers.

'Did he make any phone calls from the airport?'

'No.' She began to shake her head, and stopped.

'Did he?'

'To his hotel, that's all. He'd forgotten a pair of shoes, and he phoned and asked them to send them to him.'

He shrugged as though the call to the hotel meant nothing. 'Did they have his shoes?'

'Yes. He told me they'd found them already.'

'Told you? Weren't you with him when he made the call?'

'My God!' Her head went back on the chair, and she stared up at the ceiling, then came forward, smiling at his persistence. 'No, I was *not* with him. I waited at the check-in counter. My God! What difference does it make?'

'None.' Christ, she didn't even begin to wonder about Ross. She was so far from suspecting him that she didn't even allow herself the ragged edge of a doubt. But it was probably as instinctive for her to trust people as it was for him to doubt them. They couldn't be more unlike, he and she. 'I'm a little surprised that Ross stayed in a hotel, since you're such good friends.'

'You said you didn't want to talk about him and me.'

'I did, didn't I? Where did he stay?'

'The Ambassador.'

'Not bad for a civil-rights lawyer.'

Slowly she shook her head at him, amused. She was a lot more relaxed now than when she came in.

'Karin, you're sure you didn't tell anyone else about Hess's envelope?'

'Quite sure.'

'Of course, your father might've, in all those years.' He was sure that hadn't happened. But he wanted to move her away from Ross, now he had all he needed. He didn't want to alarm her about her friend.

'I don't think he would have done that.'

'We'll see. What kind of envelope was it—letter size?'

'No. A big brown one, for documents.'

He sat thinking about it. What the hell could be in it? 'You didn't call the police about this, did you?'

'Not yet.'

'Don't. I'll talk to a friend, and he'll take care of it.' They couldn't have the police trampling all over this. This wasn't just a simple burglary. He knew it was much more than that. Much more.

Chapter 15

On the way back to her office, she drove Strang to the Mission, and he went straight upstairs and phoned Kluger.

'You're not calling about Karin Hartmann?' Kluger said. 'I haven't had time to get out the stuff on her.'

'I'm not calling for that. She's been to see me.' He told Kluger about the burglary.

'Jesus,' Kluger said softly. 'I'd like to know what was in that envelope.'

'Maybe we'll find out. I'd like you to check on a friend of hers, an American named Ross.'

'Ross? Are-oh-ess-ess?'

'Right. First name Joseph. He's a lawyer from New York. Works in civil rights, and he was helping Karin Hartmann with the Hess appeal. He was in Berlin for two weeks.'

'Why d'you want to know about him, Phil?'

'She told him about that Hess envelope yesterday. Showed it to him.'

'Oh?'

'Yes. He's the only one she showed it to. Then they went from her office to the airport, and he got a flight out. He went back to New York, she said. I'd like you to confirm that.'

'Okay. I'll let you know.'

'And something else. She says he didn't talk to anyone, but he phoned his hotel from the airport. He told her he'd forgotten a pair of shoes, and called the hotel to send them on to him. It was the Ambassador.'

'I'll check that.'

'I'm going to ask Langley to send me what they can get on him. Let me have yours as soon as you can, Dieter.'

'Okay. You think he's up to something?'

'Only he and Karin Hartmann knew about that envelope. What d'you think?'

'I'll call you as soon as I've got some answers.'

Strang was already getting up from his desk as he slapped the phone down, and he strode out of his office, down to the communications centre, to send a message to the CIA headquarters in Langley, Virginia.

*

Twenty-five minutes later his phone rang and he snatched it up. It was Kluger.

'I sent a man to the Ambassador,' he said. 'Ross didn't leave any shoes there and he didn't call them from the airport.'

'Terrific,' Strang said quietly. Who had Ross phoned, if it wasn't the Ambassador?

'He's mixed up in something, wouldn't you say?'

'I'd say so. Have you got a file on him?'

'No, but he's in Karin Hartmann's. He met her for the first time three years ago, at an international congress in Frankfurt. And he's come to Berlin every year since then, and spent time with her, usually three or four weeks.'

'Like that, is it?'

'Seems to be. And he's been here for two weeks, as she said.'

'Anything else?'

'That's all. He flew out yesterday, all right. To Frankfurt on Pan Am, and he got a Lufthansa flight at thirteen-thirty for New York.'

'Thanks, Dieter. I'm going to wait here till I get an answer from Langley. It might take a while, but if I get anything interesting on Ross and I need your help, where will you be?'

'At home.'

'I hope I won't interrupt anything.'

'Call after dinner. Everything'll be finished by then.'

'I hope so.'

He put the phone down and sat back. If Ross and Karin Hartmann were such good friends, why had he stayed at a hotel? Why hadn't he stayed with her? Not because she'd wanted to keep him away—no, not Karin. But if it had been Ross's idea, why? Had he been keeping things from her? Maybe. But what?

80

Chapter 16

At eight forty-two in the evening two policemen in a patrol car were driving in toward the centre of the city, along Königstrasse, from the southwest boundary, near the East German border.

Passing the area of the bathing beach at Wannsee, they went around a bend and their headlights lit up a black Volkswagen beetle parked on the road.

'God in heaven!' The police driver began braking. 'If they're going to do it in a damn Volkswagen, why can't they wait till they get off the road and park it out of the way somewhere?'

'Let's get the stupid bastards out of there,' the second policeman said.

They stopped the patrol car on the side of the road, behind the Volkswagen, and stepped out. Drawing their pistols, because one could never be sure, so close to the border, they walked carefully up to it, one on each side.

The driver looked through the back window and could see no couple on the seat, no bare legs in the dark. He shone his flashlight in.

'My God! There's something in there, Horst! On the floor!'

The second policeman flashed his light in from the other side, and saw the top of a man's head and his forehead protruding from a dark blanket that covered his body.

He tried the door, and it opened. Folding the seat down, he reached over it into the back and tossed the blanket off the face. He shone his flashlight on it.

Still looking through the window, the driver said: 'That's the one we're looking for, isn't it? The one from Spandau?'

'I think so.' The second policeman tossed the blanket all the way off, and in the flashlight beam there was dried blood all over the body—the suit jacket, shirt, tie, and most of the trousers all the same rusty colour. It looked as though the man had been stabbed many times, in the chest and stomach.

'Wait, Horst! I'll get the photo.' The driver ran to their car and came running back with the picture of Lichti that had come from the Americans.

'Yes, it's the man, Horst. It's Lichti. I'll go and call in.'

'Tell them he's dead.' The second policeman held his cap on as he backed out of the Volkswagen with his head bent. 'Tell them he won't be answering any questions.'

Chapter 17

At nine o'clock the information from Langley had not arrived, and Strang sat waiting in his office. He was sure Ross was involved in this, and he wanted to know more about him, to find a lead.

The phone rang and he snatched it up.

'Yes?'

'Mr Strang?'

'Yes.'

'Colonel Goodblood.'

'Hello, Colonel.'

'Thought you'd be interested to know the civil police have found Lichti. Dead.'

'Oh, for God's sake. Where?'

'Out near Wannsee. His car was parked on the road and he was in the back. He'd been stabbed eleven times. His watch and wallet were gone.'

'You don't think that's why he was killed, do you?'

'No. Someone wanted to keep him quiet. No question in my mind about it.'

'Dammit!'

'I agree. But we'll continue to work on his background. Maybe we'll turn something up. I'll let you know if we do.'

'Thanks, Colonel.'

*

It was almost ten o'clock when a messenger came up from the communications room with a message from Langley: the information that had been gathered on Ross. All of it had come from the FBI and New York City police, and there was nothing but routine biographical details. Nothing illegal or even dubious in his background.

But he had changed his name, legally, in 1970, from Rauss to Ross. He had been born in New York City on September 4,

1948, to Otto and Trudi Rauss, who had arrived from Germany through the Port of New York as immigrants on March 11, 1948. The parents had both been born in Munich: Otto on August 7, 1910; Trudi, on October 29, 1913.

Joseph Rauss had received primary and secondary education at public schools in New York, and had graduated in law from New York University. In October, 1973, he had established his law practice, working from an office on East 48th Street, New York. He was known to accept cases primarily involving civil rights, and often to represent tenants in landlord-tenant disputes. He was unmarried and lived alone in an apartment on East 52nd Street.

His mother had died on February 15, 1968. On March 31, 1970, his father had sold the gourmet food store he had owned for twenty years and retired to a country house he had bought near Kingston, Province of Ontario, Canada, where his social security retirement check was sent each month.

Strang pushed the short strip of teletype paper aside. It wasn't much. But what there was might be interesting. It might be.

He pulled the phone across and dialled Kluger's home.

'I've got the stuff on Ross, Dieter.'

'Anything interesting?'

'No—except that he changed his name from Rauss.'

'The bastard. Honest German name wasn't good enough for him.'

'It was good enough for his father—and I'd like you to check on him. Otto Rauss, born in Munich, August seven, nineteen-ten. Look at the mother too: Trudi, also born in Munich—October twenty-nine, nineteen-thirteen.'

'Okay. When d'you want this stuff, Phil?'

'Now.'

'I'll call you back.'

*

Ninety minutes later he was still waiting for Kluger's call. The phone rang, and it was the guard at the entrance to the compound.

'There's a Mr Kluger here, who wants to come up and see you, sir. Is he all right?'

'He is if he's Mr Kluger. Let me talk to him.'

'Yes, sir.'

Kluger came on the phone.

'What're you doing here, Dieter?'

'I've got some stuff. I didn't want to give it to you on the phone.'

'Is it hot?'

'Damn right it is.' Kluger sounded excited.

'Put the guard back on.'

'Hello, sir,' the guard said.

'All right. It's Mr Kluger.'

'Someone'll bring him up right away, sir.'

He put the phone down and sat back in his chair, waiting to hear what Kluger had found.

There was a knock at the door and he called: 'Yes!'

A security guard opened the door. 'Here's Mr Kluger, sir.' He held the door to let Kluger through.

Getting up, Strang nodded to the guard, and they waited for him to get out and shut the door.

'What is it, Dieter? Sit down.' He slapped a hand on the back of a chair beside the desk.

Kluger was too excited to sit down. 'Ross's father. D'you know what he was?' He tugged a folded sheet of white paper from his pocket.

'Tell me.'

'Hess's adjutant.'

Strang stared at him, and sat on the edge of the desk. 'I'll be damned.' He got up and walked around to his chair. He couldn't believe it. 'There's no doubt about this, is there?'

'Of course there's not.' Kluger sat in the chair, satisfied with Strang's reaction. It was why he had not wanted to tell him on the phone. He had had to come, to see the effect. He read notes he had written on the sheet of paper: 'He joined the army in nineteen thirty-two and became Hess's adjutant in thirty-six. He was made a captain then.'

Strang saw how pleased Kluger was with what he'd found. He was right to be pleased. It was fantastic.

'He was his adjutant right through to May tenth, forty-one, when Hess flew to Britain,' Kluger said.

'I can't believe it,' Strang muttered.

'He was arrested after Hess flew off—Hitler arrested a lot of Hess's staff then—and he was in jail for two years. Then they released him—in August, forty-three—and sent him to the Russian front. The Russians captured him in February, forty-five. He was repatriated in July, forty-seven, and went home to Munich. He and his wife went to the States in March, forty-eight—you know that, I guess.'

Strang nodded.

'There's nothing on the wife. They were married in thirty-eight, and she never left Munich—till forty-eight.'

'We don't need anything on the wife, Dieter. What you've found on Rauss is more than enough.'

'What d'you think it means?'

'It connects Ross solidly to Hess. I think he knows something about what's happened to Hess—and I'm sure he knows something about that burglary at Karin Hartmann's.' Strang rose. 'I'm going to talk to him about it.'

'How?'

'I'm going to New York.'

Friday
April 29, 1977

Chapter 18

He landed at Kennedy at one twenty-seven in the afternoon. As soon as he cleared his bag through customs he carried it to a pay phone and, with it at his feet, found the number for Ross's office, and dialled it.

There was no answer. He stood listening to the phone ring twelve times, and there was no answer.

He phoned Ross's apartment and there was no answer.

Damn! He hung the phone up, hoping Ross hadn't shut down his office and gone out of town for the weekend. He hoped it was just that he hadn't come back from lunch yet.

He carried his bag out of the terminal, into the thin sunlight that was shining through haze. It was heavy and humid. He got into a taxi and rode downtown, sitting in the middle of the back seat with both windows half open. He felt he needed air. Last night he hadn't slept well, thinking about Ross, and he'd tried to make up for it on the plane, napping for fifty minutes, but that had made him feel worse, with the beginning of a headache.

He got out of the cab on Forty-Eighth Street at Fifth Avenue, outside the building where Ross had his office. It was an old building and Ross's office was on the fourth floor.

The office door had a pane of pebbled glass in the upper half. It was locked. Strang rapped on the glass and listened. There was no sound. Now it was almost two-thirty. Even if Ross hadn't come back from lunch yet, he must have a secretary, and she should be back. Unless they'd taken the afternoon off together.

From the office across the hall there was the sound of typing and music. He opened the door and looked in. A woman with long black hair was typing at a desk, a radio near her elbow. She looked up and smiled, turning the radio down.

'Hi! What can I do for you?'

'I'm looking for Mr Ross.' He nodded across the hall.

'Isn't he in there?'

'No. The door's locked.'

'He's working today. I know that. I saw him this morning.'

'Does he have a secretary?'

'Yes.' She looked at her watch. 'She should be back from lunch by now. But it's Friday. Sometimes they leave early on Friday. I should work for a lawyer.'

'You should.' He started to back out.

'If I see them, can I tell them anything?'

'No, thanks.'

'Okay.' She smiled. 'Sorry.'

He walked back to the elevators. They were old but they were automatic; there were no operators who might have seen Ross go out. And in the lobby there was no doorman or even a desk for one.

Another cab took him over to East Fifty-second Street. Ross's apartment building was at the corner of Second Avenue, much newer than his office building.

Strang walked down three steps from the sidewalk, and a doorman pulled open a glass door for him.

'Yes, sir. Who d'you want to see?'

'Mr Ross.'

'I'm not sure he's in. I'll check.' The doorman lifted a phone from a lighted name panel, and pushed a button beside Ross's name. It was an apartment on the sixth floor.

The doorman stood listening to the phone. He pushed the button again, and held his finger on it longer this time. Shaking his head, he set the phone down. 'Sorry, sir. There's no answer.'

Strang stood there with his bag on the floor, and looked out at the street as though he expected Ross to come in. 'He was supposed to be here. He's been away for a couple of weeks.'

'Yes, sir, he has. In Europe, I believe.'

'Yes. He should've come back the day before yesterday.'

'Oh, he did. He's back, sir.' The doorman lifted his cap up, smoothed his hair back, and lowered the cap again. 'I saw him go out this morning. Was he supposed to be here now to meet you?'

'Yes.'

'Have you tried his office?'

'Yes. There's no one there.'

The doorman turned his lips down and shrugged. 'I can't help you, sir.'

'I hope I haven't missed him. There's no chance he came back early and left town for the weekend, is there? That's what I'm afraid might've happened.'

'No, sir.' Firmly the doorman shook his head. 'I've been here since eight this morning, and he hasn't come back. If you want to wait here, you're welcome.' He held out a hand to an avocado vinyl banquette against the wall.

'Thanks, but I'll go back and try his office. Maybe he's back from lunch.'

The doorman nodded.

There was no taxi on the street, and Strang carried his bag to the corner of Second Avenue, feeling uncomfortable and clammy now, from the weight and awkwardness of the bag in the damp heat, not enough sleep, and the creased untidiness of the clothes he had sat in all through the flight.

At the corner of the avenue he got into another taxi and rode back to Ross's office building. If Ross wasn't back there by now, his secretary should be. If not. He didn't know, if not.

Again he went up to the fourth floor and tried Ross's office. It was still locked. The sound of typing still came through the music from the office across the hall. He laid his bag down and looked back and forth along the hall. There was no one. The lock on Ross's door was old and simple. Dammit, he had to be sure it was empty in there.

He took out his wallet. He never carried credit cards, but he had a thin plastic strip that he had used once or twice on doors like Ross's. He pushed the plastic in, between the door and the frame, around the hasp of the lock, and sprang it open. He carried his bag inside.

The secretary was there, on the carpet. On her back behind her desk, and her chair was tipped over, half underneath her. It looked as though she had gone over backwards on it. She had been shot in the head. In the forehead, it seemed, and the rest of her head was a bloody, bony mess.

The door behind her was wide open, and there was a man in there, in a chair behind a desk, his head back so that Strang could see only his neck and the underside of his jaw. He was barechested.

Strang walked in and looked at the face that was turned up to the ceiling. It was Ross, all right. The blond man he'd seen in Karjn Hartmann's office. He was tied in the swivel chair, arms dragged back and tied by the wrists behind it, ankles lashed to the steel base. A loosened gag hung around his neck, a twisted strip of orange and white stripes that had been ripped from a shirt on the floor beside the desk.

Ross had been shot twice in the chest, in the heart area. But first he had been tortured. Around both nipples, and precisely on the right one, so it was almost obliterated, were neat round burns, the flesh raised and red around them. They looked like cigarette burns, four or five around each nipple, and the one that had almost burned away the right.

Strang stood looking at the body. He looked back at the secretary out there on the floor. Ross and the poor damn secretary too. But she'd just been shot, not tortured. Ross, with a gag over his mouth, had been tortured. Why? Someone had tortured this poor bastard, keeping him quiet with the gag until he was ready to talk, then taken the gag down to let him tell whatever it was. Then shot him. Something like that. Probably more than one had done it. One to tie him, one to make sure he tried nothing while he was being tied.

But why? What had they wanted to know? And why hadn't anyone heard the shots? Because these people must have used silenced weapons. They were pros.

He looked at the desk drawers. They were all shut, and the top of the desk looked neat. In a corner of the office was a small box safe, shut. Books in the shelves were undisturbed. Nothing in the office seemed to have been touched. If Ross had been made to give them anything, there was no sign that it had been in this room.

Quietly Strang walked back to the outer office, picked up his bag, and stood listening beside the glass of the front door. There was no sound out in the hall. Holding the hem of his jacket in his hand, to cover the doorknob, he eased the door open and stood listening, wiping the outside knob. There was only the music from the office across the hall.

He stepped outside and gently shut the door. At the end of the hall, beside the elevators, was a fire exit. He went through and trotted down the stairs, not to risk having anyone see him now in the elevator. He didn't want any complications now.

Along the street was a pay phone, and he called an unlisted New York number, for a firm that was a CIA cover.

At once a man answered: 'Watchman Consultants.'

'My name's Strang. From the Berlin station. I flew in this afternoon and I've run into a problem.' He told what he had found in Ross's office.

'Did you touch anything in there?'

'No. Just the outside doorknob, and I wiped that.'

'We'll go over and make sure everything's clean, then give the police a call.'

'Not yet. I'm going up to Canada, to talk to Ross's father, and I don't want the police to get to him first and tell him his son's dead. I don't want him to have time to think about it before I talk to him.'

'All right. We'll wait twenty-four hours. Will that be time enough?'

'Yes. I'm going up there as soon as I can get a flight. But I'd like you to call first, and tell him I'm on my way. I want to be sure he's there and healthy, before I go. His name's Otto Rauss, and he lives near Kingston, Ontario. Tell him I've got to talk to him about government business.'

'We'll take care of it. What's your phone number there?'

Strang told him. 'It's a pay phone. If it's busy, keep trying.'

'Right. I'll check on flight times, so I can tell Rauss when to expect you. Won't be long.'

Strang hung up and stood beside the phone. He wanted to hear it ring, to know that old Rauss was safe. He didn't know why they'd killed Ross, but they could've killed his father too. He hoped not. But he didn't know why any of this had happened.

No one came to use the phone, and in seven minutes it rang. He snatched it off. 'Yes?'

'Who is this?'

'Strang.'

'It's all right. Rauss is there and he'll be expecting you. He sounded a little surprised, but he didn't ask any questions.'

'Good.'

'You can get a flight from Kennedy at five thirty-five. Air Canada. It'll get you to Toronto at seven, and you'll have to drive from there. There'll be a rented car waiting for you at Toronto. It'll be about two hours to Rauss's place. There'll be a message at the airline counter when you land, with directions for getting there.'

'Terrific.'

He hoped Rauss knew what his son had been doing, and would talk about it.

Chapter 19

From Toronto the highway ran east along the shore of Lake Ontario, and Kingston was about one hundred and forty miles along it. Strang drove the rented Chevrolet up the wide concrete strip, past small lakeside towns.

Rauss lived about ten miles outside Kingston. Beside the highway was a white mailbox with his name on it in black, and when Strang's headlights lit it up he slowed and turned beside it, down a gravel road through trees, toward the lake.

He took two shallow bends in the road, and came out into a wide clearing. In the middle of it was a white ranch-style bungalow. Lights were on at all the windows, and above the porch.

A station wagon was on the grass near the house, and Strang swung the Chevrolet in beside it. He climbed out and breathed the air. He didn't think he'd ever smelled air so fresh. In the glow of light from the house he could see the slope of the ground toward the lake. Across the water were the lights of houses on an island.

A screen door opened, the spring twanging, and in the porchlight was a bald man with a fringe of white hair, in a white turtleneck sweater.

'Mr Strang?'

'That's right.' He went up two steps to the porch. 'Mr Rauss?'

'Yes. Otto Rauss.' There was only a very faint German accent.

'I hope this isn't inconvenient.' Strang held out his hand.

'No. Not inconvenient at all.' But Rauss looked cautious and unsure. When he shook hands he did it very carefully, placing his fingers in around Strang's hand, as though he did not want them gripped, and when he took his hand away he clenched his fist lightly, curling the fingertips out of sight.

He pulled open the screen door and stood back for Strang to go in, straight into a living room. The furniture was all solid-

95

looking: two long couches and two big armchairs, all upholstered in brown wool fabric. A wide carpet of dark green covered the floor. Strang smelled old pipe smoke. It all looked and smelled like the smoking room of a men's club with a declining membership.

Rauss went to the armchair that was more worn than the other, his favourite chair. A pipe rack and tobacco jar were beside it on a table. 'Will you be seated?' He held out a hand to the couches, careful to keep it turned so his nails would not show.

Strang sat back in one of the couches. God, he was tired of sitting today.

'May I offer you something—coffee or anything?'

'No, thanks.'

'Have you come from Washington?'

'New York.'

'But you're from the federal government?'

'Yes.'

'The man who phoned didn't say what it was about. I've been wondering if there was a problem with my social security. I don't see how anything can be wrong.' Rauss was concerned about the retirement check.

'No, it's not the social security, Mr Rauss.'

'It's not?' Rauss looked relieved, but curious.

'No. I have to tell you your son's dead.'

Rauss stared at him and settled further back in his chair, opening his hands and curling his fingers over the arms.

Strang saw that all the fingernails were gone. There were just old twisted scar tissues where they had been.

It was quiet in the room.

'Was it an accident?' Rauss's voice sounded no different than it had before. Except for the fingers tensed on the chair arms, there was no sign that he had been hurt.

'No. He was shot in his office.'

'Shot? Was it one of those stupid robberies?'

'I don't know. It only happened today—probably some time this morning. There hasn't been an investigation yet.'

Rauss looked at the pipe rack beside him. He selected a pipe and sat looking at it in his hand, rubbing the smooth brown of the bowl between his thumb and forefinger.

'He came back from Berlin the day before yesterday,' Strang said.

Rauss sat looking at the pipe, rubbing the briar with the ball of his thumb.

'He was there for two weeks. D'you know what he was doing there, Mr Rauss?'

Slowly Rauss shook his head. 'No.' He set the pipe back in the rack. 'He often went there. We haven't spoken to each other for five years. We haven't been in touch at all. I almost phoned him, several times—many times—but I never did. And he didn't phone me. We're both very proud. *Were* both. But I always told myself it wouldn't go on like that forever, and we would talk to each other again. Now we never will.'

'Why did you stop speaking to each other?'

'It was my fault. I objected to something he was doing.'

'To changing his name?'

'Oh, no! No. That was a silly little thing. He did that because he thought Ross would be a better name for business. He's very conventional, in many ways.' Rauss had not adjusted to the past tense for his son. 'I didn't like it, but if he wanted to do it . . .' He shrugged.

'What was it you objected to?'

'Ah!' Grunting, Rauss sat back in the chair, stretching his shoulders and taking a deep breath, his chest rising in the white sweater. 'His friends in Germany. I objected to them. We argued about them several times.'

'What was it about his friends?'

'Their politics. They were Nazis. The National Party. Joseph was a strong supporter of those people. For years. I saw it when it began, when he came back from his first visit to Germany, when he was a student, ten years ago. We argued about it then.'

It was interesting. Ross and the Nationalists. So the phone call he'd made from the airport, which hadn't been to the Ambassador for his shoes, had been to the Nationalists, to tell them about Hess's envelope? Was that it? No doubt about it.

'Are you sure he kept his connection with the Nationalists, Mr Rauss?'

'Yes. He became even stronger and stronger for them. If he'd changed, we would have been talking again. He would have told me, if he'd changed his opinion.' Rauss shook his head. 'Joseph would never have changed.'

'Why did you object?'

'Is it necessary to ask, Mr Strang? I said they're Nazis. Isn't that enough reason?'

'You were a Party member yourself once, weren't you?'

Rauss looked guarded. 'I? I don't know why you would think that.'

'You were Rudolf Hess's adjutant. He wouldn't have had you so close unless you were a Party man.'

'Ah!' Slowly Rauss nodded. 'So you know that about me. Yes, I was a Party member. I joined when I was very young— much younger than Joseph. I think that you have to be young to believe in something like Nazism. Young or unrealistic.'

'When did you become realistic?'

'When I was still quite young. The Gestapo showed me reality.'

'The Gestapo?'

'They were the secret police we had in Germany under Hitler.'

'I know. What did they do to you?'

'Do?' Gently Rauss smiled. 'They had long talks with me, after *Der Stellvertreter* flew to Scotland.'

Der Stellvertreter. The Deputy. Strang couldn't believe he'd heard it, the quick word of German. He was sitting here, in this quiet Canadian house beside a lake, listening to an old man who still spoke of Hess as Hitler's deputy, when Hitler had been dead and Hess in prison all these years.

'Yes, I had long talks with the Gestapo. In a few weeks I told them the story of my five years as his adjutant. My God, they were persuasive.'

*

In the summer of 1936 Rauss was a lieutenant in the First Bavarian Infantry Regiment, in which Rudolf Hess had served for the first two years of World War One. Rauss's commanding officer, Colonel Boch, had been with Hess then, and had kept his friendship through the twenty years since they were together in the trenches. When Hess asked Boch if he could recommend an officer to serve as his adjutant, Boch at once named Rauss.

Rauss went to the big compound, the Rudolf Hess Settlement, which had just been built for Hess and his expanding staff at Pullach, ten kilometres south of Munich. It was a group of buildings, one-storey and two-storey, and some bunkers, all surrounded by a wall almost two kilometres around. Hess liked him at once, and had him promoted to captain.

Of all Hess's staff, including Martin Bormann, the chief of staff, Rauss was closest. He went almost everywhere with Hess: to conferences with Hitler, to all the public rallies where Hess spoke, even to Hess's home in the country for weekends.

On March 12, 1938, German troops occupied Austria, and on the same day Hess took Rauss with him and flew to Vienna to sign the declaration that united Germany and Austria.

At the huge Hitler Youth Rally at Nuremberg, on September 12, 1938, Rauss was in the group that stood around Hitler, Hess, and Baldur von Schirach on the reviewing stand.

Seventeen days later, Rauss was with Hess when he stood behind Hitler at the signing of the Munich agreement with the British and French prime ministers, Chamberlain and Daladier, which Chamberlain told the British would give 'peace in our time.'

World War Two broke out the next year, and in the summer of 1940 the German Army cut through France, and the British evacuated their troops from the beaches of Dunkirk. On June 21, 1940, when Hitler went to sign the French armistice in a railroad sleeping-car, in the forest at Compiègne, and Hess went with him, Rauss was close beside Hess.

A few days later, sitting in his office at Pullach with Rauss, Hess said: 'This is the beginning. Now that we have this armistice with the French, we can begin to develop co-operation with them.'

'But there is still England, Herr Minister,' Rauss said.

Hess, with his thick black eyebrows, blue eyes set back deep under them, wore a grey Party uniform, a black swastika on a red band on his left sleeve.

'We will make peace with the British, Rauss, just as we did with the French. We must do that. We must stand together, all of us, against Bolshevism. The Communists are the true enemies of Europe. The British must be made to see this. I am sure they will.'

'They are a tough and stubborn people.'

'But not foolish. They can not believe that we are their true enemies. The Führer allowed the British to escape from Dunkirk precisely because he did not want to destroy the possibility of an understanding with them, and an alliance against Communism. They will realise that when it is explained. You will see.' Hess nodded. 'The British will understand the vital need for an alliance. They will see the wisdom of it.'

Suddenly it all sounded like much more than speculation, and Rauss was curious. He knew of no plan to meet with the British and propose an alliance, but Hess was speaking of it so confidently, as something that was going to happen. Rauss wondered if Hitler and Hess had made secret plans for negotiations with the British. But there would be no point in asking. If Hess had not told him, it was because it was not time for him to know. When the time came, Hess would certainly tell him.

Hess sat smiling at him, his thin lips tight, and Rauss was sure something was being planned. Hess had said enough to make him wonder, and now Hess was amused, knowing that he was curious.

And as he thought about it Rauss didn't know why it should surprise him that an anti-Communist alliance with the British might be considered. It had probably been part of Hitler's master plan for a long time. For years, in private and public, Hess had spoken of the Communists as the main enemy, and Hitler's view was the same. But it was exciting to think that there might actually be such a plan.

A few weeks later, near the end of August, Rauss went with Hess to Augsburg, to the Messerschmitt aircraft plant, to talk to Professor Willi Messerschmitt about his latest fighter, the twin-engine Messerschmitt 110.

Sitting in the designer's office, watching Hess's face as Messerschmitt told him about the performance of the 110, Rauss was sure something was happening. Hess was planning something. What he could see in Hess's face was more than just pleasure from talking of airplanes, though he knew that gave Hess great pleasure. Hess had often told him how much he regretted that when he graduated as an Imperial Flying Corps pilot, in 1918, World War One was almost over, and he had made only a few combat flights in the last few days before the armistice. He had kept flying as a hobby through the twenties and thirties, and had won a racing trophy in 1934. Then Hitler had grounded him; he said Hess was too valuable to risk his life flying his own airplane. When war was declared, in September, 1939, Hess had asked Hitler to allow him to join the Luftwaffe, but Hitler again told him he was too valuable. Hess had given his word that he would not fly for a year.

But in a few days that year would be ended, and Rauss sat trying to imagine what could be in Hess's mind. Why was he here, asking about the new fighter?

When they were driving the forty kilometres back to Pullach that day, sitting in the back of a Mercedes, a glass screen between them and the chauffeur, Rauss felt Hess watching him, and turned. Hess was smiling.

'You're wondering what it's all about, aren't you?' Hess said.

'Yes, sir. I admit it.'

'Patience, Rauss. Have patience, and you will see.'

Ten days later, in the first week of September, Hess called Rauss to his office early in the morning, and said: 'We're going back to see Messerschmitt this afternoon.'

'Yes, Herr Minister.'

'You're still wondering about it?'

'Yes, I am.'

'I'm going to fly again, Rauss.' Hess smiled and showed the gap between his front teeth. He rarely smiled wide enough to show his teeth.

'But it is forbidden by the Führer, sir!'

'I promised him I would not fly for a year. The year expired yesterday. Today I fly.'

'Does he know of your intention?'

'No, Rauss, he does not know of it. It will be our secret, yours and mine—and I have told you of it precisely because I did not wish a discussion like this in front of Messerschmitt this afternoon. He is unaware that the Führer disapproves of my flying—and he will remain unaware. I do not wish to cause him embarrassment.'

'I understand, Herr Minister.'

In the afternoon they drove to Augsburg, and Hess flew a Messerschmitt 109, the fast single-engine fighter that was the main strength of the Luftwaffe fighter squadrons, and was now flying against Royal Air Force Spitfires and Hurricanes in the Battle of Britain.

In the next three months they went back to Augsburg ten or twelve times, and always Hess flew the 109.

Then, when he felt comfortable being back in the air, he took up the twin-engine fighter, the 110.

When he landed he climbed out of the cockpit and walked to the car, where Rauss had been standing with Messerschmitt, watching him. They drove back to Messerschmitt's office and sat down.

'I have some questions about your plane, Herr Professor,' Hess said.

'Yes? I shall do my best to answer.'

'What is the range?'

'Operational range, about nine hundred kilometres.'

'I have wondered if it might be possible to fit extra fuel tanks, to increase the range, without detracting from its manoeuvreability.'

'Yes, certainly, it could be done—and there would be no loss of airworthiness.'

'Where could such tanks be placed?' Hess sat with his knees crossed, arms folded, watching Messerschmitt.

Rauss was certain there was more than technical curiosity here. Messerschmitt, sitting making calculations with a pencil, was conscious of nothing but the question and the answer he would give, the problem and the solution, but Rauss knew Hess had a reason. Hess always had a reason.

'I could fit two seven-hundred-litre tanks.' Messerschmitt tapped his notepad with the end of his pencil. 'One in each wing. That would increase the range to about sixteen hundred kilometres, depending on speed and altitude.'

'And a more powerful radio, to receive navigational signals at the increased range. Could that be fitted?'

'Yes, of course.'

Hess's face showed nothing but total absorption with the technical problems. 'Could all this be done in a few days? I should like to fly the plane when this equipment has been fitted, to test its responses. Could it be done in two days?'

'Yes,' Messerschmitt said slowly. It had been in his mind, and now he decided to ask: 'May I enquire what is the reason, Herr Minister?'

'I might have need for a plane with such a range. There is a good reason.'

Messerschmitt asked nothing more.

When they got back to Pullach, Hess took Rauss to his office and, smiling, said: 'Have you guessed?'

'No, sir.'

'I'm going to fly to Britain, to take the proposal for the alliance against the Soviet Union.'

Rauss went numb.

Hess sat smiling with his lips together. 'It has been planned. I shall fly to Scotland. I can do it in the Messerschmitt, a flight of fifteen hundred kilometres, Rauss. I shall fly to Dungavel, near Glasgow, the country home of the Duke of Hamilton. He will take me to the most influential men in Britain. He has access to all of them in London, even Churchill and King George.'

'Does he know you're coming, sir?'

'No. But he has been informed by letter that a meeting between him and a German representative is desirable.' Three months ago, Albrecht Haushofer, son of Professor Karl Haushofer, who had taught Hess at Munich University, had sent a letter through a mutual friend in neutral Lisbon to the Duke of Hamilton, whom Albrecht had known before the war, suggesting a meeting in Lisbon. Hitler had approved the sending of the letter. 'The Führer agreed to that approach, you will be reassured to know.'

'And your flight is by the Führer's order, sir?' It was incredible. Rauss could not believe Hitler would want Hess to do this.

'Not by his order, but it certainly will be with his approval when he knows it has been done. I assure you of that.'

'I don't know what to say, sir.'

'Say nothing, for the moment. When the time comes, I will tell you what to say, and to whom.' Smiling, Hess said gently: 'And don't worry.'

A few days later Hess flew the twin-engine fighter with the long-range tanks. In the next few weeks he flew it several times. In January, 1941, he even tried a maximum-range flight, simulating the one he would make to Scotland, but a fault developed in an aileron, and the Messerschmitt could not climb to the altitude he needed for crossing the German coast. Two months later he tried again, flew into bad weather, and had to land again at Augsburg.

Early on the morning of May 10 he phoned Rauss at home, told him to confirm that the flying weather that day would be favourable, as it had been predicted the day before, and told him to be ready to drive to Augsburg in the afternoon.

'I feel this will be the day,' Hess said.

They drove in the Mercedes from Hess's home, outside Munich: an easy hour's drive to the Messerschmitt plant. On the way they stopped and walked together in the woods west of Munich. Hess was wearing a civilian jacket, but the rest was Luftwaffe officer's uniform: light blue shirt, dark blue tie, blue-grey breeches, and flying boots. From the side pocket of his jacket he took two sealed envelopes. He handed Rauss the first one. It was addressed to Adolf Hitler.

Rauss felt sweat running from his armpits under his uniform jacket.

'And these are your instructions.' Hess gave him the second envelope. 'Wait three hours, and if I have not returned, open the envelope, and follow them precisely.'

'Yes, Herr Minister.'

They drove on to the Messerschmitt plant, and while the fighter's fuel tanks were being filled Hess changed into a blue-grey Luftwaffe jacket with captain's rank badges on the shoulder straps and collar patches. He pulled on a fur-lined brown leather flying suit, and with a leather flying helmet in his hand he walked with Rauss out to the plane. It was five-forty in the evening, and the fighter was ready.

'Goodbye, Rauss. Thank you for your service through these five years.' Hess held out his hand.

'It has been an honour, Herr Minister. I wish you good fortune.'

'Thank you.' Hess pulled on the flying helmet, climbed up

on the wing, and swung his legs over into the cockpit. A mechanic on the wing closed the canopy.

Rauss stood back. One propeller began turning, then the other, and the fighter rolled to the end of the runway.

It took off, and Rauss stood watching it until it was out of sight in the sky about the field.

He waited exactly three hours, then opened his instructions. Hess had written that he was to phone the Luftwaffe headquarters in Berlin at nine o'clock, and have them beam a radio homing signal to Dungavel Hill, thirty kilometres south of Glasgow. Then he was to take the other envelope to Hitler at his headquarters in Berchtesgaden, in the Bavarian Alps, south of Salzburg.

Rauss phoned Berlin, and identified himself to the duty officer at Luftwaffe headquarters.

'I have instructions for you from the Deputy Führer,' Rauss said, and asked him for the beam to be transmitted.

'May I ask why this is needed?' the Luftwaffe officer said.

'The reason is secret.'

'We are sending a big bomber force over there later tonight. There can be no radio signal that might alert the British in the period before the bombers arrive. We can transmit only until ten o'clock.'

'If that is the best you can do, we shall have to be content.'

'We'll begin the transmission immediately.'

'Thank you.'

Rauss walked to the Mercedes, told the chauffeur to drive him to the Munich railroad station, and climbed into the back. All the way to Munich he sat in a corner of the seat, wondering what would happen when he handed Hitler the letter.

Hess's private railroad car was kept at Munich, and Rauss ordered it coupled to the overnight train for Berchtesgaden, which would leave at midnight. For twenty minutes he walked back and forth on the street in front of the station, the letter to Hitler in his righthand pocket. Then he went in and climbed aboard the train.

For most of the seven-hour ride southeast to Berchtesgaden he lay in one of the berths in Hess's car, with the lights out and the blackout curtains drawn back from the windows, staring out.

D* 105

At seven in the morning he stepped down to the platform at Berchtesgaden and phoned Hitler's compound, the Berghof. He asked an aide for an appointment with Hitler at once, and for a car to take him from the station.

'Why do you wish this urgent appointment with the Führer?' the aide said.

'It's for him alone. I'm afraid I can't tell you.'

'Then I'm afraid I can't arrange it.'

'You might regret it.'

'Yes, I might.' The aide was constantly being told he might be sorry if he didn't give someone or other an instant audience with Hitler. 'However, I will send a car for you now, Captain. When you arrive, I will do what I can to get you to the Führer as soon as possible.'

The car arrived from the Berghof, and Rauss sat in the back, staring out at the trees as it climbed the twisting road to Hitler's mountain estate.

When he arrived at Hitler's villa he found the aide he had spoken to from the station, and again told him it was urgent that he see Hitler as soon as possible. Now he said he had a vital message from Hess.

He waited almost three hours until Hitler, black hair combed to the side over his forehead, came downstairs in dark trousers and a grey Party uniform jacket with a swastika armband. The aide whispered something to him and, glancing at Rauss standing at attention on the other side of the anteroom, Hitler nodded and walked into his study.

The aide hurried across the room. 'The Führer will see you now.'

Rauss's palms were wet. His shirt was sticking to his back. He was shown into Hitler's study, and the aide came in behind him. Sliding picture windows were along one side of the room, sun shining through, and outside there was sunlight on the pine trees over the mountaintops. Hitler's great desk was in front of the windows.

Hitler was beside the desk, hands behind his back, looking at a big world globe. He looked across the room.

'Yes, come in, Rauss, come in.' Briefly he flicked a hand, beckoning.

Rauss marched across the deep carpet and came to attention

a pace from Hitler, right arm up in the Nazi salute. 'I have been instructed by Minister Hess to deliver this to your hand, Mein Führer.' He handed Hitler the letter.

Hitler picked up his glasses from the side of the desk, carefully slid them on, and opened the envelope.

Rauss watched his face as he read the letter. He saw the jaw muscles tighten, the corners of the mouth turn down under the square black moustache. It was warm in the room, with the sunlight through the big windows. Rauss smelled the heavy scent from a bowl of flowers on the desk. He could feel the aide standing somewhere close to him.

Still staring at the letter, his voice low and cold, Hitler said: 'Where is Hess now?'

'I do not know with certainty, Mein Führer. Yesterday evening, at precisely a quarter to six, he flew from Augsburg. He intended to go to Scotland, to the Duke of Hamilton.'

'At this particular moment in the war, that could be a most hazardous escapade.' Hitler's eyes stared through the glasses at Rauss.

'Yes, Mein Führer.'

Hitler stood reading the letter again. Hess had written of the technical details of the flight, and how difficult it would be, then explained that his mission was intended to implement Hitler's old theory of an alliance with England against Communism, to control Europe and later the world.

He began to read it aloud, very quietly, and Rauss, sweating, still at attention in the sunlight from the window, heard '. . . and if this project—which, I admit, may have only a small chance of success—ends in failure and the Fates decide against me, this can have no detrimental results either for you or for Germany: it will always be possible for you to deny all responsibility. Simply say that I was out of my mind . . .'

Hitler laid the letter on the side of the desk, not looking at Rauss. Taking off his glasses, he turned to the window and stood looking out at the mountains, hands behind his back.

The door opened and Hitler's mistress, Eva Braun, took a step into the room. She felt the tension and stopped with her hand on the doorknob.

'Lunch is ready,' she said.

Still staring out of the window, Hitler nodded.

Eva Braun backed out and closed the door.

For a few moments more Hitler stood at the window, then turned and walked past Rauss, across the big room, and out of the door.

'Come on,' the aide muttered to Rauss. 'Come and join us for lunch.'

They walked out. Men and women were coming from other parts of the villa, moving to the dining room. There were members of Hitler's staff and some officials who were there for a conference. Dr Fritz Todt, the Minister for Armaments, was there; Ernst Udet, a Luftwaffe general; Martin Bormann; and Karl Bodenschatz, adjutant to Hermann Göring, Reichsmarschall and head of the Luftwaffe.

As Rauss walked down the hall to the dining room, Bormann caught up and whispered: 'What's wrong?'

'Herr Hess has flown to Britain, to try to negotiate an alliance between us and the British. I've just delivered a letter from him to the Führer.'

'My God!' Bormann stepped back. Still backing away, he whispered: 'That's nothing to do with me. Don't involve me. I know nothing of it.' He hurried ahead of Rauss to the dining room.

The lunch was quiet, all of them seated down both sides of the long table, Hitler at the head. Hitler, vegetarian, was eating a green salad with raw vegetables and yoghurt, and drinking mineral water.

Rauss chewed some of his meat, but his throat was tight and he found it almost impossible to swallow. He was very dry, and he drank several glasses of mineral water.

Hitler finished and at once stood up, glaring down the length of the table at Rauss. 'I wish everyone to leave—except you, Rauss. You stay too, Bormann.'

Rauss and Bormann stood beside their chairs, watching the others walk out of the room. Bormann glared across the table at Rauss, blaming him for drawing him into it. Bormann, as Hess's chief of staff, thought it impossible that Hitler would not accuse him of knowing Hess's plan, and of keeping him uninformed.

Hitler strutted around the table and stood in front of Rauss.

He snapped: 'Bormann, go and bring Decker and Raab.' They were two ss officers of Hitler's bodyguard.

'Yes, Mein Führer.' Bormann marched out.

'You are under arrest, Rauss,' Hitler whispered. His fists were tight and Rauss could see he was barely under control now, his lips wet. 'You will tell us precisely what part you played in this madness of Hess's.'

'Yes, Mein Führer.'

Bormann came back with the two ss officers in silver-trimmed black uniforms.

'Take him away!' Hitler turned from Rauss.

One on either side, the two officers marched out with Rauss.

In the next two days most of Hess's staff were arrested. But not Bormann. Before the end of the month Hitler gave him all the offices and power that Hess had held.

Rauss was taken to Berlin, to the Gestapo prison on Prinz Albrechtstrasse. They kept him there for three weeks, in the torture chambers below the cells, interrogating him until they were convinced he had told them all he knew of Hess's plans. Then they confined him to prison.

Chapter 20

'Did the Gestapo do that?' Strang nodded at the tips of Rauss's fingers, spread out on the arms of his chair.

Rauss drew his fingers in and folded his arms across his white sweater. 'No. They were comparatively gentle. The fingers were done later, by the Ivans.'

'The Soviets?'

'The Russians, yes. After the Gestapo were finished with me, I was kept in prison for two years—to be precise, two years, two months, and six days. By then, I suppose, my country was finding such a scarcity of trained officers that they couldn't afford to keep me in prison. I was released on August eighth of nineteen forty-three, and sent to the Russian front.'

*

By the summer of 1943 the German army on the Russian front was crumbling. Its casualties month after month were far greater than its replacements. The morale of the troops had been broken, and though their discipline and courage were still intact they no longer believed they could win a final victory against the seas of Russian tanks and infantry that kept breaking against them and breaking against them until they flowed over and rolled on. The Germans began retreating, slowly backing west across European Russia, blowing up bridges and strong-points behind them, burying their dead in shallow graves in the dusty soil.

Rauss was posted to an infantry regiment in the Second Army, on the Central Front, and was given command of a company. He found his unit was constantly among the rearguard in their long series of withdrawing actions.

By the middle of February, 1945, Rauss's regiment, all of the Second Army, had been pushed back inside Germany and was fighting on the line of the Neisse River. In a rearguard action there on the night of February 15, Rauss's company was overrun, and he was wounded in the left leg and taken prisoner.

His wound was treated and he was questioned by an officer, who took his name, rank, number, and what he knew of his unit's movements. Then he was loaded into a cattle car with other non-walking wounded prisoners, and shipped by rail across Poland, to a prison camp on the edge of the Pinsk Marshes, in Byelorussia.

For six weeks he stayed there. His wound healed and he was able to exercise in the sun with the other prisoners, walking in circles on the thawed, muddy ground around the huts, trying to ignore the barbed-wire fence and the guards at the machine guns in the wooden towers.

Often the prisoners talked among themselves about what the Russians might do with them. All of them had seen friends shot after they were taken prisoner; the badly wounded had been shot on the ground where they were captured, and many of the unwounded had been killed during the march across Poland to the camp. They wondered how they would be treated now. Rauss listened and never said anything. Since the night he was captured he had been asking himself what would happen to him when the Ivans discovered he had been Hess's adjutant. The battlefield interrogation had been nothing, just a unit intelligence officer taking down the routine details to send back to Moscow. That had been nothing. But what would happen when the people in Moscow came to his name among the hundreds of thousands of other German prisoners, the millions, checked it against their records and realised who he was and what he had been?

They came for him in the middle of the first week of April. A Red Army sergeant and two soldiers with tommy guns marched into the compound while he was sitting in the sun with a group of other men, all in a row with their backs to the wall of a hut, faces to the sun. They dragged him up, out of the compound, and marched him five kilometres down the road to a village: a few small houses on either side of the road, their roofs patched but the walls still chipped and holed by the shells and bullets of months before.

One house was undamaged, except that the windows were all

111

gone. They took him inside. There was only one room, where a Red Army major sat behind a plain wooden table. His uniform was clean and well-fitted, and under the table his black kneeboots, crossed at the ankles, were polished bright. The soldiers marched Rauss up in front of him and stopped at attention.

The major's cap was at the side of the table, and his black hair was combed straight back, cut so that his head looked square at the sides. In good German he said: 'Captain Rauss, my name is Major Galkin. I am from the GRU. Do you know the GRU?'

'No, sir.' But Rauss knew. The GRU was the Chief Intelligence Administration of the General Staff. Two or three times before the war their agents had been arrested and executed in Germany. All these weeks he had been hoping the GRU would not find him.

Galkin sat staring at him. 'I think you must know. We know you.' He opened a file. 'Tell me about your former superior, Rudolf Hess.'

'I know nothing of him, sir. He deserted my country almost four years ago. He flew to the British, as you must know.'

'Yes, I do know that. Tell me why he did it.'

'I don't know that, sir.'

'You were his adjutant.'

'Yes, sir, but there were many things he didn't tell me.'

'On the contrary, I think he told you most things. You were close to him for five years, Rauss. I think you know why he went to Britain. Tell me.'

'I assumed it was because he thought Germany could not win the war, sir.' Rauss could see Galkin didn't believe that, but in his torn, filthy uniform he felt at a disadvantage, with Galkin in his polished boots. 'I assume he wanted to join the winning side.'

'In May of nineteen forty-one? You were winning everywhere then, Rauss. It was not until six weeks later that it became obvious that you must lose—when you so treacherously attacked my country.'

Rauss stood at attention and said nothing.

'Do you know the Messerschmitt one-one-oh, Rauss?'

'Yes, sir.'

112

'You have seen such a plane many times, I expect.'

'Yes, sir.'

'You saw Rudolf Hess fly one?'

'Yes, sir.'

'Many times.' Galkin said it flatly. It was no question.

They knew all about him. Rauss was sure they did. They knew exactly how much he had known of Hess's plans.

'A number of times, sir, yes.'

'And when you were with him at Augsburg, at the Messerschmitt factory, Hess told you why he was spending so much of his valuable time flying that plane. Not so, Rauss?'

'He said it was for a long flight, sir. No more than that.' It couldn't go on like this. They had him in their filthy country, and they could do anything they wanted with him until he told them all he knew.

Galkin sat back in his chair, stretching his shoulders against the straight wooden back. He sounded very patient. 'Rauss, we know he went to Britain to try to persuade them there to join an alliance with you Hitlerites against us.'

'It sounds incredible, sir.'

'Does it? True, nevertheless. Do you know how we have this information?'

'No, sir.'

'Our allies, the British, told us. More than three years ago they told us what Hess, the anti-Communist, wanted them to do.' Galkin folded his arms. 'Now you can be our ally. Tell me if Hess made his flight because of an order from Hitler.'

'I don't know, sir.'

'When you went to Hitler the morning after Hess left Augsburg, what did he say to you?'

'Very little, sir.' So they knew he'd gone to Berchtesgaden. They knew it all. 'I don't remember in detail. He was not pleased.'

'And what did you tell the Gestapo, when they questioned you?'

'There was little I could tell them, sir.'

'Did they question you as I am questioning you now, Rauss —or were they more brutal, more German?'

'They were pigs, sir.'

'Perhaps you would be more informative if we treated you as

113

the Gestapo did. Perhaps the Gestapo were pigs dealing with a pig.'

It was going to begin. Rauss had been waiting for it every day, all these weeks, and now it was going to begin. It was going to be difficult for him to hide anything from them, because they already knew much more than he had believed they could. They probably knew too much for him to mislead them.

They kept him in the house for two days without food, and the guards came in relays to beat him with fists and clubs. The beating did not stop when the major left to eat, or at night, when he left to sleep. It never stopped. When they beat him unconscious they threw water on him to revive him, then began again.

After the two days he told Galkin what Hess had told him of his reason for flying to Britain. Since the Ivans knew it anyway, there seemed no reason not to tell them. But, for pride, he had made them work on him before he gave it to them.

But they were not satisfied. They took him out of the house, threw him into the back of a truck and, with six guards, drove him to a military airfield. They flew him to an airfield outside Moscow, and in the back of another truck took him into the city. He saw nothing from inside the truck, lying on the floor in manacles and leg irons, but where they took him was the GRU headquarters on Arbat Square, on the other side of the Kremlin Palace from Lubianka, the headquarters of the GRU's rival intelligence organisation, the KGB.

They dragged him down long flights of stone steps and along a corridor where the sound of his chains rattling and hitting the stone floor echoed along between the bare walls. They opened a steel door and dragged him into a room with bright lights in the ceiling. When they lifted him and sat him on a wooden chair he saw it was a torture chamber. What had happened with Galkin was nothing. In this place they would never stop until they had squeezed everything from him.

Rauss never knew the name of the interrogator. He was a colonel, who walked with a cane, with an artificial leg that was propped out rigidly in front of him when he sat down. He had a black patch on his left eye. From the beginning Rauss could see that the man hated him, just because he was German.

For days and nights the colonel questioned him about Hess's

reasons for flying to Britain, and whether it had been Hess's idea or whether he was simply following an order from Hitler. Rauss told him what he had told Galkin, but they tortured him for days because the colonel wanted to be sure there was nothing more.

They shocked him with electrodes on his genitals. They strapped him on his back on a bench, draped a thick woollen cloth over his face, and poured water on it until he was breathing water through the cloth and thought he would drown.

After days of it they saw he could take no more, and dragged him off to a cell and left him untouched for a few days and nights, feeding him enough to keep him alive, then took him back to the chamber and began it all again.

When the colonel was satisfied that Rauss had told everything he knew of the reason for Hess's flight, and that it had been made without Hitler's knowledge, he began to ask what else Hess had done because of his hatred for Communism and the Soviet Union.

Rauss said he knew of nothing else.

They tortured him for days and he told them nothing. For a few days they brought him into the chamber early in the morning, strapped him into a dentist's chair, and slowly drilled his teeth, three or four a day. He said nothing, and kept saying nothing until there were no teeth left to drill.

Next day they pulled out his fingernails, and he told them nothing.

Then the next morning they brought him into the chamber and he saw a movie screen had been set up, and a projector with a reel of film spliced into it. The colonel was sitting in a wooden armchair in front of the projector, his left leg straight out.

Rauss wondered what was going to happen.

'You did not know it, but yesterday was a historic one for my country,' the colonel said. 'The date, for you to remember as long as you might live, was the Eighth of May. Your leaders signed an unconditional surrender to the Red Army in Berlin.'

Rauss did not believe it. This bastard was lying to him and hoping it would break him down.

The colonel said something in Russian. The lights went out and the screen was white in the beam of the projector. The film began: Russian tanks moving down the wide avenues of Berlin, machine guns hammering bursts at snipers; squads of infantry scrambling over piles of brick and splintered wood that had been houses, firing tommy guns and tossing grenades. A Soviet flag was flying on top of the Brandenburg Gate, blackened and broken, but still standing. Two Russians in boots and baggy uniforms were dragging a woman off the sidewalk on to the churned-up grass of a garden or park.

The film went on, but Rauss could think of nothing but the Ivans with the German women. He wondered if the pigs had got as far as Munich, and his wife.

The film ended and the lights came on.

'You see how it is now,' the colonel said. 'We are doing to your women what you were doing to ours for four years. How does it make you feel?'

Rauss said nothing.

'No?' The colonel pushed himself to his feet, leaning on his cane. 'You still have nothing for me? The war is over. You are free to tell anything. It can do your damned country no harm now.' He sat behind his desk. 'So tell me: what else did Hess do because of his hate for my country? What else is he guilty of?'

It was not a trick, Rauss thought. If the Ivans were in Berlin —and that film had certainly been Berlin—the war was over, and there was no reason not to tell this pig what he wanted to know. The man he had been protecting was almost certainly an Ivan himself, and his only value had been that he was working for Germany. Now the war was over, and the damned Ivan could protect himself.

So Rauss told the colonel about Mikhail.

Mikhail was, he said, an agent that Hess himself had recruited, because he wanted his own source of information on the Soviet Union, to use at Hitler's cabinet meetings. Partly he had wanted to impress Hitler with his own information, but mainly he had not trusted the reliability of many of the reports that came from the military intelligence service, the Abwehr, and from the ss foreign intelligence service; he had suspected that each of them wrote their reports largely from imagination, shaping the facts to satisfy the bias of the General Staff, and of ss Reichsführer Heinrich Himmler. The generals and the ss leader both wanted to influence the cabinet in their own directions, almost always different directions.

'Who is this Mikhail?' the colonel said. 'Is it his real name or a codename?'

'I don't know. I always assumed it was a codename.'

'Is he a Russian?'

'I don't know.' But I hope so, and I hope you find him and give one of your own what you've been giving me.

'But you are sure it is a man—not a woman?'

'A man. Hess referred to Mikhail once as "him." I remember that very well.'

'And is it just one man—or could Mikhail be the codename for a group?'

'I don't know. I heard only the reference to Mikhail.'

A stenographer beside the colonel's desk was taking it all down.

'When did you first hear of him?' The colonel brought his cane up from where he had been holding it across his knees, and laid it on the side of his desk.

'In nineteen thirty-nine. March or April, I'm not sure.'

'You heard it from Hess?'

'Yes. He was pleased with a report that had come in.'

'How long had these reports been coming in?'

'I had never heard of Mikhail before. Perhaps this was the first contact. Perhaps that was why Hess was so pleased.'

'And how was the contact made?'

'By radio, to Hess's headquarters at Pullach.'

The colonel moved his cane in his hands, and looked as though he was going to reach across and swing at Rauss with it.

'By radio to Hess's headquarters.' He held the cane in both hands over his desk. 'And you, Hess's adjutant, tell me you know nothing but the codename Mikhail? Did you never speak to the radio operators, and ask them about this Mikhail? Have you no curiosity?'

'It was always the same operator who made the contact. That was all he did. He was an officer, a lieutenant, chosen by Hess and sworn to secrecy. If anyone had asked him, he would never have said anything.'

'What was his name?'

Rauss wished he were able to refuse to answer this, but by

now it was easier to speak. Nothing seemed important, now that the war was lost.

'Lieutenant Gunther Langkau, a signals officer.' He hoped Langkau was dead, or captured in the west, so these pigs would never get him.

'How did Hess recruit this Mikhail?'

'I don't know.'

'I ask you again.'

'I don't know.'

The colonel nodded as though he had expected that answer, and Rauss knew that that was a question they would return to sometime, and this pig would ask it and ask it until he was sure he had the truth.

'Did this Lieutenant Langkau also encode and decode the messages to and from Mikhail?'

'No. Hess did that himself.'

'So. You tell me Hess trusted no one among his staff?'

'Not with that information. Not with anything concerning Mikhail.'

'What manner of information did Mikhail supply?'

'I don't know.'

Slowly the colonel swung the tip of his cane around until it was touching Rauss's chest. He jabbed sharply, pushing Rauss back.

'Tell me what kind of information it was—trivial or vital?'

'I never saw any of the messages, even in code, and Hess never spoke of their contents to me. Never.' Rauss knew this pig would not be satisfied with it.

There were many more days and nights of questioning in the GRU torture chamber before the colonel was satisfied that Rauss had told him all he knew about Mikhail.

When they were finished with him they sent him back to a prison camp. He stayed there for two months, until he had sufficiently recovered from the weeks in the GRU cellar, then he was crowded into a cattle car, on a train with hundreds of other prisoners, and sent to work in northern Russia, rebuilding roads that had been destroyed during the war. He worked on road-building in north and south Russia until July, 1947, when he was repatriated.

'Did you really not know how Hess recruited Mikhail?' Strang said.

'Mr Strang, if I had known, I would certainly have told the Ivans. No, I didn't know.'

'When the Gestapo interrogated you in forty-one, did you tell them about Mikhail?'

'Yes. There was no reason not to. We were all on the same side, after all. At least, we were fighting the same war, even though I didn't care for the way the Gestapo were fighting it.'

'D'you think someone would've taken over the control of Mikhail after Hess was gone and you and the others on his staff were arrested?'

'I assume that would have happened. I assume the Abwehr would have taken control. The Gestapo would have found the codebook at Pullach. And Lieutenant Langkau would have told them the times and frequencies for radio contact. He might not have told them easily, but they would certainly have found out.'

'D'you think the GRU suspected someone like Mikhail existed, when they interrogated you?'

Rauss sat filling one of his pipes. 'I thought about that many times, after they sent me back to a camp. I can't be sure, Mr Strang. I remember having the feeling that, yes, they were looking for something in particular. They kept asking me if *Der Stellvertreter*, because of his anti-Communism, had done anything else against them.' Thinking about it, he nodded. 'Yes, I had the feeling that they were looking for something. Perhaps they suspected that the reason for our great victories over them in the first period of Barbarossa—and they were great victories, Mr Strang, which no one can deny—could only be explained by the fact that we were receiving information on their plans. The Ivans would have wanted to believe that—anything rather than admit that they were simply no match for us, which was the truth.'

'But they suspected something.'

'Yes.' Rauss struck a big wooden match and held the flame to his pipe, puffing clouds of smoke. 'Yes, I would say so.' He blew the match out and dropped it in the ashtray on the side table.

'When you went home, in forty-seven, did you tell anyone this?'

'Yes. I was questioned at a West German reception centre for returning prisoners, and I told them all about the entertainment the GRU had provided for me. Later, when I had gone home to Munich, a man came to ask me more about it—he was German but he said he was working for the American Army, and this was true because I confirmed it with your Army before I told him anything. He asked me, as you just have, whether the Ivans might have suspected the existence of Mikhail before they interrogated me. I told him what I've told you.'

'It'd be interesting to know who Mikhail was.'

'I've often wondered.' Rauss puffed. 'Often.'

'Yesterday afternoon in Berlin, I was told about an envelope that Hess gave his lawyer at Nuremberg in forty-six. D'you have any idea what might be in it?'

'My God! No!' Vigorously Rauss shook his head. 'At Nuremberg in forty-six? No, I can't imagine what's in it. Is it not possible to open it?'

'No. It was stolen from his lawyer yesterday.'

'And the lawyer had never opened it?'

'Hess's instructions were that it shouldn't be opened till after he was dead.'

Rauss sat drawing deeply on his pipe. 'Is this why you came to see me, Mr Strang? Did you think I might know something of this stolen envelope?'

'I wasn't sure about you, Mr Rauss, but I'm sure your son knew something.'

Saturday

April 30, 1977

Chapter 21

Strang stayed overnight at a motel near the Toronto airport, and in the morning he bought a ticket on an American Airlines flight to Washington. Before he left he phoned Langley and asked for a car to meet him at Washington National.

The driver was waiting for him at the arrivals gate, and they went out to the car. It was more than three years since Strang had seen Washington, and he sat looking across the Potomac at it as they moved northwest along the Washington Memorial Parkway, around the curve of the river.

They turned off the parkway, down the road past the high chain-link fence that surrounded the woodland site of the CIA. At the gate the guard checked them, and they drove down the twisting road among the trees to the great concrete headquarters building.

Strang got out at the entrance, walked through the wide lobby, and went down to the data centre. He asked for a printout on German anti-Soviet intelligence operations from the middle of 1940, when Hitler was preparing for the invasion of Russia, through the post-war years to the end of June, 1955.

After the war the German intelligence organisation that had specialised in the anti-Soviet operations had, almost intact, with all its wartime files, been absorbed by the United States—first by Army Intelligence, then, in June, 1949, by the CIA, which financed and controlled it for six years, until July, 1955, when West Germany, which had become fully independent two months before, took it over and called it the Federal Intelligence Service, the *Bundesnachrichtendienst*, known as the BND.

All the history of the war time and the ten years after were in the CIA data bank: the daily record of all operations, the names of agents and their codenames, and of the German officers who had controlled them. All this Strang got from the computer, and sat down to read through it, looking only for one name.

When they were planning Operation Barbarossa, the invasion of Russia, Hitler and his generals based their strategy on evaluations of Soviet military strength and ability that came mainly from an intelligence section of the German Technical Staff called Foreign Armies East, which had been formed for this work late in 1938.

By the end of 1941, when their armies had been inside the Soviet Union for six months, the generals saw that their operations were not running as fluidly as they had expected. Progress was slower than they had planned. The fault was in their intelligence reports, which had been inadequate and inaccurate.

Colonel General Franz Halder, the Army Chief of Staff, took action against Foreign Armies East. At the end of March, 1942, he dismissed its head and replaced him with Lieutenant Colonel Reinhard Gehlen.

At once Colonel Gehlen began reorganising and expanding the section. From all branches of the army he began drawing officers with knowledge of the Soviet Union, building a younger and more energetic staff at his headquarters in the forest southwest of Angerburg, East Prussia.

The Abwehr was co-operating with Gehlen, principally with a unit commanded by Major Erich Lansdorff, who was controlling agents who had been parachuted behind the Red Army front, many of them Russian prisoners who had volunteered to work for the Germans.

In the spring of 1943 Lansdorff, operating from a base in Vinnitsa, in the Ukraine, transferred from the Abwehr and he and his staff were added to the personnel list of Foreign Armies East. By now his unit was controlling agents and groups of agents in Soviet factories and offices, among partisan groups in the forests, and in Red Army headquarters and the Communist Party administration in Moscow.

Soon after Lansdorff had transferred, and his unit's reports began appearing in detail in the records of Foreign Armies East, the name of Mikhail appeared for the first time: June 4, 1943. In a message from Moscow, Mikhail had reported recent changes of officers in the General Staff of the Red Army.

All through 1943 and 1944 Mikhail was mentioned many times as the source of information from Moscow. Almost every week, sometimes two or three times a week, there was a report from Mikhail. Several times there were messages from Gehlen to Lansdorff, congratulating him on the quality of Mikhail's information. But there was never any mention of Mikhail's real name. All through the records of Foreign Armies East were periodic entries that showed where names had been deleted from the list of agents, where someone had broken contact, presumably killed or captured; names were added, when new agents were recruited. The lists gave codenames and, beside them, actual names. Mikhail appeared on every revised list, but only the codename.

From the time of the great German defeat at Stalingrad, January 31, 1943, it had been clear to the officers of Foreign Armies East that the Soviet strength was too great for the German Army to resist, and the estimates of Soviet intentions that they sent to the General Staff, almost always totally accurate, were more and more pessimistic. And Hitler became more and more impatient with the reports and with Gehlen.

At the end of March, 1945, when the Red Army had been fighting on German soil for two months, Gehlen, by now a major general, prepared a report that said massed armies under Marshal Zhukov and Marshal Koniev were preparing for a major assault aimed at Berlin. A general took it to a conference with Hitler, who screamed and stamped and said he would not tolerate reports like this from Gehlen.

For months General Gehlen had been making his own plans. Since the spring of 1942 he had been studying estimates of United States military power and had become convinced that it would be too much for Germany. He was also convinced that when the war was over the west would need Germany as an ally against the Soviets.

He told it all to Lansdorff, who was now a colonel, and said they should make plans to move the staff of Foreign Armies East and copies of all their records from their headquarters near Zossen, twenty kilometres south of Berlin, to the southwest, toward the advancing American forces.

Gehlen, slim, with thin dark hair brushed back, said: 'We

must microfilm everything and be ready to take it to the Americans.'

'The damned ss are watching us,' Lansdorff said. 'They've got their people everywhere. If they once suspected anything like this, they'd shoot us all at our desks.'

'I have taken care of the ss. I've told them we must prepare for the possibility that Germany will be occupied by the enemy, and in that case it will be necessary for an intelligence service to continue to function underground.' Gehlen smiled. 'I have pointed out to them how essential it is for us to have duplicates of all our files on microfilm, so that if the originals are destroyed or captured we can continue to operate.'

'It will be a huge task. It will take time.'

'Yes, but as little as possible. Those damned Ivans won't wait.'

By the beginning of April, 1945, the work was finished and Gehlen ordered the duplicate files packed ready for shipment. There were fifty steel chests filled with microfilmed reports and intelligence evaluations, aerial photographs, a biographical index of every senior Red Army officer from brigade commanders up, and a list of every agent operating through the Soviet Union. Among the list of agents was Mikhail, still sending reports to Lansdorff.

On April 9 Hitler, who could tolerate no more of the impossibly bad news in Gehlen's reports, dismissed him from command of Foreign Armies East. The new commander was one of Gehlen's officers, and the plans for moving to the Americans went ahead. By April 19 the time had come. With Berlin almost surrounded by Soviet troops, Foreign Armies East evacuated Maybach Camp, outside Zossen, and moved into Bavaria, toward the American advance, with the chests of microfilm loaded aboard trucks.

In a fieldcar Lansdorff travelled at the head of the truck convoy. It had been planned that Gehlen would meet them in Bavaria and take command again, but Lansdorff thought it might not happen. Now it was twelve days since Gehlen had left Zossen, and the roads into south Germany were under constant enemy air attack. Anything moving on them could be bombed and strafed at any time. It could have happened to Gehlen. If it had, Lansdorff would be in control of a store of intelligence

126

that would be invaluable to the Americans. He believed he was a better intelligence officer than Gehlen. Gehlen had a talent for impressing his superiors, but Lansdorff was convinced that he himself was the better man and would certainly be accepted well by the Americans—if only Gehlen was not there to attract attention to himself.

But in late April, when they were driving through the wooded terrain of Lower Bavaria, Lansdorff saw Gehlen's car ahead, stopped at the side of the forest road, with Gehlen and two other officers standing beside it.

Lansdorff signalled the trucks to stop, and climbed out of his fieldcar, saluting and smiling.

'It's good to see you again, General.'

'And it's good to see you, Lansdorff. Was there any difficulty?'

'No, sir.' Lansdorff nodded back at the trucks. 'We have everything here.'

'Excellent work, Colonel.' Gehlen climbed into his car. 'Now follow me, and we'll hide ourselves and our microfilm until it's time to come out and talk to the Americans.'

They drove into the Bavarian Alps, south of Munich, and near Valepp they buried the fifty steel chests. Gehlen, Lansdorff, and six other officers climbed up through the trees, to a hut in a mountain clearing. They planned to wait there until they were sure that the area was in American control and would stay under American, not Soviet, occupation after Germany surrendered—and they were sure that would be soon.

On the morning after they arrived Lansdorff went outside the hut and began working on a routine of callisthenics. For years, even in the busiest times through the war, he had exercised for ninety minutes every day, including thirty minutes of running.

On the grass outside the hut, the sun on his back, he began a quick series of pushups.

'Colonel Lansdorff!'

Lansdorff had counted to fifty-two pushups and, holding himself up from the grass on his taut arms, he looked over his shoulder. Gehlen was standing at the door of the hut. Lansdorff pushed himself up and stood at attention. His wide, hard chest was not moving; he was not even breathing heavily from the pushups.

'Yes, General?'

'What in the name of God are you doing?'

'Exercising, General.'

'Come in, man, come in!' Gehlen motioned into the hut. His face, his body were stiff with anger.

Lansdorff walked in past him, into the dimness inside the hut. Inside was one big room—for cooking, eating, and sleeping—and the other officers were standing at the far end, trying to isolate themselves from the scene that was coming.

'What was in your mind, Colonel?' Gehlen shut the door and stood with his back to it. 'Did it occur to you that by showing yourself out there you were risking all of us? There could be American patrols anywhere out there.' He pointed to the window, and through it, beyond the meadow around the hut, were the pines sloping up the valley on all sides. 'Our plan is to surrender when the time is right for us—when *we* choose it—not to be captured and perhaps handed over to the Ivans. We've planned it for months, and you would risk it because you want to'—he tossed out a hand at Lansdorff's bare chest—'build your beautiful muscles.'

'I must object to that as an unnecessary personal remark, sir.'

'I note the objection, Lansdorff, and I order you not to leave the hut again to repeat your exhibition. Until we decide to surrender, we all stay under cover. You understand?'

Lansdorff clicked his heels. 'Yes, Herr General!'

From then on they both knew there was strain between them. All through their years together Lansdorff had never let Gehlen see how he resented the authority of a man he considered his professional inferior. Now, in the days they spent in the mountains, the hostility could not be hidden.

Reports began coming to them that American troops had moved through, heading further east, but Gehlen told them they should wait until American control was consolidated. He did not want to surrender to the first troops they saw, and be shut in a prison camp. He wanted to surrender to a general, who would understand their value.

At the end of the first week of June, a month after the German surrender, Gehlen was satisfied that it was time; the

US Army had a firm hold on the area. In the evening all of them took their rank badges off their jackets and the red stripes of the General Staff from down the sides of their trousers. In the morning they walked down the mountain and surrendered to the Americans.

They were loaded into jeeps guarded by MPS, driven into Miesbach, and marched before a captain commanding a Counter-Intelligence Corps unit. All of them stood in front of a wooden table that the captain was using as a desk.

'I am head of the section called Foreign Armies East in German Army headquarters,' Gehlen said.

'You were, General,' the captain said. The CIC was hunting for war criminals and former Nazis, and the captain was suspicious of every German who was brought in to him.

'I have information to give of the highest importance to your government.'

'That's what they all say.'

Lansdorff saw Gehlen was not going to be able to convince the American. Gehlen was used to being accepted without question. He had no experience of dealing with anyone like this American, who had never heard of him and was not impressed.

Lansdorff said: 'Captain, this officer is General Reinhard Gehlen and we are officers of his staff. It is most vital that you take us to a senior officer, so that we may be given an opportunity to explain our value to your country.'

The captain looked at him, then across the room at an American sergeant sitting at another table. 'Sergeant, take these people's details and have them sent over to Salzburg.'

'Yes, sir.' The sergeant waved a hand at Gehlen and the other officers. 'All come this way.'

Gehlen first, they all filed by the table, answered the sergeant's questions and stood watching him write the answers. MPS took them all out again to the jeeps and drove them to a prison camp at Salzburg. Sitting with Gehlen in the back of a jeep, Lansdorff did not look at him. He was disgusted at the way Gehlen had led them, and he wanted to let Gehlen see it.

But Army Intelligence officers were looking for Gehlen and the staff of Foreign Armies East. They had been looking since

E

the third week of May, after they heard reports that Red Army officers were asking for them. The search went through prison camps packed with Germans in uniform and among the millions of civilian refugees moving through the German towns and countryside, some of them wanted war criminals who had hidden their uniforms and hoped to escape.

It took Intelligence until the middle of July to find Gehlen, in a prison camp at Oberursel, in the Taunus Mountains, north of Frankfurt, where he had been transferred from Salzburg. At last Gehlen was taken to an American general: Brigadier General Edwin Sibert, senior intelligence officer in the US zone of Germany. They talked for several days, and Gehlen took a party to dig up his chests of microfilm from their hiding place in the Bavarian Alps. Lansdorff and other officers of Foreign Armies East were found in the prison camps where they had been sent. They were brought together and went to work reassembling their files on the Red Army.

In August they were flown to Washington, and stayed there ten months, conferring with Intelligence officers at the War Department, making plans for the creation of a German intelligence service to work against the Soviet Union, financed by US Army Intelligence.

Early in July, 1946, they flew back to Germany and set up their headquarters in a US Army base at Oberursel. With an American liaison team they began to rebuild their anti-Soviet intelligence organisations. It became known as the Gehlen Organisation.

When they had been at Oberursel a few days Gehlen called Lansdorff to his office. Since their disagreement in the mountain hut they had been cool to each other, but now Gehlen was smiling—and Lansdorff was cautious.

'Colonel, we are at the beginning of a new career—together,' Gehlen said. 'I want to assure you that I have the greatest respect for your professional ability, for your skill in the collection of information. My own expertise is in the evaluation of that information. I need your talent. The organisation needs the skills of both of us. I believe we can work together. Do you agree?'

'Yes, sir.' For the moment. Lansdorff thought. Gehlen certainly needed him, or he wouldn't be making this speech of friendship, but why would he necessarily need Gehlen? He himself was at least as capable as Gehlen of running this organisation for the Americans.

'It is vital that we rebuild our sources of information. Where do you propose to begin, Colonel?'

'I should like to establish contact again with all the wartime agents we had inside the Soviet Union.'

'Can it be done, do you think?'

'I'm sure we won't be able to raise them all, but some, perhaps many of them.'

Gehlen nodded. 'Go to work on it. Find all your old staff; tell them we need them.'

The Gehlen Organisation spent months looking for former members of Foreign Armies East in the prison camps in the western zones of Germany, arranging their release, and putting them to work. By January, 1947, Lansdorff was ready. His radio operators began calling their old contacts inside the Soviet Union, on the old frequencies, on the old transmission schedules, hoping the agents would still be listening.

There were very few replies, but there was one from Mikhail. He answered immediately.

Lansdorff sent test messages for two weeks, sending questions and studying the replies, until he was certain it was Mikhail and not a Russian operator trying to trick him. Then he told Gehlen that contact had been re-established.

'Excellent, Colonel! That one alone is worth a hundred of our other agents.'

'I wish I knew who Mikhail was,' Lansdorff said.

'The information's reliable and always of high quality. That is the most important thing, Colonel.'

Later in 1947, in the summer, the Russians began sending home their German prisoners, and Gehlen sent teams of officers to the West German reception centres to interview them and gather all the information they had brought back. There had been more than three million of them, working in agriculture, industry, every area of the Soviet economy: they added much to Gehlen's store of information. One of them was Captain Otto Rauss, who told of his interrogation by the GRU, and how he had at last revealed the existence of Rudolf Hess's agent, Mikhail.

131

A report of the interview was passed to Lansdorff, and it shocked him. He went to Gehlen and told him about it.

'Did you know that Hess had recruited Mikhail?' Gehlen said.

'No, of course not. I had no idea.'

'How did he come under your control originally?'

'From the Gestapo.'

'The Gestapo?' Gehlen came up straighter in his chair.

'Yes. It was early in the Russian campaign, when I was still with the Abwehr, before I transferred to Foreign Armies East. July or August of forty-one. A Gestapo officer came to me with the instructions for contacting Mikhail—the radio frequencies and the receiving and transmitting schedules—and the codebook.'

'Just that? Did the Gestapo not tell you Mikhail had been recruited by Hess?'

'No—and of course I didn't ask anything.'

Gehlen picked up the report of the interview with Hess's former adjutant. 'Do you believe this, Lansdorff? Can it be possible that Hess recruited Mikhail?'

'I suppose it's possible. When the Gestapo came to me it was two or three months after Hess flew to the British. They would have had time to interrogate his staff and get this information.'

'This man Rauss has gone home to Munich.' Gehlen laid down the interview report. 'I'm going to send someone to talk to him again, in more detail.'

'If he can tell us anything about Mikhail, I'd be interested to hear it,' Lansdorff said.

Gehlen sent an officer to Munich, and he spent a day at Rauss's home, questioning him minutely for any clue to the identity of Mikhail. But Rauss knew nothing more than he had already told.

Gehlen and Lansdorff read the second report a few days later, in Gehlen's office.

'So the only one who knows about Mikhail is Hess,' Lansdorff said. 'And he's been in Spandau for two weeks and will probably be there for the rest of his life, watched by the Ivans.'

'I'm not sure that you should continue to use Mikhail.' Gehlen looked worried.

'I don't understand.'

'I think it's very obvious, Colonel.' Gehlen was impatient that it was necessary to explain it. 'I'm already being criticised by some of them in Washington, and some in the American Army here, for bringing so-called former Nazis into the organisation. What if they hear that one of our principal agents was actually recruited by a convicted war criminal, Rudolf Hess? The Americans are still very suspicious of us, you must know. They need us to work for them against the Ivans, but they are very far from trusting us.'

'Mikhail is an excellent source of information. That should be all that concerns us.' Lansdorff told himself he should have expected this from Gehlen, that he would think of the political complications, when they should be concentrating on gathering intelligence. 'It seems to me irrelevant, how he came to be in our service.'

Gehlen said nothing, but he looked displeased.

'Do you wish me to stop communicating with him?' Lansdorff said. He knew Gehlen wouldn't want that; they couldn't afford to lose Mikhail.

'No, no.' Impatiently Gehlen shook his head. 'Continue to use him. Continue.'

Lansdorff maintained contact with Mikhail, and the reports came in every week, once or twice a week, from Moscow. In June, 1949, the Gehlen Organisation moved from the authority of Army Intelligence and became controlled and financed by the CIA. Nothing changed. Messages continued to come in from Mikhail. All the information continued to be highest quality. Mikhail was the CIA's most valuable source of information from inside the Soviet Union.

It went on until March 10, 1952, when Lansdorff's operator listened at one of Mikhail's scheduled transmission times, and there was no message. The operator listened at the next scheduled time, and there was still nothing. Lansdorff told him to send a message, to try to make contact. There was no response.

Lansdorff told Gehlen.

'He must have been discovered,' Gehlen said. 'Close down the circuit.'

'I should like to keep trying.' Lansdorff thought Gehlen was relieved to have Mikhail gone. Even now, after five years,

Gehlen seemed uneasy about that memory of Hess. 'Something might have happened to his transmitter. There might have been any kind of accident. I want to keep trying.'

'Very well.' Gehlen did not like it. 'But keep me informed.'

For two months, on every scheduled transmission period, Lansdorff's operator tried to re-establish contact with Mikhail. Then Gehlen ordered the circuit to shut down. Mikhail was recorded as lost.

Sunday
May 1, 1977

Chapter 22

Strang flew back on a Lufthansa flight that landed at Frankfurt a few minutes after eight in the morning, and while he waited for the connection to Berlin he phoned Karin Hartmann at her apartment and said he wanted to see her.

'Yes—but when? Where are you now?'

'Frankfurt.'

'My God, what're you doing there?'

'Coming back from New York.'

'New York! You move fast. I didn't know you'd even left Berlin. What time will you be back here?'

'Ten-fifteen.'

'Oh. It's not going to be easy to see you. I have to go out at ten-thirty, and I'm not sure when I'll be back. Quite late, I think.'

'Damn.' She lived in the Tiergarten district, several kilometres from the airport. He couldn't get there in time.

'Are you going straight home from the airport?'

'Yes.'

'I could meet you and drive you home. I have to go very close to where you live. We could talk on the way. Would that be all right, Philip?'

'Perfect. I'll be in on Pan Am.'

'At ten-fifteen.'

'Right.' He wondered how she'd be when she heard what he had to tell her.

She was not in the terminal when he landed at Tegel, but when he walked outside she was running from the parking lot, her blonde hair bobbing and swinging around her head in the sunlight. She was wearing a light blue jean suit, the jacket open and flapping as she ran. It'd be damn nice to go with her, he thought, wherever she's going today.

'Sorry.' She stopped, panting, smiling. 'I thought I had more time. You weren't waiting long, were you?'

'I just got here.'

'Good. My car's over this way.'

It was a light blue Porsche. 'I'm on my way to meet a friend.' She swung down into the low seat, in behind the wheel. 'We're going to picnic in the Grünewald.'

'Lucky friend.'

She was backing the Porsche out of the parking space. 'She thinks so.'

He smiled.

'Why did you go to New York in such a hurry? But that's an indiscreet question, I suppose.'

'I can give you a discreet answer. I went to talk to someone.' He didn't like having to tell her about Ross.

'I see.' She swung south on the road from the airport, in the stream of traffic.

She'd guessed it was Ross he'd gone to talk to. He could see that.

'Karin, Ross is dead.'

She frowned at him, her lips tight, then looked back at the road.

Strang sat watching her, saying nothing, waiting for her to absorb it.

'What happened, Philip?'

'Someone shot him, in his office.'

'My God! Why?'

'I don't know. I think someone wanted something from him.'

'You mean it was a robbery?'

'No, I don't think it was that. He'd been tortured, and . . .'

'Tortured?'

'Someone was trying to get information from him—and I think they got it.'

'About what, Philip?'

'I can't be sure.' He didn't want to tell her what he thought it was—what he was sure it was. He didn't want to tell her about Ross—but, God, he had to.

'It must've been robbery.'

'No, Karin. Nothing was moved in his office. I think someone wanted to know something about that envelope of Hess's.'

She jerked her head around to him, flicking her hair out of her eyes with a hand. 'What could Joe have known about that?'

'He was very close to the Nationalists.'

'Joe? Oh, no.' She shook her head. 'No, that's impossible.'

'I spoke to his father. He told me about it. They'd argued about it. His father's name is Rauss. Did you know he'd changed his name?'

As she drove she was slowly shaking her head. She could not believe what she was hearing.

'It's true, Karin. His father emigrated to the States in forty-eight. Did he tell you his father used to be Hess's adjutant?'

'No!' She was startled. 'My God, no!'

'Since you were both so interested in Hess, don't you think he might've mentioned that—unless he was hiding his German connection?'

'Yes. I suppose so.'

'His father had a bad time with the Gestapo during the war. He knows his Nazis. That's why he fought with Ross over the Nationalists.'

They were on an expressway, moving fast in the traffic heading downtown, and she said nothing, watching a Volkswagen ahead of them, glancing at the rearview mirror, waiting for a chance to pull out and overtake. She eased her foot down and the Porsche swung out and passed, swung in ahead of the Volkswagen, and she slowed.

'I can't believe it about Joe,' she said. 'I can't.'

'How much did he help you with Hess's appeal?'

'Very much. He circulated a petition in America. A lot of influential people signed it.'

'Did he suggest it in the first place?'

'The appeal?'

'Yes.' It must've happened that way. Ross, fronting for the Nationalists, had persuaded her to do it.

'Yes, he did. He wrote to me last year, in the autumn, and suggested it. Why?'

'No reason.'

She looked quickly at him, and back at the traffic. Now they were moving through Zehlendorf, not far from Strang's apartment house.

'You think it was all arranged, after all, don't you?' she said. 'You think the Nationalists had Joe persuade me to make the appeal, for their political reasons.'

'I'm sure of it. And when it didn't work they hired someone to kill Hess.'

'I think you might be right,' she said quietly.

'I think so—and I think Ross helped them steal that envelope.'

'But how, Philip?'

'He told them you had it. That phone call he made from the airport wasn't to the Ambassador. We checked and they had no call from him, and he didn't leave any shoes there.'

They stopped outside the apartment building and she switched off the ignition, turning to him in her seat. 'You've been busy.'

'There's been a lot to do.'

'And you think Joe was killed because of the envelope?'

'Yes. They happened too close together—it was stolen, then he was killed. Yes, I think they're connected.'

'But if the Nationalists took it and he helped them, why would he be killed?'

'I can't imagine. I don't know what the hell's happening. You're sure he didn't see what was in the envelope?'

'Of course I'm sure! I didn't open it. I told you!'

'I know.' He opened the door. 'Enjoy your picnic.'

'I won't. I don't feel like it now.' She switched on the engine. 'But I've got to go.'

'I'll call you if I hear anything that might interest you.'

'Thank you, Philip. But please make it good news.'

'I hope I can.' He got out.

She waved as she drove off, and he stood watching the Porsche moving fast down the street. She'd asked a good question and he wished to God he had the answer: if Ross had helped the Nationalists get that envelope—and he certainly had—why had they killed him? And tortured him. Had he been keeping something from them? Or from someone else? Was it possible that someone else had tortured him and made him tell them something about Hess's envelope? How could it be possible? Who else could've known it existed?

Chapter 23

It was a red brick house with a wide garden around it, on a prosperous street at the edge of the Grünewald. Strang got out of the cab and walked up the short concrete path from the sidewalk, and rang the bell.

A woman opened the door. '*Ja?*' She was tall, about thirty-five, and wore a beige silk-knit dress that clung to her.

'I'd like to see Colonel Goodblood.' He didn't know anything about Goodblood's life—whether this was his housekeeper, wife, or little friend. But she was attractive.

'Is he expecting you?'

'I phoned twenty minutes ago.'

'You are?'

'Strang.' Whoever she was, Goodblood had her trained to be cautious with strangers at the door. Goodblood would do that.

'Ah!' She smiled, suddenly friendly. 'Yes, Mr Strang. Please come in. My husband's expecting you.' He stepped into the hall and she shut the door. 'He's in the garden. Please follow.'

He walked behind her down the hall. In the knit dress she moved sensationally. It surprised him to see anyone like this here. With Goodblood, he'd never have suspected it. Old Goodblood.

Behind the house was a long stretch of lawn with rose bushes around the sides. Out behind it were the tops of the trees in the Grünewald. Goodblood was walking down from the end of the garden, wearing a pair of suntan trousers and a red shortsleeve shirt, open at the neck, but he was holding himself very upright and it was as though he was still in uniform, with his steel-rimmed glasses and short grey hair.

His wife led Strang out on the lawn to him.

'Walter, here's Mr Strang for you.'

'How are you, Mr Strang?' Goodblood looked curious.

'Fine, Colonel. Sorry to disturb your Sunday afternoon.'

'It's nothing at all.' Goodblood brushed away with a hand.

141

'Sunday afternoon's much like any other. This lady's my wife. Gudrun, this is Herr Strang, from the Mission.'

She took his hand with a strong grip. She was more than half a head taller than Goodblood, altogether bigger.

'D'you want to talk out here?' Goodblood said. 'We can get some sun at the same time.'

'Perfect.'

'Gudrun, would you please excuse us?'

'Of course. Nice to meet you, Herr Strang.' She walked back to the house.

While they strolled back and forth on the lawn Strang told what had happened to Ross, and about his neo-Nazi sympathies and his part in the appeal for Hess's release.

'I'll be damned,' Goodblood murmured. 'It was all a setup by the Nationalists?'

'Yes.'

'This connects them to the attempt on Hess. They wanted him out alive or dead. Is that the way you see it?'

'I don't think there's any question about it, Colonel.'

Goodblood rubbed his right eye behind his glasses. 'They're desperate sons of bitches. To have done all that, and killed that man Lichti, to make sure he stayed quiet. I wonder if they think it's worth it all?'

'If they could put us into confrontation with Moscow over Spandau, they'd consider it worth everything they've done.'

'I'm sure they would. They're crazy enough.'

'Is there anything new on Lichti's murder, Colonel?'

'Not a thing. But now I'm going to have the civil police look at some of the senior National Party people. I want to know which of them had dealings with Ross. If we know that, we might know who's in this damn plot. Then we might be getting somewhere.'

'The civil police might be nervous about checking on the Nationalists, Colonel. They're a legal political party.'

Goodblood stopped and looked at one of the rose bushes. 'It'll be delicate—but, dammit, there's nothing legal about murder and attempted murder. If they're responsible for it, we've got to know. The civil police'll have to get to work on them.' He looked at his watch. 'I believe I'll go over to the Mission and make a call.'

142

'There's something else.' Strang didn't think he should say much about it. Not yet.

Goodblood stood waiting.

'Ross's father told me about an intelligence operation Hess was involved in during the war.'

'Intelligence?' Goodblood stood staring up at Strang through his steel-rimmed glasses. 'Is it something significant?'

'I'm not sure. I'm going to look at it. If it turns interesting I'll tell you.'

Chapter 24

The Kurfürstendamm was the big Berlin shopping street. Berliners called it the Ku-damm, and after dark it was a wide, bright strip of lighted store windows, moving traffic, coloured neon, and streetlights that arched high above and glowed down on all of it.

When Strang got out of a cab on the Ku-damm, at the corner of Fasanenstrasse, the afternoon crowd filled the wide sidewalk: standing at store windows and strolling. A lot of them looked like tourists. He walked among them, moving toward the round tables of a sidewalk café, and when he was a few paces from it, looking beyond the rows of tables for Kluger, he saw him coming the other way, head and shoulders above the people around him.

There was an empty table against the window of the restaurant, at the end of a row, and Strang sat at it, hands flat on the checkered red-and-white cloth.

Kluger walked between the rows of tables, pulled out a chair beside him, and sat with his back to the restaurant window, where he could look over the other tables.

'Christ, Phil, I hope this is important, on a Sunday afternoon. Irene says you're starting to come between us.'

'Tell her that doesn't sound like my kind of fun.'

A waiter in tight black trousers came to them, wiping a small round tray. They ordered lager.

Kluger watched him go, prancing among the tables. 'What did you get from Ross?'

'Nothing.' He told him how he had found Ross and the secretary.

'My God!' Kluger began to say something else, saw the waiter coming with the tall, slim glasses of beer on the tray, and sat watching him, impatient.

The waiter set the glasses down on the checkered tablecloth and was gone.

144

'Why was he tortured, for God's sake? Who wanted to make him talk, and about what?' Kluger picked up his glass and drank half of it.

'I've been all over that for hours. I don't know. But he was working with the Nationalists. I had a long talk with his father, and he told me all about it. The appeal was his idea. Karin Hartmann told me he suggested it to her. He was using her for the Nationalists.'

'So that's who he phoned from the airport.' Licking his lips with the tip of his tongue, Kluger set his glass down.

'Yes. They've got Hess's envelope, all right.'

'What the hell could be in it?'

Strang sipped his lager. 'I've been thinking a lot about that too. Ross's father told me something else—about Hess.' He told Kluger about Mikhail.

'I'll be damned.' Kluger sat looking at his glass, slowly turning it on the cloth with his thumb and forefinger. 'Gehlen's people ran Mikhail all that time and didn't know who he was?'

'Or whether it was he, she, or they.'

'It'd be very interesting to know, wouldn't it?'

'Very.'

Kluger's glass was empty, but he picked it up and put it to his lips, head back to let the last trickle of foam run into his mouth.

'There's something I'd like you to do, Dieter.'

'What?'

'From the time Hess flew to Britain, Mikhail was always run by the same man, an officer named Lansdorff—he ran him for the Abwehr, Foreign Armies East, then the Gehlen outfit after the war. All the time, till Mikhail broke contact. I checked on Lansdorff, and he was with the BND till sixty-five. He resigned early, as vice-president, a brigadier general.'

Crumpling a gum-wrapper into the ashtray, Kluger slipped the stick into his mouth. 'This is Erich Lansdorff you're talking about?'

'Yes. D'you know him?'

'Not exactly, but I know about him. And I've met him a couple of times. He had a big fight with Gehlen. That's why he retired early. They kept it very quiet, but that's the real story. He and Gehlen were both power-hungry bastards, but Gehlen was a lot shrewder. He played better politics. Lansdorff's an egotistical old bastard, and he wanted to be president of the BND; he couldn't stand being second man to Gehlen. His son told me the story.'

'You know his son?'

'Sure I know him. He's with us, Internal Security. He's in Hamburg now. That's how I met old Lansdorff.'

'I'd like to meet him myself. I'd like to talk to him about Mikhail.'

'Is that what you want me to do—arrange it?'

'Yes.'

'That shouldn't be a problem. He lives outside Stuttgart. I'll call him when I get home. You want it as soon as possible, right?'

'That's right.' After all these years, there couldn't be much about Rudolf Hess that was unknown. Not much except Mikhail. Just Mikhail and whatever Hess had sealed in that envelope all those years ago. Yes, he wanted to know all he could about Mikhail, and he wanted it fast.

Monday
May 2, 1977

Chapter 25

Strang and Kluger flew to Stuttgart in the morning, rented a car, and drove south from the airport into bright sun. Lansdorff lived about thirty kilometres out, in a house on a hill above the Neckar River.

'He's got a hell of a nice place there,' Kluger said. 'I just hope I can remember how to find it.'

'Oh, that's beautiful. Why didn't you check it before you left the airport?'

'Don't get excited. I know where it is. Knowing where it is and finding it aren't quite the same. I've only been here once, and his son was driving. I should've paid more attention. His place isn't designed to be conspicuous. He likes privacy, old Lansdorff. No one here knows who he is. He calls himself Schmidt.'

'Oh, Christ.'

Kluger shrugged. 'He took his work seriously. Or maybe he thinks someone might still be looking for him, because of something he did while he was with Gehlen. Maybe someone is. I don't know. You'll see. He's a character.'

'Does he live alone?'

'No. With his daughter. Ingrid. And that's interesting too.'

'Why?'

Kluger shook his head, chewing gum, looking mysterious. 'They've been living together for a long time. He and his wife were divorced about twenty years ago, and he and Ingrid've been living together ever since. Klaus, the son, doesn't like it.'

'It sounds as though Klaus is missing a lot of action.'

'I think that's why he doesn't like it.'

'Dieter, what the hell're we getting into?'

Kluger chuckled. 'I shouldn't've told you. They're just like any other couple.'

'I'll try to think of them that way.'

149

'All right—but don't let them know that. Don't call Ingrid anything but Fräulein Lansdorff.'

'Jesus.'

Kluger turned on to a narrow road among tall chestnut trees, driving carefully. When they were about three kilometres down it, the dirt road speckled with sunlight and shadows of leaves, they saw sunlight in a clearing ahead, and some houses. Wooden houses with low, ridged roofs.

'Here's the problem,' Kluger said. 'On the other side of the village, the road forks. I remember that. What I don't remember is which one goes to Lansdorff's place.'

'Ask at the village.'

Kluger began slowing, watching the houses on either side of the dirt road. A man came out of one ahead of them, walking away. Kluger eased the car alongside him, leaning out, and said: 'Please'.

The man glanced at him and walked on.

'Please,' Kluger said.

Still walking, the man looked at him again. '*Ja?*'

Kluger pointed down the road, where it forked among the trees. 'Which is the road to Herr Schmidt's house?'

'The left.' The man walked on, not looking at him.

Kluger pulled his head in, muttering. 'Swabian bastard! Christ, they're surly bastards in this part of the country. You can't get anywhere with them, if they don't know you.'

'It can't be an accident that Lansdorff lives here.'

'No, it's no accident. They leave him alone and he leaves them alone.'

Beyond the village, they took the left fork, and the road began rising gently through the trees. Kluger took the car slowly around a shallow bend, the road still rising, then another bend, and ahead of them was a long straight stretch rising for about two kilometres. At the top of the hill they could see the sun bright on a red rooftop.

'That's the place,' Kluger said.

As they climbed higher they saw more of the house: all the slope of the roof and then, when they were less than a kilometre away, a row of windows in a yellow-washed wall under the red eaves.

Then, at four or five hundred metres, they saw a man

standing in front of the house, suddenly visible when they drove over a rise in the road. His hands were raised to his face, elbows jutting.

'That's Lansdorff,' Kluger said. 'The bastard's got glasses on us. He's probably been watching us all the way up.'

Strang sat watching Lansdorff as they drove up the last stretch. He was wearing a pale pink shortsleeve shirt and white shorts.

At the top of the hill Kluger swung the car gently off to the grass beside the road, and as they got out Lansdorff came forward to them, the glasses he had been using bobbing on his wide chest from the strap around his neck.

'Good day, General.' Kluger held out his hand. 'Kind of you to let us come.'

'Good day, Herr Kluger. It's my pleasure to meet you again.'

Kluger introduced Strang, and Lansdorff shook hands. He had a square hand and a thick, strong-looking arm. He was darkly tanned: face, arms, chest in the shirt that was open to the navel, and bare legs below the shorts.

'Will you come to the other side?' Lansdorff waved a hand out to beyond the rooftop. 'We can sit there and be comfortable.'

They followed him around the side of the house. It was two-storey stucco, and there were red shutters hinged back from all the windows. At the back was a wide stone patio, a flat lawn and flower beds beyond it, sloping off to pastureland. Below the pasture were thick trees down the hillside, and out beyond the treetops the Neckar was blue-green in the sunlight.

'It's a beautiful view, isn't it?' Lansdorff said.

'Yes.' Strang looked along the hillside and saw no other houses. There was just one across the river, downstream, among the trees there. 'It's quiet too.'

'That's an attraction for me.' Lansdorff held out a hand to a group of long chairs on the patio. 'Please. Let's go and sit.'

A woman came out of the house as they stepped on to the patio. She had long blonde hair tied back, and her legs were long and brown in a pair of light blue shorts, very short and close-fitting. Above the top of the shorts was a brown strip of flat belly, where the ends of her yellow shirt were tied together. It was a man's shirt, very loose on her shoulders, the sleeves rolled high.

'Let me introduce you to my daughter, Herr Strang.' Lansdorff held out a hand for her. She came and took it and they stood holding hands. 'Ingrid, you've met Herr Kluger in the past.'

'Yes. It's a pleasure to meet you again, Herr Kluger.'

'A pleasure for me, Fräulein.'

'And this is Herr Strang.'

'Charmed to meet you, Fräulein Lansdorff.' He was too. She was very attractive and well-built, and looked about twenty-eight. But, then, Lansdorff himself, with his black hair combed back from his low forehead, no sign of grey in it, didn't look more than forty, and he had to be at least sixty-five.

'I'll go and leave you, gentlemen,' she said. 'Is there anything I may bring you?'

'Yes. Please,' Lansdorff said to them. 'Anything at all to drink —or perhaps something to eat?'

'Please, a lager,' Kluger said.

'The same,' Strang said.

'Good! I'll have one too, dear. Three Löwenbräu.'

As she walked back into the house they sat in three of the long chairs, Strang and Kluger side by side, Lansdorff facing them, lifting the glasses from around his neck and setting them down beside his chair.

'I believe you want to talk to me about some of my wartime activity, Herr Strang.' Lansdorff laid a hand on his bare, hard-looking chest. The hair on it was all black too, and he seemed very proud of it.

'Yes. Wartime and after the war. I'm interested in an agent you used to control. Mikhail.'

'Ah, yes.' Lansdorff sat nodding slowly. 'Mikhail. I remember well. But why do you say *an* agent? I was never certain of that.'

'Did you think there were more than one—that it was the codename of a group?'

'Quite possibly. In fact, more than possibly. Judging from the quantity and quality of the information, I often thought

152

it must be a group.' Lansdorff looked across to the house.

Ingrid was coming out with three tall glasses of beer on a tray, walking with her back very straight, feet bare.

The three of them sat waiting for her, not talking.

She handed cool, moist glasses to Strang and Kluger. When she went to Lansdorff she stood very close to him and he took the lager with one hand, quickly brushing her thigh with the other, smiling up at her. It was done very briefly and secretly, and she smiled at him as she turned away. He sat watching her walk back across the patio, into the house.

Kluger raised his eyebrows at Strang.

'Prosit!' Lansdorff raised his glass to them.

'Prosit!' they said, and sipped the cool lager.

Strang leaned down and stood his glass on the stone of the patio. 'I've studied the operational records, General. Mikhail was referred to in the lists of agents only by the codename. Always. Did you know who he was—or they?'

'No. I never knew.'

'What about the codename? D'you remember being told why that particular one was chosen? Did it have some significance?'

'Not to my knowledge.' Lansdorff set his glass beside his chair, and sat back gently stroking the hair of his chest. 'I suppose old Hess chose it for some reason, originally—but we had no system for allotting codenames to agents or groups working inside the Soviet Union during the war. There were so many of them. Thousands. Groups and single agents. Some of them were Russian-speaking Germans that we infiltrated, but very few. They were mostly Ivans. Anti-Communist refugees who had escaped before the war or anti-Stalinists who surrendered to us in the first weeks, and volunteered to go back and work for us. Thousands of them.'

'But you knew the names of all of them. Their real names were all known.'

'Correct.' Lansdorff reached down for his lager and sipped some more. 'Mikhail was the only exception.'

'Did you ever talk to Lieutenant Langkau about this, General?'

'Langkau? Langkau?' Lansdorff cocked his head back, trying to associate the name.

153

'Gunther Langkau. He was a signals officer that Hess assigned as Mikhail's radio operator.'

'Ah, yes!' Lansdorff snapped his fingers as he remembered. 'Of course. Gunther Langkau. I heard this name for the first time after the war, in forty-seven. To be more precise, I didn't hear it but read it, in the report of an interrogation team at one of the reception centres for our returning prisoners from Russia. The man who had been Hess's adjutant—and his name was Rauss—spoke of Langkau. I remember it well now, because we tried to find Langkau. I had been curious for years about the identity of Mikhail.'

'Did you find Langkau?'

'No. We examined the old Gestapo records that we were able to gather, and found that he had been arrested on . . .' Lansdorff tried to remember the date but shook his head. 'I can't remember, but it was very soon after Hess flew to Scotland. Sometime in May of forty-one. There was no entry that showed Langkau had been released by the Gestapo and no record of what might have happened to him. Not uncommon practice for the Gestapo, I regret.'

'It was the Gestapo who came to you and gave you Mikhail, and the instructions for contacting him, wasn't it, General?'

'Correct. One presumes that they extracted this information from Langkau, the poor fellow.' Lansdorff sipped his lager.

'He might've known something about the identity of Mikhail?'

'Possibly—but I suspect that the only one who ever knew that was Hess. Incredible. I wonder how many secrets are lost in the crazy mind of that poor old man.' Lansdorff shook his head. 'It would be fascinating to know the answer to this one. Herr Strang, you've made me think about something that used to occupy my thoughts very much. I often wondered about Mikhail. That group—you see I still think of it as a group—was one of our very best sources of information. Perhaps the very best.'

'Was it?'

'Oh, yes. I remember that some time in forty-three—in the late summer, I think—our master, the great Gehlen, instituted a system of grading the quality of reports from agents. There were five ratings: reliable, credible, possible, questionable, and improbable. Mikhail was always stamped reliable. Always. Not that the reports were given the attention they deserved.' Lansdorff's lips pressed together and he looked bitter.

'Why not, General?'

'Why?' Lansdorff snorted. 'Because our leader, Adolf Hitler, was a paranoiac who would believe nothing that was unfavourable. He would allow no shadow of truth to distort his insane unreality—especially in forty-four and forty-five, when things were obviously going badly. Fortunately for us, Stalin was equally insane—because we know now that the Ivans were receiving information from a very high source on our side—someone in the Supreme Command, it's believed, whose identity is unknown to this day. Not in the General Staff of the Army, you understand, but in Hitler's Supreme Command. Like Hitler, Stalin disregarded most of that information.' Slowly he shook his head, wondering at it. 'Two certifiable maniacs, and how many did they kill? My God.'

'Do you think it's possible that Mikhail was on the Soviet General Staff? Is that what you believe?'

'My dear Strang, that has been my personal opinion for many years. The quality of the information forced the conclusion, inevitably, that it was coming from the General Staff level. At least that. Either that or from someone at the political level, in the Military Council, because the information often concerned the Air Force, also, not just the Army. That implied Mikhail was a group of staff officers of the Army and the Air Force, or a political official with access to such information.'

Strang glanced at Kluger and saw how closely he was concentrating on Lansdorff. It was an interesting suspicion of Lansdorff's.

'Which would you say was more likely, General—Army and Air Force officers, or a politician?'

Lansdorff drank the last of his beer and, setting the glass down, said: 'As I've told you, I always thought it must be a group. I still do, thinking about it as we speak now. Always the information was very fresh. We would be told of plans as soon as they had been made. If that information had come from the political level it would often have been older—by the time it had gone through the staff officers, through the layers of bureaucracy to the politicians.' He nodded, stroking his chest. 'My belief is that it was a group of senior officers.'

'Would it have been possible to recruit a group like that?'

Lansdorff grunted a quick laugh. 'Possible? Oh, yes, my dear Strang. In the Red Army, particularly, there was very deep opposition to Stalin, all through the officer corps, because of his purge of them in thirty-seven and thirty-eight. That paranoiac thought they were becoming too powerful; so he slaughtered about thirty-five thousand of them—half of all the officers of the Red Army. That was one of the reasons for our great success against them in the first stage of Barbarossa, that their Army had no effective officers. Yes, it would have been possible to recruit them.'

'And after the war they went on working against him?'

'Of course. In forty-seven, when we began to call up all the wartime radio links, Mikhail was one who responded immediately. Very few did—many of them had undoubtedly been caught by then, others cut themselves out, I'm sure, because they had lost hope, believing that the Communists were so strong that the west could never challenge them'—Lansdorff smiled a quick, sour smile—'or would never have the will. So they undoubtedly decided there was no gain in risking their lives further. One finds it hard to condemn them for it. But Mikhail answered our call at once, and worked as devotedly as during the war.'

'Until the tenth of March, nineteen fifty-two.'

'Correct.'

'And why d'you think they broke contact then—because Stalin died?'

Lansdorff looked thoughtful. 'Possibly—except that Stalin's death was not until the following year.' He burst out a quick laugh and at once jerked out a hand to Strang, to soothe. 'Forgive me! I didn't intend to laugh.'

Strang smiled and said nothing. 'Why d'you think they broke contact?'

'Since they obviously weren't discouraged after the war, as so many of the others were—since they worked for more than five years after the war—I would say it's unlikely that they voluntarily cut themselves out.'

'They were captured, you think?'

Lansdorff stroked his chest. 'Captured and executed.'

*

When they drove away Lansdorff stood at the top of the hill, watching them down the road.

Glancing into the rearview mirror at him, Kluger said: 'How did you like the history lesson?'

'I'm never going to forget the year Stalin died.'

'You should've seen your face when he laughed. I thought you were going to choke him.'

'I thought so too.'

'Don't blame me. I didn't say he was diplomatic; I said he was egotistical. You wanted to see him.'

'It was worth it, Dieter.'

'D'you think he's right—it was a group of Army and Air Force officers? Staff Officers?'

'How could I argue with General Lansdorff? He's had years to think about it. Yes, he could be right.'

'And old Hess recruited them. Wouldn't that be something?'

'Yes, it would.' Strang was thinking about Hess's envelope, and what might be in it. 'And what if he'd written a list of their names?'

Hands together on top of the wheel, Kluger was unwrapping a stick of gum. He glanced at Strang. 'Is that what you think's in that envelope?'

'It could be. At Nuremberg in forty-six, when he saw the Soviets wanted to hang him, he had nothing to lose. A list of names like that, all senior officers, would've turned Moscow upside down if it'd been published. It still would, even if they were all executed in fifty-two. It'd be dynamite, that a group like that worked against their country for all those years.'

Kluger concentrated on taking a bend in the narrow road, and when he was around it he said; 'Phil, if the Nationalists have that list, they could make bad trouble with it. If they make it public, it'll do more than turn Moscow upside down. It'll make a lot of tension between them and us—Germany. It makes no difference that it happened thirty years ago; they know we still feel the same about them and we know they feel the same about us. It'll be bad.'

'I know, Dieter. I know how bad it'll be.'

157

Chapter 26

General Igonin had asked for another meeting of the Kommandatura to discuss the Hess case, and again the western allies had agreed, but an hour before they went to it the British and French commandants drove to the United States Mission and talked with General Benson.

'We all know why they want this meeting,' Benson said. 'They're going to want Hess returned to Spandau at once. They know he's much improved and they're going to insist we send him back. We can't agree to it that easily, of course.'

'Absolutely not,' Henshaw said.

Bourdais shook his head firmly. 'Harry, I would never submit to that.'

'But the best we can do is settle for a compromise,' Benson said. 'We can't keep him out of Spandau for ever—though God knows I'd like to. What I want us to agree on, here and now, is how much longer we can delay sending him back. It can't realistically be more than a few days—not without involving ourselves in a very hot argument with the Soviets.'

'I am not intimidated by the possibility of an argument with the Communists,' Bourdais said. 'I think we should not allow our decision to be affected by the thought of that.'

Henshaw smiled, and it was twisted by the scar across his left cheek pulling at the corner of his mouth. 'I'm sure we both share your feeling, Claude.'

'Yes, we do,' Benson said. 'The question is: how much discomfort can we give Moscow at the least cost to ourselves? We should make the strongest gesture we can, but let's not forget it's no more than that. Nothing but a gesture. We don't want to have them closing off access routes to the city or playing any of their other damn games, if it's a question of keeping Hess in hospital for another week or sending him back to Spandau at once.'

'But we must not capitulate,' Bourdais said. 'We *must* not!'

'Oh, absolutely not,' Henshaw said. 'I'm sure that isn't what Harry's suggesting.'

'It's not,' Benson said. He slashed one of his heavy black lines across the notepad in front of him, and sat filling in an arrowhead at the end of it. 'I'm aiming for an acceptable compromise with them. One that'll make it clear that we don't intend to have them dictate to us. But I'm not going to see us involved in a confrontation over this. I don't intend to have it go so damn far that we or they won't be able to back off without a loss of face. You're with me on that, aren't you, Claude?'

Bourdais sat brushing his white moustache with both hands, the tips of his fingers stroking it left and right, away from the centre. He looked reluctant, but he nodded.

Benson sat looking at him, to be sure Bourdais was agreeing without reservation.

'But we must make it clear that we are not capitulating,' Bourdais said.

'It'll be clear,' Benson said. 'If I don't make it clear enough, you may tell Igonin whatever comes to your mind. All I ask is that you don't talk us into anything we might have to shoot our way out of. If that ever comes, I'd like to be prepared for it.'

'You know how I feel about the Communists, Harry—but you may be sure I will say nothing foolish.'

Benson nodded. 'I know that. Now let's decide how much longer we're going to insist on keeping Hess in hospital. Peter, what's your view?'

'He's really quite all right now, isn't he?' Henshaw said. 'I mean, he could go back today, if he had to, without any risk to his health?'

Benson nodded.

'Quite. Then why don't we suggest keeping him in hospital for another two days? Is that agreeable?' Henshaw looked at Bourdais.

'I would agree to that—but I think we should tell Igonin that we intend to keep him there for another week.' Bourdais shrugged. 'Then if we come down to two days he will be convinced he has won a victory.'

'It's not a bad idea,' Henshaw said. 'I think perhaps we should do a spot of haggling. What d'you say, Harry?'

Benson nodded. 'Certainly would've proposed it myself, if no one else had. I wouldn't go into that room with Igonin without having a primary position to fall back from. Certainly we'll tell him we want to keep Hess in hospital for another week.'

'Good!' Henshaw slapped his hands on his knees. 'Shall we go and talk to him now?'

*

General Igonin sat with his fists on the edge of the table, on either side of his microphone, looking as though he had come prepared to beat down any opposition.

'It is now six days since the prisoner Hess was taken into the American hospital,' he said. 'My country's jailers who are at the hospital report that he is sitting up and is walking in his room. This is true, is it not, General Benson?'

'It's true, General.'

Igonin nodded, satisfied that they agreed this far. 'My country's director from Spandau visited the hospital yesterday, as you must know, and it is his opinion that Hess is fully recovered and is fit to be returned to prison immediately. This is the desire of my government, and I am instructed to present it here this morning.'

Benson sat drawing a heavy black slash and tipped it with an arrowhead.

'It's out of the question, General Igonin,' he said into his microphone.

'But my country's director says Hess is completely fit to leave hospital now.'

'I heard you say that—but I read a report from my chief medical officer this morning, and he doesn't agree with your director's medical opinion.' There had been no report. 'We believe Hess should stay in our hospital for at least another seven days.'

Igonin hunched cautiously forward, knowing the battle was beginning. His head began drawing down toward his shoulder boards, and he sat trying to gauge the determination of Benson, Henshaw, and Bourdais.

'It would not be your intention to keep Hess at your hospital for the indefinite future, General Benson?' he said into his microphone, not looking at Benson. 'That could not be your intention?'

'No, it's not, General. Neither is it my intention to send him back to Spandau so long as there's the least risk to his health and his life.'

Igonin sat back slowly, arms folded. 'You say Hess should remain in hospital for at least another seven days?'

'That's right,' Benson said.

'Are you gentlemen agreed on this?' Igonin looked at them.

'It sounds eminently reasonable,' Henshaw said.

'I agree,' Bourdais said.

Igonin stared coldly at the three of them. 'Hess is assured of good medical attention in Spandau. In view of this I would agree to one more day in hospital. No more than one additional day.'

'That's unacceptable,' Benson snapped.

'Unthinkable,' Henshaw said.

Bourdais said nothing, but sat staring across the table at Igonin.

'I cannot agree to a week,' Igonin said. 'My superiors would not accept to have him remain out of Spandau for seven more days.' He was asking them to be reasonable.

'Hess's health should concern you at least as much as it does us,' Benson said. 'I'm sure your government wouldn't want to put it at risk.'

'No, of course not, General Benson.' Igonin sat leaning to his microphone, considering. 'I think I could agree to let him remain for two more days. Not longer than that.'

Benson sat looking as though he was giving it thought. 'Would you gentlemen agree to this? General Bourdais?'

'I would accept it with reluctance.'

'General Henshaw?'

'I too—also reluctantly.'

'I'd like to call a five-minute adjournment,' Benson said. 'I'm going to phone my chief medical officer and ask his opinion of this, General Igonin.'

'With pleasure,' Igonin said.

Benson walked out to an anteroom, phoned the Army hospital, and spoke to the Garrison Surgeon.

F 161

'How would it be for Hess if we sent him back to Spandau the day after tomorrow?' he said.

'No harm, sir. He's healthy. There's no danger now.'

'You're sure? The Soviets want this, but I don't want to go along with them if there's the slightest doubt here. I've already told them you recommend keeping him in hospital for another week.'

The doctor chuckled into the phone. 'I'm prepared to say it if that's what you want, sir. It'd certainly do Hess no harm.'

'No, that's not necessary. So long as you're sure he's fit to go back in two days.'

'Completely sure, sir.'

'All right, Colonel. Let's say he'll be moved from the hospital at oh-eight hundred, day after tomorrow.'

'He'll be ready to go, sir.'

Benson walked back into the conference room and sat at his microphone.

'My chief medical officer says that if you insist on having Hess returned to Spandau in two days, your country will have to accept the medical risks. Are you willing, General Igonin?'

'Yes. I am authorised to agree to that.'

Benson nodded. 'I've instructed that Hess be ready to leave hospital at oh-eight hundred hours the day after tomorrow.'

'This is good, General.' Igonin nodded. 'Perfectly acceptable.'

'There's still the question of his safety in the prison,' Bourdais said. 'I do not speak of his health but of his life. There was an attempt to murder him—we all agree to that now—and it has not yet been determined who was responsible.'

'The kitchen worker, Lichti, who was himself murdered, was undoubtedly guilty,' Igonin said.

'Not undoubtedly—possibly,' Bourdais said. 'And none of us believes that he acted because of personal feelings against Hess. Obviously he was paid by someone. That must be obvious to anyone.'

'If it is obvious to you, General Bourdais, I agree with you,' Igonin said smoothly. 'I agree it must be obvious to anyone.'

Benson saw the deepening colour in Bourdais' face, and said heavily: 'The risk that General Bourdais refers to is a real one, General. We still don't know who wanted Hess killed. Lichti

162

was merely hired to do it, and there's no question about that, it seems to me.'

'Someone wanted Hess dead, yes,' Igonin said. 'It may never be known who that was. It can be said with certainty that my country has no wish to see him murdered.'

'Do you mean to imply something, General?' Henshaw said, the scar pulling tightly at the corner of his mouth.

Igonin leaned in on the table, close over his microphone, shoulders hunched, square-looking with the shoulder boards. 'I will say it very clearly. I wish to say that your three countries have for many years wished the release of Hess. Your countries are the ones who would gain from his death—your countries and the regime of West Germany, which pays for the maintenance of Spandau. For years you have been pressing my government to agree to his release.' As he spoke he became less controlled. 'It would satisfy the west to have him out of Spandau, dead or alive.' He looked at Benson. 'Perhaps the Americans' investigation should concentrate in the areas where the motive is the strongest.'

Benson's face was very white and taut. His voice low, he said: 'There's no reply possible to a statement like the one you've just made, General Igonin. If this conference is to continue, I believe you should withdraw it.'

Bourdais and Henshaw said nothing, but sat staring at Igonin, waiting for him to answer.

Igonin sat back, folding his arms, and said carelessly: 'Of course, there is no evidence to support my remarks. Possibly I should not have made them at this stage of the investigation.'

The others said nothing.

'In any case, there is nothing more to be said here today,' Igonin said. 'Except to advise you that my government would interpret it as an unfriendly act if there should be any delay in returning Hess to Spandau.'

'I've told you when he'll leave the hospital,' Benson said. 'There's nothing further to discuss.'

Chapter 27

They flew back to Berlin in the early afternoon, and Strang took a taxi to his apartment. When he walked into the lobby, Karin Hartmann was sitting there.

She was on her feet at once, hurrying to him in quick, long strides across the marble floor. He could see there was trouble.

'Oh, Philip!' She stopped in front of him, trying to control her lips as they trembled.

'What is it?' He put out a hand to her shoulder.

'Oh!' She stepped in close and laid the side of her face against his chest, holding him around the waist.

He put his arms around her and stroked her hair. 'What is it?'

'They're going to send him back.'

'Who? Hess?'

'Yes.'

'When?'

'The day after tomorrow.'

He stepped back, hands on her shoulders. 'Are you sure about that?'

'Yes, yes.' She was not crying but her eyes were shining and her lips were pressed tight together.

'Come upstairs.'

Going up in the elevator, they stood together, saying nothing. As they walked down the hall he said: 'How long were you waiting downstairs?'

'Not long. Thirty minutes.'

He opened the door and followed her in, through to the living room.

'D'you want anything?' he said. 'Are you hungry?'

'No. I had lunch before I heard about this.' She sat in an armchair, leaning forward, staring at the toes of her shoes.

'I'm going to check it, and make sure you're right.' He picked up the phone. 'When're they supposed to move him?'

'The day after tomorrow. They're taking him from the hospital at eight in the morning. It's true, Philip.'

'All right, but I'll check it.'

He phoned the Mission, Goodblood's office.

'I hear Hess is going back to Spandau, Colonel. Is he?'

'Yes.' Goodblood was surprised. 'They're taking him out of the hospital at oh-eight hundred, Wednesday.'

'What's the hurry?'

'The damn Russians've been pushing for it. There was a special meeting of the Kommandatura with their representative this morning.'

'Is it safe to send him back, Colonel? Dammit, we still haven't proved the Nationalists hired Lichti. They're still loose. They could hire someone else.'

'You don't need to tell me.' Goodblood sounded weary. 'I don't like it, but what the hell can we do? The Russians know the risks.'

'Christ,' Strang said softly.

'That's what I said when they told me. How did you hear about it? I didn't know myself, till a couple of hours ago, and we're keeping it wrapped up very tight. There's heavy security.'

'I was talking to someone at the hospital. Nothing to worry about, Colonel. The security's good.'

'I hope so.'

Strang put the phone down, looking across the room at her. 'Who told you about this, Karin?'

She looked up from her shoes, leaning back in the chair. 'A friend.'

'Who?' He sat in a chair near her. 'It wasn't decided till this morning. The military police didn't know till two hours ago.'

'Someone at the hospital phoned and told me. Oh, Philip, it's nothing sinister. It was someone who doesn't think he should go back. They haven't told anyone else, and neither have I.'

He sat back. There was nothing wrong here. She was all right—just very worried about Hess.

'Do you suspect me of something?'

'No.'

'Philip, for God's sake—I came here to ask you to help me.' Hands on the arms of the chair, she tensed forward to get up. 'I didn't expect to have to explain myself.'

'Wait a minute.' He put out a hand. She sat still. 'Help you with what?'

'I don't want him to go back to prison. He'll die if he goes back there, and it's inhuman to send him. You agree, don't you?'

He said nothing. What the hell was she going to ask him to do?

'I want him kept out. Your people could do it. It would be easy. You could fly him out of Berlin. What could the Russians do?'

'They could do almost anything—including take West Berlin.' He could see she was serious, but it was incredible. 'I don't know what they *would* do, but that's what they *could* do.'

'Let them go to hell.'

'It's a nice thought, but it's not practical.'

'Philip, he's been very ill and he obviously must've been weakened. It's not right to send him back now.'

'We wouldn't let him go back if we didn't think he was well enough.'

'But his safety can't be guaranteed. Someone tried to kill him. Someone can try again.'

'I don't think that'll happen. Everyone'll be watching too closely.' He hoped he was right about that.

She jerked forward to the edge of her chair and reached a hand out to him. 'Why send him back? What's the point?'

'No point. There's no point, Karin. But what the hell d'you imagine I can do? The military control Spandau, and they're sending him back.'

'Yes, but the decision's really a political one. You—the CIA —can influence people in Washington.' Her eyes were beginning to fill as she sat on the edge of the chair.

He took a deep breath. He couldn't do any of this, what she was asking. She wasn't being reasonable at all.

She pounded a fist on her knee. 'At least keep him in hospital until I can make another appeal. I'll start it at once. He's ill now, and it'll make the case stronger. Please! Ask them!'

Shaking his head, not wanting to look at her eyes, he muttered: 'Dammit, Karin, there's nothing I can do. They'd think

I was a bloody idiot.' He pushed himself up out of the chair. 'And they'd be right.'

'I didn't think you cared what people thought.'

'I care enough not to want to look stupid—and I would if I did what you're asking.'

She sat looking at him, eyes red and filling up.

Quietly he said: 'Will you, for God's sake, cry, if you feel like it. I can't take the suspense.'

She opened her mouth to laugh, then, shaking her head jerkily and pounding her fists lightly on the chair arms, not wanting to cry, began to, bending forward with her face on her knees.

Watching the back of her head and her quivering shoulders, he sat on the arm of her chair. He laid a hand on her shoulder and sat saying nothing.

When she began to stop, taking deep, shuddering breaths and sniffing, she leaned her head against his side and said softly: 'Dammit,' and rubbed her eyes with the back of her hand.

'Why don't you come and lie down, and take it easy?'

Her head jerked up at him. 'What?'

'Why don't you come and lie down, and take it easy?'

'Is this because I'm crying?'

'No. Because I like you and I think you like me, and it'd be a good thing.'

She smiled. 'I don't think you'd take it very easy.'

'You set the pace and I'll follow.'

She chuckled.

'Come on.' He stood, holding out a hand for her.

Chapter 28

In the evening, when they were lying side by side, the phone rang beside the bed. He felt for it in the faint light from the window and snatched it up.

'Yes?'

'It's Dieter. Am I disturbing you?'

'Yes, but what is it?' He picked his watch off the side table. It was ten-twenty.

'A man named Becker's been shot—a writer with *Der Kurier*. He was in his apartment with two fellows from the National Party. They were shot too. All dead.'

The *Kurier* was a weekly news magazine: right-wing, anti-government. 'Does it mean something, Dieter?' He knew it did, or Kluger wouldn't be interested in it. It would be a routine piece of business for the police.

'I think so. I'm going over to the *Kurier*, to talk to the editor. D'you want to come?'

'Yes.' As he held the phone he was strapping on his watch.

'I'll pick you up. In twenty minutes?'

'I'll be waiting.'

Karin Hartmann was sitting up when he looked around, putting the phone down.

'Is something wrong, Philip?'

'I've got to go out. That's wrong.'

She stroked his back.

Slowly he drew away, and stood beside the bed. 'Sorry, Karin.'

'It's all right. I'll get dressed. Is there a light here?'

'Watch your eyes.' He switched the light on. 'Will you stay here till I get back?'

'How long will you be?'

'I don't know.'

'I'll go. I should go home. I've got a lot of work tomorrow and I must be up early.'

They dressed and went downstairs, out to her Porsche.

As she unlocked the door she said: 'May I drive you somewhere?'

'Thanks, but someone's coming for me.'

She stood with a hand on top of the open door. 'Where are you going, so urgently?'

'Why did you ask me that?'

'To annoy you.' She smiled. 'I wouldn't expect you to reveal anything.'

'You're strange, Karin.' He shook his head at her. 'Strange.'

Bending in to the seat, swinging her legs in under the wheel, she said: 'Why don't you call me, when you feel like it?'

'Why don't you call *me*, when you feel like it?'

'I will.' She shut the door.

He watched her tail lights down the road and stood looking after they were gone, waiting for Kluger.

Two or three minutes later headlights came around the bend down the road, and when they were closer he saw it was the silver-grey Audi.

Kluger stopped beside him and he got in.

'Who're these Nationalists who were shot, Dieter?'

'Hans Lotz, the party secretary, and Werner Brandt, chairman of the security committee.'

'God.'

'Did you know them?'

'I've met them. Brandt was a tough bastard.' He'd had to be, to be chairman of the security committee, the Nationalists' hard edge. There were squads of tough bastards in the security committee. 'If the Nationalists sent anyone to take Hess's envelope, it was Brandt. Why d'you think they were with this writer?' He knew why. So did Kluger. That was why they were both here now.

'Phil, if there was something in that envelope that would make trouble with Moscow, Becker would've been the one to take it to. Anyone on the *Kurier*, but especially Becker. He was a Nationalist member himself. A real damn Nazi.'

'When did this happen?'

'The police went into Becker's apartment and found the bodies about three hours ago. The *Kurier* phoned and asked them to go and look, because they couldn't get Becker on the phone and he'd been supposed to go in and write something this afternoon.'

'Write what?'

'I don't know. I got that from the police. I thought we should talk to the editor ourselves. I hope he can tell us more.'

'So do I.'

Chapter 29

The editor was Dr Bruno Schenk. He was a small man with a round bald head that reflected the white light from the neon strips across the ceiling of his office. It was a neat, cold-looking room, with a dark brown rug on the floor and Scandinavian furniture.

When his secretary showed Strang and Kluger in, Schenk was standing at a tilted drawing board at the side of the office, reading some page proofs. He looked rushed and nervous when he turned to meet them.

Kluger introduced Strang as Ritter, and told Schenk they were both from Internal Security. They had decided it was best not to let the *Kurier* know that the United States had an interest in what had happened.

'This is a terrible thing. Poor Becker.' Schenk sat with his elbows on his desk, shaking his head. 'I've told the police what I could. I know very little, and . . .'

'We might be looking for something different from the police, Herr Doktor,' Kluger said.

'Yes, yes, of course. Anything I can tell you, I shall be most pleased. What reason could there be for such a thing—killing three men like that? Do you think there's a political reason? Is that why you're here?'

Kluger seemed not to have heard. He said: 'You called the police and asked them to go to Becker's apartment—is that so?'

'Yes.'

'Why?'

'The deadline for the week's issue is tonight, and I was expecting something from Becker. He called me at my home yesterday afternoon and said he was going to have something interesting. He said he'd be in by early this afternoon, at the latest, with everything written.'

'What was it?' Kluger unwrapped a stick of gum.

Schenk shook his head, exasperated that Becker had told him so little. 'He said it would be politically important.'

'Embarrassing to the government, Herr Doktor?' Kluger dropped his wrapper into Schenk's ashtray and slipped the stick of gum into his mouth.

'Not to ours. He said it would make a great deal of trouble in Moscow.'

The phone rang and Schenk snatched it up as Strang and Kluger looked at each other.

'*Ja?* No, no. Not now. Tell him I'll call back. I'm busy now. Put no more calls through until I say so.' He slapped the phone down. 'Pardon.'

'What else did Becker say?'

Schenk smoothed a hand across the top of his head. 'He said it was something to do with German espionage work against Russia—during the war years. It didn't sound particularly exciting to me, and I asked him to tell me more about it before he went too far, but he wouldn't tell me anything. He told me to wait until I saw the finished story.' He spread his hands. 'That's all. And he said it would make trouble with Moscow.'

'*With* Moscow or *in* Moscow?' Strang said.

Schenk looked startled that Strang had spoken. He had been concentrating on Kluger. He stared at Strang, not understanding.

'Two minutes ago you said Becker told you it would make trouble *in* Moscow. Now you said *with* Moscow. Which did he say?'

Schenk raised his eyebrows as if it was unimportant. He looked at Kluger for support.

'Which was it?' Kluger said.

'He said *in* Moscow.' Schenk was impatient with it. 'Yes. In. He was very excited about it.'

'Was he usually excited about what he was working on?' Kluger said.

'Not usually. Not unless it was something really good. Becker was a very good and experienced journalist. A very disciplined man. It would have to be something unusual, to excite him. He was not a sensation-seeker, but a hardworking, highly intelligent journalist.'

172

'It sounds as though he had something sensational yesterday,' Strang said.

Schenk looked at him and said nothing.

'Did he tell you he was going to meet anyone from the National Party?' Kluger said.

'No. He said nothing about that. Do you think they had some connection with the story—Lotz and Brandt?'

'I asked simply if he had mentioned them, Herr Doktor.'

'No, he didn't.' Schenk shook his head. 'I still can't understand who could have killed him, and why.'

'Those are questions the police are trying to answer,' Kluger said.

*

They walked out and got into the Audi, on the street outside the *Kurier* office.

'What d'you think?' Kluger said.

'Lotz and Brandt had Hess's envelope—or what was in it—and they went to Becker with it. And someone else knew about it.'

Kluger nodded. 'Maybe the police've found something by now.' He looked at his watch. 'They've had time to get things together now. D'you want to come and talk to them?'

'Yes.'

*

The detective in charge of the case was a sergeant named Tillich, a small man in his middle thirties, with a heavy black moustache.

'They were all shot once,' he said. 'Each one shot in the head with a nine-millimetre pistol.'

'Is there an estimated time of death yet?' Kluger said.

'About twenty-four hours ago. Yesterday evening sometime.'

'Where did Becker live?'

'In an apartment in the Hansa quarter.'

'And none of the neighbours heard anything?' Kluger chewed quickly.

Tillich shook his head.

'Unusual, isn't it?'

'It's unusual to fire three shots and make no noise, yes.'

'Not with a silenced weapon,' Strang said.

'Exactly,' Tillich said. Kluger had introduced Strang as a CIA man, and Tillich wondered why the CIA was interested in this, but he did not ask. He knew there would be no useful answer.

'Was anything taken from the apartment?' Strang said.

'There was no sign of it. Nothing looked as though it had been disturbed. All three of them had money on them. It wasn't touched.'

'Had Becker or the others been hurt before they were shot?'

'Hurt?'

'Tortured,' Strang said.

Tillich did not understand. 'Tortured? No. Just killed. One shot each. Finished.' He snapped his fingers. 'Like that.'

Strang looked at Kluger and nodded. There was nothing more he wanted to hear.

'Thanks for your help, Sergeant.' Kluger got up.

'Is there anything you can tell me about this?' Tillich looked from one to the other, but stopped at Strang. 'Is there a reason why they might've been tortured?'

'Only if whoever shot them had been looking for something and hadn't found it easily. Since they weren't tortured, I think he found it—then shot them.'

'What was it?'

Strang shook his head. 'I don't know. We're looking for it too.'

*

When they were in the car Kluger sat sideways, against the door, an arm along the back of the seat, and said: 'D'you know what the hell's happening?'

'No. Only that what happened to those three is a lot like what happened to Ross. Except that whoever killed him was looking for information. I think they made him tell them who had Hess's envelope.'

'D'you think that? And Ross told them?'

Strang nodded. 'Whoever killed him must've known he was connected to the Nationalists. All they had to do was make him tell which one of them had the envelope. Then someone took it in Becker's apartment.'

'But why were these three shot?'

'To keep them from telling what was in the envelope. I can't think of another reason. Can you?'

'No.'

'But who killed them all, Dieter? Christ! The Nationalists stole Hess's envelope, but who took it from them? Who was able to kill Ross in New York and these three here in Berlin?'

Tuesday
May 3, 1977

Chapter 30

Usually he fell asleep as soon as he went to bed, and slept for seven hours. Tonight he lay awake for two hours in the dark, looking at his watch every fifteen minutes to see how much time he was wasting by lying here and trying to get to sleep. And when he at last fell asleep, eyes sore and red-feeling, he woke twice in the dark, slept again, and woke finally at five-twenty, more than an hour earlier than he normally did, and feeling more tired than he had when he went to bed. Dammit, he couldn't stop thinking about what had happened to Ross and those three men. He couldn't understand how anyone could have connected Ross to Hess's envelope. There was only one explanation and that was too unbelievable. Yet there was no other way to explain everything that had happened.

For fifteen minutes he stood in the shower, turning it to cold and standing under it to freshen himself, letting the cold water spray into his face and his red, half-shut eyes. But when he stepped out and stood drying himself he still felt God-awful.

He sat in his bathrobe in the living room, thinking, waiting till Karin Hartmann would probably be awake and he would call her. By seven-thirty he could wait no longer, and phoned.

She sounded bright and alert.

'Did I wake you?' He didn't think he had.

'No. I've been up since seven.'

Christ, and he'd been sitting here waiting. 'I want to talk to you.'

'I'm listening.'

'Not on the phone.'

'Do you want to come here—or to my office?'

'I'd like you to come here.'

'But, Philip, I don't think I can. I've got a busy . . .'

'Karin, it's important. Very.'

There was silence. 'All right—but I'm not dressed. I can't be there in less than forty-five minutes.'

'I'll wait.'

He dressed slowly, waiting for her. He didn't feel like hurrying. It was almost an hour before she arrived.

'You look tired.' She touched a fingertip under his right eye.

'I feel it.' He held her by the hand and led her into the living room.

'There's something wrong, isn't there?' She sat watching his face.

'Yes.' He told her of the murders of the man from *Der Kurier* and the two Nationalists, and that he thought Hess's document had been taken from them. 'That was why Ross was tortured—to make him tell who he'd spoken to about the envelope. Someone knew he was with the Nationalists—and you didn't know it, but anyone who was keeping them under surveillance would've. They'd have seen Ross with them.'

'But how could anyone have known Joe knew of the envelope?'

'That's the question, isn't it?'

'Yes.'

'What did you say to him, when you showed it to him in your office?'

She sat back, trying to remember.

'Did you mention Hess at any time?'

'Yes, I did. Yes. I showed him the envelope, so that he could read the instructions written on it, and said it was something Herr Hess had left with my father at Nuremberg. I said it was obviously a document of some kind.'

'And you asked whether he thought you should open it, since it seemed that Hess was going to die.'

'Yes. That's right. He advised me not to do anything.' She shook her head, thinking how wrong she had been to trust Ross. 'Oh, my God, I was so stupid.'

'No, you weren't. And that's not important now. Did you tell anyone else about the document?'

'No.'

He sat going through it all again in his head. It had to have happened this way. Nothing else was possible. 'Someone else knew about it, Karin.'

'How could that be?'

'They heard you tell Ross.'

180

'But there was no one else there—except Greta, and she was outside. Do you mean Greta . . .?'

'No. I mean someone bugged your office.'

She stared at him.

'There's no other way. Someone was able to hear what you told Ross. They'd bugged your office. Your apartment too, probably.'

'Is that why you didn't want to come and talk there now?'

'Yes.'

'Are you sure about this, Philip?'

'No, but it'll be simple to prove it—one way or the other.'

'Do you know who might've done it?'

'No. I'm not even sure it's been done. That's the first thing I want to do—make sure. I'd like to have some people look at your office. D'you mind?'

'No, of course not. If anyone's put a bug in my office, I want to know.' Now, as she sat thinking about it, she was becoming angry that someone might have done this, invaded her privacy.

'And I'd like them to go to your apartment.'

'My apartment! Do you seriously think there could be something there too?'

'Yes. I think someone's been watching you—listening to you, at least. I don't know why it's been done, but I think it has.'

Chapter 31

From his apartment Karin Hartmann phoned her secretary at home and told her not to go to the office until after lunch. Then Strang called Kluger and asked him to send an electronic detection team to her office.

'What's it all about?' Kluger said.

'I think someone's bugged the place.'

'What!'

'That's the only way anyone could've known she told Ross about that document of Hess's. Someone heard it.'

'I guess that's so. When d'you want the detector there?'

'As soon as possible. I'd like her apartment checked too.'

'All right, Phil. I'll meet you at her office with the team at ten o'clock. How's that?'

'Perfect.'

He put the phone down.

'When are they going to do it?' Karin Hartmann said.

'They'll be there at ten. Then they'll go to your apartment.'

She sat in the chair, still not completely accepting what was happening. 'It's hard to believe.'

'I know. Let's go over to your office and wait.'

When they got there it was just after nine-thirty, and they sat waiting in the outer office, not talking, thinking of the bugs that might be hidden there. A few minutes before ten Kluger came with two men and their electronic detection equipment in a suitcase.

'We should start in there, I suppose,' Kluger said softly, gesturing to the padded leather door to Karin Hartmann's office.

Strang nodded.

They opened the padded door and the inside door, and the two men with the detection equipment went in. Strang and Kluger stood with Karin Hartmann in the doorway, watching them.

One man took a transmitter-receiver from the suitcase and stood it on the floor, putting on a pair of headphones. He switched it on and sent out a hum that would be picked up by any bug that might be in the room. The second man uncoiled wires from the receiver to a metal wand, a receiving antenna, and began sweeping it around the room. The man at the receiver sat listening for the hum to be picked up and retransmitted by the bug.

The man with the wand passed it slowly across the desk, holding the wires clear of the top, not to disarrange papers or files.

The wand made a slow pass down the left side of the desk, then past the drawers on that side, and up underneath. The operator at the receiver put up a hand to one earphone, listening hard. He hissed, tugging gently at his end of the wires.

The man with the wand looked under the desk, bent and reached in, and came up holding a small bug, the short wire of an antenna trailing from it. He tossed it across to the doorway and Kluger caught it, tugging out the antenna.

'I'm still getting a signal,' the man with the headset whispered. 'There's another one here somewhere.'

Kluger signed to them to go on searching.

They swept around the drapes and windows, then below the sills, and in one of the big plotted plants, just under the soil, found another bug, the thin wire of the antenna hidden behind the stem of the plant. They passed it out to Kluger.

They searched everywhere: walls, behind picture frames, bookshelves, and even under the carpet, and found nothing more.

'Try out there now,' Kluger said, nodding through the door to the outer office.

While the men searched outside, Strang and Kluger sat with Karin Hartmann at her desk.

Strang looked at one of the bugs. It was American.

'It's one of ours,' he said.

'This one too.' Kluger laid the other bug on the desk.

Strang felt her looking at him. 'It doesn't mean anything, Karin. Anyone could've bought these things.' Especially someone who wanted to leave a false trail, who wanted Americans blamed if the bugs were found.

Kluger held up one of the thin wires. 'They'd transmit for blocks with this antenna.'

'I know how far, Dieter. The question is: how long? How long've these things been here?'

Karin Hartmann sat staring at the two transmitters on her desk. 'To think that someone's been listening to everything I've said. My God.'

One of the men looked in from the outer office. 'Just one out here.' He held it up. 'Under the secretary's desk.'

'That's so they'd hear the names of people coming in to see you, Fräulein,' Kluger said.

She looked even more miserable and angry.

'We'll go and find the bad news in your apartment now, Karin,' Strang said.

He drove with her in her car, and Kluger and his two men followed, to her apartment in Tiergarten.

They found another bug in the living room, behind one of the drapes; and one in the bedroom, under the bedside table. Both were American, the same type as the three in her office.

Kluger set them side by side on a coffee table in the living room.

Karin Hartmann sat on the couch, far back from them, looking at them as though they were obscene.

'Is there anywhere else you want us to look, Phil?' Kluger said.

'No. Thanks, Dieter.'

'We'll move along. Talk to you later.'

Karin Hartmann walked to the door with Kluger and his men, and when she came back across the living room she had her arms folded, gripping her elbows as though she was cold. She sat on the couch, not looking at the bugs on the coffee table.

Quietly, sounding numb, she said: 'Who could have done this?'

'It wasn't the Nationalists. They had Ross close to you. They didn't need more than that.'

'But whoever did it are the ones who killed Joe. Is that what you think?'

'Yes. And Lotz and Brandt, and the man from *Der Kurier*, Becker. And they've got Hess's document.'

'But why did they kill Joe? How did anyone know he was

184

involved? They heard me tell him about it, but how did they know he was involved in—stealing it?' Even now it was not easy for her to say that about Ross.

'Because they went to your office after it was gone.'

'What!' It was too much for her, that someone else had broken into her office.

'Someone else went to get it and found it was gone. Ross was the only one you'd told about it. Obviously he was involved. They must've gone for it later the same day, last Thursday. You found it was gone when you came back from lunch. They probably went for it in the evening. And Ross was killed in New York next day.'

'Why? Why would anyone have done all this? All for that document? Is that it, Philip?'

'There's no other reason.'

'But why would anyone do all this for something like that— after all this time? It had been in the safe for more than thirty years. What value could it possibly have? Why did no one steal it before this?'

He sat staring at the bugs. 'I don't know, Karin.' Unless no one had known about it, all those years. Was that possible? Was it possible that the people who'd taken it hadn't known of it till now?

'What are you thinking?' she said.

'When was it you went to Spandau to see Hess?'

'To talk about the appeal? In January.'

'Did he say anything to you about this document?'

'Yes, he did. And I was surprised. I expected, from all I'd heard, that he'd never have remembered anything from so long ago. I expected him to be vague and not able to remember anything.'

'What did he say?'

'He asked me if I had the envelope he'd given my father at Nuremberg. We'd never met before, and I suppose he wanted to be sure my father had left it and I knew about it.'

'Is that all he said about it?'

'Yes. I told him I had it and he smiled and nodded. That's all.'

Christ! Was this it? Had it really happened like this? 'Where did he say this, Karin?'

'In the visiting room. That's the only place where one can see him.'

'Were there jailers in the room?'

'Yes. Two, I think.'

'D'you remember what they were?'

'What do you mean?'

'American, French—what?' There was something here. He felt it. This was how it had to be done.

'I can't remember.' She thought, and shook her head. 'I really can't.'

He sat watching her trying to remember.

'One was French, I think. I remember Herr Hess saying something to one of them in French. The other was English, perhaps, but I'm not sure.'

'Only those two?'

'Yes. I'm almost certain.'

'When Hess said this about the document, could one of them have heard it?'

She shook her head. 'No. I almost didn't hear it myself. Herr Hess said it very quickly and almost whispered it.' She smiled at the eccentricity. 'He was very conspiratorial. He leaned to me across the table—there was a table between us, and he was on one side of a wall and I was on the other, and we spoke through a square hole—he leaned over and whispered this. Very quickly. I'm sure no one heard. I looked at one of the jailers and he seemed uncomfortable that he hadn't heard. I suppose they have orders to listen to everything.'

'But no one at Spandau asked you what Hess had said?'

'Oh, no! I wouldn't have told them, of course.'

He smiled quickly. 'Of course. But someone must've heard.'

'Why do you say that?'

'Because someone put these things around you.' He nodded at the bugs on the coffee table.

She stared at them from the couch. 'Do you think this was done then—after I spoke to Herr Hess in January?'

'Yes.'

'They've been here all that time,' she whispered to herself. 'And you think it was done because he spoke to me about that envelope?'

'Yes. Maybe the jailers didn't hear it, but someone did.'

186

Chapter 32

When he had explained what he wanted to do, Goodblood lifted off his glasses and dropped them on his blotter, sitting back and rubbing his eyes as though he was just waking and had not clearly heard it. Without the glasses his face looked softer and vulnerable.

'If you're serious about wanting to do this, I think you're a candidate for the psycho ward. I don't enjoy saying it.' Goodblood picked up his glasses. 'God dammit, Strang, we can't go in there and do that.'

'What's the alternative—to let this thing go on? To send Hess back there, not knowing who tried to do this or why— and let them try again? Next time he might die.'

Carefully Goodblood lifted his glasses back on, winding the wire earpieces over his ears, giving it all his attention, not to have to answer Strang.

'We have to do it, Colonel. We've got to know if it happened as I think it did. When we know that, we might be closer to finding out who tried to kill Hess.'

'But we can't go into Spandau and do what you're suggesting.' Goodblood laid out an open hand on his desk, palm up, to show how understanding and patient he was, to be discussing this at all. 'We're not even in control out there now.'

'Who is?'

'Who comes after us?' Goodblood flicked a glance at the ceiling. 'The British. It's a British month now.'

'And they've got troops out there?'

'Of course they've got troops out there.'

'But Hess is in the hospital, for God's sake!'

'Yes, he's in the damn hospital, but the normal guard complement's on duty there—on the gate and in the towers. Guarding a prison without a prisoner.'

'My God.'

'I agree. But the Russians insisted on it. D'you begin to

187

understand what I mean when I say your suggestion's insane?'

'You've still got your investigators out there?'

'Yes.'

'We can go in and do it as part of the investigation.'

Goodblood looked doubtful.

'The British will co-operate, Colonel.'

Goodblood sat with his forearms on his desk, looking at Strang as though he was seeing him for the first time and not finding him pleasant.

'Will you ask them?' It didn't surprise him that Goodblood was taking it like this, and he didn't blame him for it. What he was suggesting was desperate—but everything that had happened in these few days was desperate.

'They wouldn't do it. They'd think I was out of my mind.'

'Colonel, for God's sake—ask!'

Goodblood sat unmoved, his face stiff.

'Which is easier: to go out to Spandau and do this, or have Hess go back there and take the chance there'll be another attempt to kill him? Those are the alternatives, Colonel. And if he's killed, we begin the dogfight with Moscow over whether they should go on sending their guard into an empty prison.'

Very slightly, almost unconsciously, Goodblood began to nod, beginning to agree as he thought what Hess's death could mean.

'I'm going to try it.' He put out a hand for the phone. 'I'll talk to the British director.'

'Have him come here. We shouldn't take a chance with this on the phone.' He was relieved that Goodblood was going to do it. But if he hadn't been able to convince him, he'd have gone to General Benson, or all the way to Washington if necessary.

'All right. I'll invite him down here.' Goodblood called Spandau and asked for the British director. He hung up. 'They're all at the hospital, visiting Hess—all the directors.'

'Call him there, Colonel.' Dammit, he could see Goodblood still wasn't enthusiastic about it.

'I'll get Colonel McCubbin—he's the American director. He can talk to the British director and bring him over here.' Goodblood called the hospital and asked them to bring Colonel

McCubbin to the phone. 'Colonel, it's Colonel Goodblood, at the Mission. I'm well, thank you. And you? Good. Colonel, there's something I'd like to discuss with Colonel Dampier. No, I can't tell you about it on the phone, but it's very important. Could you bring him over here? I'd appreciate it if you'd do that. Tell him it's urgent and top priority. How long will you be there at the hospital? Fine, Colonel. If you can do that, it'll be fine. Appreciate it.' Looking relieved, Goodblood put the phone down. 'He's going to bring the British director over in a few minutes. He was curious about it.'

'I think we can satisfy the curiosity—so long as they get here.'

In twenty minutes they came. McCubbin was overweight and had a red face, with high spots of colour on the cheeks, almost purple. He had a deep voice, and he looked and sounded like a good-natured salesman.

Dampier looked as though he did not approve of McCubbin. He was a tall, slim man, with yellow hair, and his eyebrows were so light that they were almost invisible. His eyes were very pale blue and fixed-looking, points of light. He had two rows of medal ribbons and carried a leather-covered swagger stick.

'This is Mr Strang's idea, Colonel Dampier,' Goodblood said. 'I'll let him explain it to you.'

Dampier turned to Strang with his bright stare, and held on his pale tan corduroy Norfolk jacket and blue paisley ascot and Strang saw he disapproved of him too. It wasn't just McCubbin. Dampier was a man who was accustomed to disapprove. It might not be easy to convince him of what they had to do at Spandau.

'Last week a document was stolen from the office of Hess's lawyer, Miss Hartmann. It had been held for Hess since nineteen forty-six. He gave it to Miss Hartmann's father, his lawyer at Nuremberg, to make it public after his death. It had been held all those years, but last week it was stolen. This morning we searched Miss Hartmann's office and her apartment, and found bugs there, electronic listening devices. Someone's been listening to her, and I'm sure it was because they wanted to know about that document. The question was: why now, after all these years? She's told me Hess mentioned it to

189

her when she went to see him in Spandau last January. I think someone heard what he said.'

'There were jailers in the visiting room, of course.' Dampier had a high, thin voice, and spoke sharply, in sentences that were short bursts of words.

'Two, Miss Hartmann said.'

'Quite. They're there to monitor conversations between Hess and any visitor.'

'I know that, Colonel.'

'But one of them spoke of it to someone outside? Is that your implication?'

'She says neither of them could've heard. Hess spoke very quietly, and it was a quick reference to his document. She thinks it was impossible for either of the jailers to hear.'

'You're suggesting—what?' Carefully Dampier crossed his knees, and held his swagger stick in both hands, rested across his thigh.

'I think there's a bug in the visiting room at Spandau.'

Dampier tightened the grip on his swagger stick, raising it off his leg and flexing it in his hands.

'Jesus!' McCubbin rumbled a low, nervous laugh, and glanced at Goodblood, but Goodblood was watching Dampier.

'Why?' Dampier snapped. 'Why would anyone put a bug there?'

'To hear Hess's conversations with his visitors,' Strang said. 'There's no other reason.'

'What could he say that would interest anyone?'

'He said something in January, Colonel. I'm convinced his lawyer was bugged because of that, and the document was stolen.'

'This document—d'you know what it is?'

'No. And I can't imagine who wanted it or why. But I think the same people tried to kill Hess—in case he remembered what was in it.'

Gently Dampier tapped his swagger stick on his thigh. He turned to Goodblood. 'What d'you think of this, Colonel? Might there be a bug?'

'Nothing's impossible, Colonel.'

It surprised Strang to hear how Goodblood sounded. A lot less doubtful now than he'd been forty minutes ago, when they were talking of it together. Now Goodblood, the professional investigator, was supporting him. Maybe because he'd had more time to think about it, maybe just that it was one professional investigator supporting another.

'You think it'd be helpful to search the visiting room?' Dampier said.

'If Mr Strang proved right and we found a bug there, it certainly would,' Goodblood said. 'It might help us determine who tried to kill Hess.'

'If it were to be done, would your investigators do it?'

'I'd send a detection team out there. They'd work with the investigation unit there now.'

'The Russians wouldn't have it.' Dampier was still lightly tapping his stick on his thigh. 'They wouldn't stand for it.'

'Would they have to know, Colonel?' Strang said.

Dampier flicked his sharp blue eyes to him.

'The Soviet director's going to be at the hospital until this evening.' McCubbin said. 'He's keeping an eye on the preparations to move Hess back to Spandau.'

Strang saw McCubbin was with him. 'How many Soviet jailers are out at Spandau now?'

'Only three,' McCubbin said. 'Half of them are at the hospital. We've been moving teams of jailers to and from there, to maintain the watch on Hess around the clock. The jailers left at Spandau have nothing to do.'

'Would it be possible to keep the Soviets away from the visiting-room area for an hour or so?' Strang said to Dampier.

'Yes. Could be done. That could be done.' As he tapped with his swagger stick, Dampier was considering it, and he snapped to Goodblood: 'When could your people be there, Colonel?'

'Within an hour.'

'Would the two of you want to come with them?'

Strang nodded to Goodblood and Goodblood said: 'Yes. There'll be the two of us and two of my men.'

'Very well.' Briskly Dampier nodded. 'Very well. I'll lay it on. There's always one jailer on duty with the military guard at the gate. The one there when you arrive won't be Russian. Will you, Colonel, get out of your car and identify yourself to him? I'll give the word to expect you. Colonel McCubbin and

191

I will see there's no Russian jailer near the visiting room while you're there. Not likely there will be, anyhow. Been taking it easy for the past week, keeping to their quarters most of the time. But we'll see to it that he's diverted, if one of them looks like walking in that direction.' He gave a sharp, final tap with his swagger stick on his thigh. 'I'll trot back. Get things organised. By the way, Colonel, it might be advisable if you and your men wore civilian clothes, as your investigation people at Spandau are now. Make you less conspicuous, in case one of the Russians should see you moving about.'

'We'll do that,' Goodblood said.

Dampier looked at Strang, at the paisley ascot. 'This gentleman is already in civilian clothes. Very much so.' He rose, very erect, tucking his swagger stick under his left armpit, and snapped to McCubbin: 'Coming, Colonel?'

McCubbin pushed himself heavily to his feet.

Chapter 33

Goodblood sat with Strang in the back of an unmarked car from the Mission, and two of his plainsclothesmen were in front with their detection equipment.

They turned off Wilhelmstrasse, down the cobbled driveway to the entrance to Spandau, and stopped two paces from the green-painted gates in the high wall.

Goodblood climbed out and pressed the bell-push beside the gates, taking his billfold from his hip pocket. A shutter in a gate opened and a jailer's face was at the small barred window. A man in late middle age.

'Yes?' The jailer sounded American.

'Colonel Goodblood.' Goodblood held his Army identification in the billfold up to the bars, and the jailer stared at it, at Goodblood's face, and back at the photo on the identification.

'That looks okay, Colonel. Will you please step aside, so I can see how many there are in the car?'

Goodblood turned sideways from the grille.

'Four of you altogether?' the jailer said.

'That's right.'

'Okay, sir. Colonel Dampier said to expect four. If you'll get back in the car, and tell your driver to come on slowly, and stop again right inside.'

As Goodblood climbed back in beside Strang the big gates began swinging open.

'Drive in slowly, Jordan, and stop right inside the gates.'

'Yes, Colonel.'

Slowly the car drove in, and stopped. The gates closed behind them. They were in a short, dim tunnel with an arched roof. In front of them was a British military vehicle, a Land Rover. Beyond it was another pair of closed gates.

The jailer came to the car with a British lieutenant, who saluted Goodblood and said: 'May we see the identification of the rest of your party, sir?'

Strang and the two plainsclothesmen held out their open wallets, with their identification. The jailer and the officer examined them, comparing the photographs with their faces.

The jailer nodded and the lieutenant stepped back, slammed his heels together on the cobblestones, and saluted Goodblood again. 'It's all in order, sir.' Pointing at the gates ahead, he said to Goodblood's driver: 'When those gates open, please follow my vehicle.'

The driver nodded.

In a cubicle at the side of the tunnel, the jailer did not log them in the visitors' register. Colonel Dampier had given orders that there should be no record of their visit for the Russians to find. He pushed a bell button, giving a code of rings, the signal to open the inner gates.

The British lieutenant sat at the wheel of his Land Rover, watching the steel gates. They swung open and, glancing back to see the American car was following, he drove out of the tunnel, past British troops with automatic rifles in front of the guard hut beside the inner gates. The car followed him out across the cobbled courtyard and stopped behind him, at the door to the administration block.

Strang and Goodblood stepped out to the cobblestones, and the two plainsclothesmen lifted out their detection equipment. The British lieutenant led them in along a high-ceilinged corridor to a small office. Dampier and McCubbin were in there, standing at a desk, talking.

The lieutenant stiffened to attention, heels clashing on the floor, and saluted. 'Coloned Goodblood and his party, sir.'

'Ah, there you are, Colonel. Thank you, Lieutenant.' Elegantly Dampier returned the salute, right palm casually up to his right eyebrow. 'Carry on.'

The lieutenant stiffened to attention, heels clashing on the floor, and saluted. 'Colonel Goodblood and his party, sir.'

'All right. Let's get to work.' Dampier picked up his swagger stick from the desk. 'I'll take you along to the visiting room in a moment.' To McCubbin: 'Colonel, will you go along now and stop and chat to any of those Russians chaps you might see coming our way?'

'I'll take care of it.' McCubbin grinned at Strang and Goodblood. 'Good luck, gentlemen.'

Dampier stood waiting a minute after he was gone, then tucked his swagger stick under his left armpit, holding it lightly at the tip. 'Shall we go?'

They followed him out, down a corridor to the visiting room. It was small, with bare walls that were painted light green on the lower half, cream on the upper. The high ceiling was white. In one wall was a wide square opening, with a narrow table under the bottom edge, built into the wall. Two straightback wooden chairs were set against the wall, one at either end of the table. At the side of the room was a small square table and a chair, for the jailer who would sit there listening to everything that was said when Hess had a visitor.

Strang leaned across the narrow table and looked through the square opening. Below it on the other side was another narrow table built against the wall, a chair at either end of it. In there was another small room, with another table and chair for a jailer. There was a door, where Hess would come in to see his visitor.

'Used to be a sort of wire grille here.' Dampier pointed with the tip of his swagger stick around the square opening. 'Taken out years ago. Nothing to keep a visitor from the prisoner now but these.' He tapped lightly on the narrow table and the one on the other side.

Goodblood glanced around the bare room, and through the opening at the room on the other side. He drew his head back and said to Strang: 'Not many places here to hide a bug. Where d'you want to start?'

'If there's anything, this'll be the place for it.' Strang swung a hand around the square opening and the tables on either side of it.

'All right,' Goodblood said to the plainsclothesmen. 'Make a start here.' He tapped the table on their side of the wall.

Strang and Goodblood stood with Dampier, watching one of the plainsclothesmen sweeping slowly with the detector wand over the table. The other man sat at the side table, wearing headphones, listening at the receiver.

Almost at once, as the wand moved down one side of the table, the man at the receiver bent to listen more closely. 'I'm getting something,' he said softly, and made an adjustment to his tuning.

The man with the wand passed it under the table.

'It's there,' the man at the receiver said.

The man with the wand bent and looked under the table, probing further under with the wand. 'I think I've got it.' He laid the wand on the table and reached in under with both hands. On his knees, voice rumbling under the table, he said: 'Here it is.' His body jerked as he tugged, and he backed out holding a bug with a thin antenna dangling. He handed it to Goodblood.

'I'm damned!' Dampier muttered.

'So am I,' Goodblood said. 'You were right, Mr Strang.'

Strang said nothing. The bug, under the table, against the dividing wall, had been directly under Hess when he leaned forward to whisper to Karin Hartmann.

'It's American,' Goodblood said, and tugged out the antenna. Dampier's blue eyes were on them both at once.

'So were the ones we found this morning,' Strang said. Like the others, this one could have transmitted for several blocks with the antenna, some distance from Spandau.

'I'm not hearing any more transmission, sir,' the man at the receiver said.

'Make sure,' Goodblood said. 'Maybe there was only this one—but make sure.'

Strang thought there was only the one under the table. It had been put there to hear Hess and no one else.

The men swept the rest of the room, then climbed through the opening and swept the other room. There were no more bugs. They all walked back to the office with Dampier, and Goodblood sent his two plainsclothesmen out to wait in the car.

'I'll go and tell Colonel McCubbin you're finished,' Dampier said. 'Shan't be more than a moment.' He walked crisply out.

'What d'you think about this?' Goodblood was tossing the bug lightly on his palm. 'Who the hell d'you think put it there?' He was keeping his voice low, still thinking of what the bug had been able to do.

Strang stood looking at it bouncing on Goodblood's hand. He didn't think there was any doubt who'd put it there. Not now. But there was still too much he couldn't begin to understand.

Nodding at the door where Dampier and McCubbin would come in, he said: 'I think we should talk to those two. They might be able to help us with who put it there.'

'I hope so.'

'But we should do it back at the Mission.' Strang looked around the room. 'I'd like to be able to talk without wondering who's listening.' He didn't think there were more bugs here, but he didn't feel comfortable.

'I'll tell them.'

Dampier and McCubbin came in, both looking solemn.

'This is serious business, gentlemen,' McCubbin said.

'Yes.' Goodblood was still speaking softly and, gesturing with a hand around the room, said: 'We'd like to talk to you about it—but at the Mission.'

'Yes. Quite.' Dampier glanced at the walls. 'Now?'

'If that's convenient.'

'Yes. Absolutely. We can both go in my car, Colonel,' he said to McCubbin.

They drove down to the Mission, Dampier's car following Goodblood's, and went up to Goodblood's office.

'D'you actually think there might be more bugs at Spandau?' Dampier said. It had been worrying him all the way down in his car.

'Probably not,' Strang said. 'There's no reason for it. Someone wanted to hear what Hess said to his visitors—that's why the bug was in the visiting room.'

'Who d'you think put it there?' Dampier said.

'We hope you gentlemen can help us answer that.'

'We'll do what we can, of course,' Dampier said.

'The jailers have access to the visiting room at any time, I suppose?' Strang said.

'Yes.' Dampier rested the tip of his swagger stick on his crossed knee. 'Any of them could, in theory, drop in there and place a bug. Are you thinking of any national group in particular—French or Russians, perhaps?'

'Not necessarily, Colonel. Anyone could be bought—just as Lichti was.'

Dampier sat gently tapping his knee. He did not enjoy the suggestion that one of the British jailers could be bribed. 'Any of the staff could've gone in there—one of the cleaners, for

197

example. One doesn't like to think it; they've been there many years, most of them. Loyal people. Don't you agree, Colonel?'

'I do,' McCubbin said.

'Have there been any new personnel in the past few months —some time before January?'

McCubbin shook his head.

'No,' Dampier said. 'No staff changes for several years.'

'What about the military guard? Are they always the same men?'

'The officers and NCOs are, as far as possible. Each of the Four Powers makes an effort to send the same officers and NCOs, since they know the routine. The men, the other ranks, aren't always the same, of course. But you must understand'— Dampier wiggled the end of his swagger stick at Strang, and lowered it when Strang glared at it—'none of the military guard has any responsibility for security inside the prison building, therefore no legitimate reason to go inside. Their duty is solely the security of the perimeter—to man the gates and the guard towers.'

'Would it have been impossible for one of them to go in and plant that bug?' Strang said.

'Not impossible. But risky, one might say. He would most certainly have had to explain his presence, had he been seen inside.'

McCubbin put out a hand to Dampier. 'There was something like that, d'you remember, Colonel—with a Soviet officer?'

Dampier looked at him, trying to recall it. 'Yes.' He tapped his swagger stick into the palm of his hand. 'Now, yes, there was. Last November, was it?'

'That's right,' McCubbin said.

'What happened?' Strang heard how controlled his voice was. He didn't feel controlled; he felt on the edge of something.

'The Russian officer commanding their guard unit was found wandering through the administration wing. One of the French jailers, I think it was, saw him—isn't that so, Colonel?'

'That's right,' McCubbin said.

'It was reported to a meeting of the prison directors, but we didn't regard it as significant. The officer was new, and the

198

Russian director, who was in charge that month, simply mentioned it to him and asked him not to do it again.'

'The officer was new?' Strang said. 'Was he at Spandau for the first time in November?'

'First and only time. For at least two years the officer commanding the Russian unit's been a chap called Sobennikov, a captain. Pleasant enough chap. He brought their unit there again in March, as usual.'

'Who was the officer who replaced him in November?'

Dampier gave a little grunt, impatient. 'Shouldn't think that's important, is it?'

'D'you remember, Colonel, or not?' It wasn't important, but he liked to keep Dampier off balance.

'Damned if I do.' Dampier tapped his swagger stick on his thigh. 'D'you, Colonel?'

'No.' McCubbin shook his head. 'I only talked to him once —or tried to. He didn't speak much English. But the name would be in the records at Spandau.'

'And Sobennikov's been commanding their guard detail for two years?'

'Yes,' Dampier said. 'Slightly longer.'

'Never any interruption, for taking leave or any other reason?'

'Usually the chaps arrange to take their leave in the months when they're not at Spandau. Not hard to do, of course; they come to Spandau only one month in four.'

'Did anyone ask Sobennikov why he wasn't there in November?'

'I did,' McCubbin said. 'He told me he was called to Moscow. I guess it was to take some kind of course, but he didn't say and I didn't ask. D'you think there's something strange about this, Mr Strang?'

'It's something to think about.' He looked at Goodblood. 'Agree, Colonel?'

'I do,' Goodblood said.

*

When Dampier and Goodblood had left, Goodblood said: 'You think this Russian captain put that bug in the visiting room?'

'I'd bet everything on it. I don't know why it was done in November, and not thirty years ago—but that Soviet captain did it, all right.'

'To pick up Hess's conversation with his visitors?'

'Colonel, that's the only time Hess might say something worth hearing, when he's talking to a visitor. That's the only time he might say anything confidential. The Soviets heard him mention that document and they went after it. The Nationalists were never involved, except that they stole it when Ross told them about it. They just got in the way. for a few hours. But they didn't hire Lichti. It's been a Soviet operation from the beginning. They hired Lichti and killed him—him and the others. All for that document.'

'And you think they're the ones who tried to kill Hess?'

Strang nodded.

'But for God's sake why? Moscow's got every reason to want to keep him alive.'

'It makes no sense, Colonel. I agree with you, it makes no sense—but they went after that document, and they wanted Hess dead because there was a chance he might remember what's in it.'

'And what *is* in it? What the hell is it that Moscow's gone to so much trouble to keep hidden? What could be more important to them than keeping Hess alive in Spandau?'

'I think it's something Hess did before the war, early in thirty-nine. Something about a group of Soviet officers who worked for German intelligence. I think that's Hess's secret, Colonel.'

Chapter 34

Goodblood had not wanted to come, but Strang had convinced him that they had to know if there was even the frailest chance of learning what Moscow had judged was so vital—so vital that they had taken such risks for it.

'But I don't trust psychiatrists,' Goodblood had said. 'I've got no confidence in them. None. Not that I've had any personal experience with them, God knows, but I don't like them —and I don't think this man will say anything that means a damn.'

'I don't have any faith in them either, Colonel, but I think we should go and talk to Edison about this. Last week, when we thought Hess might've tried to kill himself, Edison told me he didn't think so. He was right about that. He might have some ideas about this too—and I'd like to hear them.'

Goodblood had looked unimpressed.

'Colonel, this is important. It's too important to overlook a chance.'

At last he had persuaded Goodblood to come with him to the hospital and hear what Captain Edison thought, but now, sitting in Edison's office, he could see Goodblood was still doubtful. He was sure Edison could see it too, but he seemed untroubled by it.

'Could Hess remember, Captain? That's what we want to know.'

Edison leaned back in his chair, hands behind his head. 'You say he actually wrote this in forty-six?'

'That's when he gave it to his lawyer. I'd guess he wrote it then, while he was at Nuremberg. If he'd done it before, in England, it would've been found on him when he was taken to Nuremberg.'

'And it's about something that goes back to thirty-nine?'

'Yes.'

Edison took a deep breath and stroked his blond moustache.

He was not wearing his uniform jacket, and Strang had seen when they walked in how Goodblood disapproved of the way he looked, with his shirt cuffs turned back and his tie off, collar open.

'If he wrote it at Nuremberg, there's no reason why he shouldn't be able to remember it,' Edison said.

'Why?' Goodblood said sharply.

Goodblood was going to fight this all the way, Strang could see. He was going to question everything Edison told them, and if all his questions were answered he still wouldn't be convinced.

Resting a knee on the edge of his desk and rocking his chair gently back and forth, Edison said: 'He began complaining of amnesia at the end of forty-one, about six months after he landed in Britain. But if he still remembered something in forty-six, there's no reason why he shouldn't remember it now.'

'He spoke of this document to his lawyer, four months ago,' Strang said.

Edison stopped rocking. 'He did? What did he say?'

'Just asked her if she had it.'

'Did he say anything about it—about the contents?'

'No. He asked if she still had the envelope he gave her father at Nuremberg.'

'That's all?'

Strang nodded.

Edison began rocking again. 'It's enough. There's no question he remembers the document. My guess is he'd certainly remember what he wrote in it.'

'After thirty years, Captain?' Goodblood, rubbing his eye behind his glasses, looked ready to laugh.

'Yes, Colonel.' Still with his hands behind his head, Edison smiled slightly, knowing what Goodblood was thinking, unaffected by it. 'If he remembers, after thirty years, that this document exists, I have no doubt at all that he remembers what he wrote in it.'

'Then there's something I'd like you to explain to me.'

'What's that, Colonel?'

'If this document described something that happened in thirty-nine, how could he have remembered it and written about it in forty-six, if he lost his memory in forty-one?'

Nodding gently, as though he had expected Goodblood to ask

it, Edison came forward in his chair, feet on the floor and elbows on his desk, looking businesslike. 'Last week, when Mr Strang and I were discussing old Hess, I gave my opinion that most, maybe all, of his psychological problems were self-induced. I think his amnesia, if it's real at all, is highly selective.'

'You do?'

'Yes, Colonel. I think he's simply decided to forget what he wants to forget, which is a great deal. But anything else, I've got no doubt he remembers. This document of his sounds like something he certainly wants to remember.'

'D'you think he'd talk about it, Captain?' Strang said, and from the corner of his eye he saw Goodblood's head come around instantly, and felt him staring, but he said: 'Would he tell what he'd written in that document?'

'That's another question. I think it might be very hard to persuade him.'

'Why?'

'I don't know what this document is, but he's had strong motivation, all these years, to say nothing to anyone about it, and to remember it. If his instructions were, as his lawyer told you, that it should be made public after his death, he's probably had it in his mind constantly, all his thirty years in Spandau. He must've had a very strong reason for that. Can you make a guess about what might be in it?'

'I think it's about a group of senior Red Army officers who worked for German intelligence during the war. Hess recruited them, some time early in thirty-nine.'

Edison pushed out his lower lip, up on to his blond moustache. 'Wow!' he said quietly. 'I'm not sure he'd talk easily about that. Not at all.'

Strang felt Goodblood still watching him, but did not look at him, and said: 'Why not?'

'I imagine his reason for giving it to his lawyer at Nuremberg, and for the instruction to publish it posthumously, was that he was convinced he'd be executed. He knew that was what the Soviets wanted. And he wanted some revenge against them. Revenge would've been his motive. A document like that, about a group of their senior officers, would've been pretty explosive stuff in Moscow in forty-six, wouldn't it?'

Strang nodded. 'It still would.'

203

'I'm sure you're right. And I'm sure Hess realises it too—which is why I think he'd be unwilling to talk about it. Considering the old boy's psychology—all his pride, that massive ego—I'd say his desire for revenge against the Soviets, who've been responsible for keeping him locked up so long, must be very strong. Very strong.' Edison shook his head. 'God, that must be all he lives for.'

'So you think it'd be hard to persuade him to talk?'

'He's had a powerful reason to keep this secret, all these years. You'd have to give him an equally powerful one to share it with you.'

*

When they were riding down in the elevator Goodblood said nothing, nor when they were crossing the hospital lobby, where the MPs on duty came to attention and saluted him, but all the way Strang was waiting for Goodblood to say what he had been thinking, the last ten minutes in Edison's office.

They walked out, and along the front of the hospital two more MPs saluted Goodblood. Impatiently he returned the salutes. He wanted to get into his car. He could not wait. Strang could see it and feel it.

They walked along the line of parked cars behind the hospital, and Goodblood got in behind the wheel, slamming the door. At once he turned in his seat, one hand on the wheel, one along the back of the seat, and said: 'All right, what was all that about?'

'What was all what about, Colonel?'

'You know damn well what I'm talking about. Why were you asking whether Hess might talk?'

'Because I want to talk to him.'

Goodblood had known it, but even now, now he heard it, he could not believe it.

'I've got to, Colonel.'

'You're out of your damn mind. The Russians'd never let you go out to Spandau and talk to him.'

'In here.' Strang nodded to the hospital. 'I can talk to him here.'

'They've got their jailers watching him here. He might as well be in Spandau. They wouldn't let you close to him.'

204

'It can be done, Colonel. I've got a plan.'

'But, dammit, Strang, there's no time for plans. He leaves here tomorrow morning. At oh-eight hundred he goes out of there and back to Spandau.'

'It can still be done. I think we should go and talk to the commandant about it.'

'General Benson?' Goodblood eased his cap off his forehead, looking oddly at Strang, moving a little away from him, until the back of his cap was against the side window.

'With or without you, I'll go and tell him about this. I've got to talk to Hess before he gets back inside Spandau. We've got to know what was in that document of his, Colonel. The Soviets killed six people to get it, and they tried to kill Hess to keep him quiet. Anything they worked that hard for is something we should know about.'

Chapter 35

It was early evening when they got to the commandant's residence. Goodblood had insisted on going home from the hospital, to change into a fresh uniform before they went to see General Benson, and Strang had gone with him. All the way to his house, and while he was changing his uniform, Goodblood had argued with him, trying to convince him how damn stupid it was to suggest getting in to talk to Hess this way, and how much trouble there would be with the Russians if it were done and they heard about it, and finally how General Benson would think they were both crazy if they went to him and suggested it.

Strang had said it had to be done, and if Goodblood did not want to come with him to Benson, that was understandable, but would change nothing. He would still go. All of it was, anyway, his responsibility not Goodblood's, and Goodblood should not feel involved, whichever way it went.

But Goodblood had not wanted to let it go. Not agreeing with it, he had still insisted on going with Strang to see General Benson, and Strang saw at last that he wanted to be there only to make it clear to Benson that he disapproved. He also saw that Goodblood did not want to miss a chance to present himself to his commanding officer, even a chance like this. He had not been pleased to see that in Goodblood. He never liked to see it, in anyone.

It was there, though. When they rang the bell at Benson's front door and stood waiting, he saw how Goodblood was tidying himself: tightening the knot of his tie into his collar, tugging and smoothing the skirt of his uniform jacket. Strang wished he hadn't seen him like this.

A corporal opened the door. He came to attention for Goodblood. 'Good evening, sir.'

'Good evening, Corporal. We've come to see the general.'

'Yes, sir. Will you come in, gentlemen? I'll get his aide.'

They stepped into a wide, square hall, and the corporal led them into a waiting room at the side. 'I'll get Captain Wylie, gentlemen.'

Strang stood with his back to a marble fireplace. Goodblood sat in an armchair. Strang had noticed that about him: he never stood if he could sit, especially if it meant standing with people who were much taller than he was. He hoped Goodblood wasn't going to complicate it for him with Benson, and make it harder than it had to be.

Captain Wylie came in, and Goodblood introduced him to Strang.

'Why d'you want to see the general, Mr Strang?'

'It's delicate, Captain. I'm sorry. I can't talk about it to anyone but him. But it's urgent.'

'We've got a couple of people from Washington—a couple of senators—and the ambassador's in from Bonn.' Wylie looked at his watch. 'They'll be going in to dinner in a few minutes. It's too bad you didn't phone before you came.'

'It *is* very delicate. I didn't want to use the phone.'

'You know how it is with the CIA, Captain.' Goodblood chuckled, sounding very nervous.

'Yes, sir.' Wylie looked again at his watch. 'I'll go and tell the general, Mr Strang. Maybe he'll come out for a few minutes before dinner.'

'I hope he can.'

'Yes, sir. Excuse me.'

When the door shut Goodblood sat again and Strang stood at the fireplace. They did not speak or look at each other. Strang hoped Benson would come out now, before dinner, but if not he would wait as long as he had to. Some time tonight he would get to Benson.

With the silence, it seemed that they waited a long time, but it was less than five minutes when the door opened. Benson walked in.

Goodblood snapped out of the armchair, holding himself at attention. 'Good evening, sir.'

'Evening, Colonel.'

Goodblood introduced Strang, and Benson said: 'I think we've met once, haven't we, Mr Strang?'

'About a year ago, sir.'

'I don't have much contact with the Agency unless it's real trouble. Wylie told me this was urgent.'

'Yes, sir. I want to talk to Hess before he goes back to Spandau.'

Benson took it well. He showed no surprise. Carefully he linked his hands behind his back. 'You know he goes back at oh-eight hundred tomorrow?'

'Yes, sir.'

'Why d'you want to talk to him?'

Strang told him about the document, and all Moscow had done to get it.

'And you think Hess would remember what he'd written?' It was not that Benson was questioning that Hess might remember; he was genuinely curious about his memory.

'The psychiatrist, Captain Edison, thinks so, sir.'

Benson stood studying Strang, then glanced at Goodblood, and Goodblood looked neutral, as though he did not know Strang and had never heard of him until now.

'I guess the Soviets must think he'd remember too, if they tried to kill him,' Benson said.

'That's right, sir.'

'It must be something damned important, if they're willing to kill Hess to make sure he doesn't talk about it. Until now, I'd have said Moscow would do all they could to keep him alive for ever. It sounds incredible.' Again Benson looked at Goodblood, looking for agreement.

'It does, sir,' Goodblood said, not looking at Strang.

'But it's happened,' Strang said sharply, glaring at Goodblood. 'It took an organisation to move so fast on this—to get to that man in New York, the morning after they decided he had the information they wanted. And it was the Soviet officer who bugged the visiting room; there's no question about that.'

Benson nodded. 'I'm prepared to accept it all as you tell it, Mr Strang, and I'd like to co-operate with you—but there's no way for you to get to Hess. The Soviets would never agree.'

'It'd have to be done without their knowledge, sir.'

'I'd have no objection to going behind the bastards' backs, but it'd take time to arrange something like that—and we don't have it. Hess goes back at oh-eight hundred, and that's the way it has to be.'

'It can still be done, sir.'
'Mr Strang, d'you have a plan?'
'Yes.'
'I'd like to hear it.'

Wednesday
May 4, 1977

Chapter 36

Two American soldiers with rifles slung from their shoulders stood at the head of the corridor that had been cleared for Hess and his jailers. Down the corridor, outside Hess's closed door, another soldier sat with his rifle across his knees. Across from him was the open door to the room that was being used as an office by the jailers, and one of them, a Frenchman, was on duty, on a chair inside the doorway, watching Hess's door.

At six-twenty in the morning one of the nurses who had been assigned to Hess walked past the guard and down the corridor to Hess's room. Smiling, the guard at the door got up from his chair, and she smiled at him and went in, carefully closing the door.

The guard stood stretching his shoulders, then sat again. As he leaned back, settling his rifle across his knees, there was a hum from loudspeakers along the corridor and all along the connecting corridors, and then a voice began calling urgently, a woman's voice, echoing and crackling from the loudspeakers. The guard could not make out the words, but he came upright in his chair, looking along the corridor at the guards there.

The loudspeakers cut off, and around the corner, past the guards, doctors and nurses came running, pushing a wheeled stretcher and a cart with gleaming equipment. They ran down the corridor.

The guard outside Hess's room jumped to his feet, and the jailer stood and looked out of the doorway.

The doctors and nurses came running. One of the doctors pushed open Hess's door and they rushed in with the stretcher and the equipment trolley. The door swung shut.

'What is it?' the jailer said. 'What is happening?'

'I don't know.' The guard stood with his rifle in both hands, looking at the two men at the head of the corridor, who were standing staring at him. None of them knew what was happening.

Another jailer, an Englishman, stepped out of his bedroom, buttoning his shirt. 'What is it, Henri?'

The French jailer shrugged. 'I don't know. Some doctors have gone into Hess's room.'

The Englishman darted across the corridor, rapped on the door of another bedroom, and looked in, calling: 'Something's happened to Hess!'

A Russian jailer rushed out, pulling on his trousers with one hand, his other arm in the sleeve of his shirt.

All of them stood together, staring at Hess's door.

'What is happening?' the Russian said.

'Doctors went in there,' the Frenchman said.

'We must go in.' The Russian tucked his shirt into his trousers.

'Hold on!' The Englishman jerked out a hand. 'We can't go barging in there. We don't know what they're doing.'

'We must look.' The Russian took another step.

Hess's door was tugged open and the stretcher came wheeling out fast, a doctor and nurse pushing it, Hess covered with a blanket to his chin, eyes closed. Another doctor and two nurses came after them, hurrying with the equipment trolley, past the jailers, down the corridor.

The Russian jailer took a step after them. Then another doctor swung out of Hess's room and the Russian blocked him, a hand on his arm.

'What is happening?' the Russian said.

The doctor jerked his arm free. 'He's had a cardiac arrest!'

'What is this? He is going from here in one hour and a half. What is this cardiac arrest?'

'His heart's stopped!' The doctor stepped past.

'Wait!' Again the Russian grabbed his arm.

Violently swinging his arm free, turning on him, the doctor snapped at the other jailers: 'Keep this man out of my way! Hess won't be going anywhere but the cemetery if we don't move fast! We've revived him. Now we've got to keep him alive.' He jerked a thumb at the Russian. 'Explain it to him — and keep him the hell out of my way!' He pushed past the Russian and ran down the corridor, around the corner after the others.

The Russian darted for the door of the office. The British

jailer went in ahead of him, reaching for the phone on the desk.

'I must call my director!' the Russian shouted. 'I must have the phone!'

'I'm calling my director first, Sergei!'

The Russian grabbed for the phone and the Englishman jumped back with it.

'I must have it!' the Russian yelled.

'After me!' The Englishman gripped the phone in both hands. 'The British're in charge this bloody month and Colonel Dampier's got to be told first.'

The Russian stood there. 'All right, George. All right. But please be fast.'

Around the end of the corridor, the cardiac-arrest team wheeled the stretcher and their equipment into an elevator. It went down one floor and they wheeled out, trotting down a corridor, into the intensive-care unit, and the double doors swung shut behind them.

Four MPs stood inside. One of the doctors locked the doors and the MPs stood on either side of the doorway, backs to the wall. Two of the doctors wheeled the stretcher across the room, around an operating table, and out through a door on the other side, into a small storage room.

Strang was waiting there. He got up from a wooden chair when the stretcher wheeled in. Hess's eyes were open now, and he was up on one elbow, looking around. His blue eyes were almost hidden, set so deeply under the heavy black eyebrows.

'No trouble?' Strang said to the doctors.

'Not a bit.' One of them smiled. 'One of the guards went a little wild—I guess he was Russian—but no trouble.'

'How long have I got?'

'Oh, you're good for an hour. If you need more, let me know. I'll be outside.'

The doctors went out and the door closed.

'What is happening?' Hess muttered. His voice was deep. Now he was sitting up on the stretcher, legs over the side, dressed in shirt and trousers, the shirt open at the neck. With his hands he smoothed his white hair where it was wild over his ears.

'Herr Hess, I'm from the United States Mission. My name is Strang.' He showed his identification and Hess sat reading it

215

carefully, and handed it back. 'I want to talk to you. Would you be more comfortable in one of those chairs?' Three straight-back chairs were against the wall.

'Yes. I think so.' Hess slid cautiously off the stretcher. 'What is it that you wish to talk about?' He sat on one of the chairs.

'About the document you gave your lawyer in nineteen forty-six.'

Hess had moved a chair in front of him and was swinging his feet up on it. He looked sharply at Strang. 'I know of no document.' He rested his legs on the chair and leaned back, alert and cautious, his eyes now hidden in shadow under the thick brows.

'You spoke of it in January, Herr Hess.' Strang drew up a chair and sat close to him. 'You spoke of it to Fräulein Hartmann, when she came to Spandau.'

'No, no.' Heavily Hess shook his head. 'I remember nothing. Why have you brought me in here to ask me about this?'

Strang leaned forward with his hands on his knees. 'Herr Hess, it's very important that you remember.'

Hess folded his arms, sitting upright on the wooden chair, jaw out.

'We brought you here because it's important for me to talk to you without the Soviets' knowledge. At eight o'clock you were to go back to Spandau. But I had to talk to you about your document.'

Hess said nothing and did not look at him.

'Herr Hess, I know it's something that could embarrass them in Moscow.'

There was a movement on Hess's face, a twitching around his mouth, the beginning of a smile.

'It's so, isn't it?' Strang said.

Slowly Hess turned his head and looked at him from the deep-sunk eyes. 'Yes, this is so. It will cause very much embarrassment to the Russians, but I can tell you nothing of it. It will be used only after my death. It will be my revenge on the Russians. They have insisted that I must stay in Spandau. If it were not for them, your government and the others of the west would have set me free years ago. But the Russians hate me, because I was the deputy to the Führer. They wanted to kill me at Nuremberg and they have never forgotten. They want to keep me in prison until I die.' He jabbed a long finger at his own chest. 'A man of eighty-three years, and still they have no mercy.' He folded his arms again, looking firm and stubborn. 'When I die, the contents of my document will become known. That will be my revenge on the Russians.'

Looking at him, so confident at the thought of his document, Strang hated to tell him what had happened to it.

'Herr Hess, your document's been stolen,' he said quietly.

Hess sat very still.

'This is not so,' he said in his deep voice. 'Not so.'

'It's true. The Soviets stole it.'

Hess sat staring at him, looking for a trap.

Strang hoped he could take the shock. It had been a bad one for him, and he hoped he was going to be all right.

'They killed six people to get it—and they tried to kill you, because they think you might remember what you wrote in it. They're the ones who poisoned you.'

Slowly Hess shook his head. 'No. I remember nothing. They are wrong. I remember none of it.'

'They think you do.'

'Is it true? Did they honestly do that—poison me?'

'Yes. A Soviet officer put a listening device in the visiting room. They heard you ask Fräulein Hartmann about the document. Yes, they poisoned you.'

'They would do it. They are animals.'

'Tell me what was in the document, Herr Hess. If it can be used against Moscow, we'll use it. We'll give you your revenge.'

Hess sat staring at his upright feet in bedroom slippers, together on the chair in front of him.

'It's about Mikhail, isn't it?' Strang said.

The sunken eyes stared. 'What do you know about Mikhail?'

'Nothing. No details. I'd like you to tell me.'

'If I do, will you use it to do the utmost damage to the Russians? Will you promise this?'

'Yes. I promise you that.' Strang shifted in his chair, glancing at the door of a closet behind Hess, where they had a microphone feeding into a tape machine. Behind the ceiling panel above Hess's head was another, just to be sure.

'I hate the Russians so strongly. They have made me suffer so

217

much for so many years. They have kept me from my wife and son, and made us all suffer.'

'Tell me about Mikhail,' Strang said gently.

*

From the beginning of 1933, when Hitler took power in Germany, Stalin and the Communist party leaders began watching the growth of German military strength, and very soon they were convinced that war must come between the Soviet Union and Hitler's dedicated anti-Communist state. By the end of 1934 Stalin had begun expanding the Red Army.

Since 1920, the end of the Russian Civil War, the Red Army had had little prestige in Soviet society and the officer corps had lost influence to the political commissars. As the Army expanded, the officers' confidence began to grow again, and they were given some freedom from the control of the Communist party, including immunity from arrest by the civil power, unless there was authorisation from the Commissar for War.

But as the Red Army expanded Stalin grew more and more uneasy. Almost twenty per cent of the officers were men who had fought through the Civil War, many with commissioned or noncommissioned ranks in the Czar's army, and they held almost all the senior commands. Very few of them had been given their position by Stalin and had no reason for loyalty to him. They could not be relied on to support him against any other power group that might form within the Communist leadership.

In 1936 there were reports in Moscow that many senior Red Army officers favoured Nikolai Bukharin, an opponent of Stalin and his enforcement of the Communist system with mass arrests and executions.

In January, 1937, Bukharin was arrested for treason, and through the spring there were signs that Stalin was preparing to move against the Red Army. On June 11, 1937, the commander-in-chief, Marshal Tukhachevsky, and seven other senior officers were arrested and tried for treason. Next day they were executed. It was the beginning of the Great Purge of the Red Army.

Through the rest of 1937 and all the next year officers were arrested and executed, and at the end of it half the officer corps had been shot: 35,000 men. All eleven Vice Commissars for War were gone, seventy-five of the eighty members of the Supreme Military Council, three of the five marshals, thirteen of the fifteen army commanders. The firing squads had swept through all levels of command down to the brigade.

All of it was watched by German intelligence. But there was little information coming out of the Soviet Union. Through the 1920s, after the Treaty of Rapallo, there had been close co-operation between the German and Soviet armies; German officers taught in Red Army academies and Soviet officers took German staff courses. But Hitler, with his anti-Communism, ended it all when he took power. So through 1937 German intelligence knew hardly more than they read in press reports of the purge of the Red Army. Most of the agents they had had in the Soviet Union were officers who had been killed in the purge. Now their information came almost exclusively through ex-Czarist officers in Germany and France, and the reliability of their sources was unknown.

On an afternoon in early September, 1938, the low quality of the intelligence sent Hitler into one of his uncontrolled rages. At his villa in the mountains above Berchtesgaden a group waited for him around the long table in the conference room. Hess was there; Göring; Admiral Wilhelm Canaris, chief of the Abwehr; and Himmler, the ss leader.

The door opened and Hitler walked in carrying two slim folders. All of them came to attention on both sides of the table, right arms stiffly out in the salute. Hitler, eyes down, stalked to the head of the table and stood glaring from side to side. Abruptly he snapped his right hand up, returning their salutes, and they all lowered their arms. But he did not sit, and they stood at attention, waiting.

Lips tight, turned down at the corners under his black moustache, Hitler glared at Canaris, and flicked open one of the folders. He held up some typewritten sheets, an Abwehr intelligence report on the Red Army.

'This is yours!' Holding the report out over the table at Canaris, Hitler shook it.

Canaris, white-haired, in his braided admiral's uniform, stood looking at the papers fluttering in Hitler's hand, and said nothing. What Hitler had said sounded like an accusation, not a question, and there was nothing to say.

219

Hitler jerked the report aside and the sheets scattered across the carpet behind Canaris.

No one moved.

Hitler opened the other folder and held out the typewritten sheets to Himmler, across from Canaris. 'This is yours, Himmler!' It was a report from the foreign intelligence of the ss Security Service.

Himmler, in his black ss uniform, round-faced, squinted through his pince-nez and said: 'Yes, Mein Führer.'

Hitler flung the sheets aside.

No one moved. Hess, at attention on Hitler's right, saw the bright red on his cheeks. He thought Hitler was right to be angry. He himself had spoken twice to Hitler in the past five or six weeks about the need for better intelligence on the Soviet Union.

Hitler was still glaring back and forth from Canaris to Himmler. Then he turned away from the table and began stamping on the scattered sheets of Himmler's report, turning his heels on them and ripping them on the carpet, kicking the pieces, shouting: 'This is what your report is worth, Himmler! It's not fit to read! It's for wiping shoes!'

Himmler stood stiffly and did not turn and look to see what Hitler was doing to his report.

Hitler walked back to the head of the table, dragging his chair in close. He sat, motioning the others down with his hand. They all sat. Hess glanced again at him and saw he was breathing heavily, but he looked calmer and was bringing himself under control.

More quietly now, Hitler said: 'Understand this, Canaris—and you, Himmler. We all know what is happening in Russia. That pig Stalin is tearing his army to shreds, destroying his officer corps. We know this. But we must know accurately how badly they are damaging themselves.' He pounded his fist on the table. 'We *must* know! In a few years we shall be at war with these Bolsheviks—that is a certainty—and if Stalin has left any of his army officers alive it is vital, absolutely vital, that we know the state of their morale. This is obvious. Not so?'

'Yes, Mein Führer,' Canaris said.

'Completely understood, Mein Führer,' Himmler said.

'If it is so, and it is completely understood'—Hitler pounded the table—'why am I *not* getting this information?'

Canaris said: 'My service had informants among officers of the Red Army, Mein Führer, but they were, unfortunately, among those whom Stalin has liquidated. Among those who survive, it is extremely difficult to find anyone willing to speak. They are afraid that everyone who approaches them is an agent of Stalin's secret police.'

Hitler waved a hand at him. 'I know the excuses. I've been hearing them for months. It's the same with you, Himmler—the same alibi?'

'The problem is the same for my service, yes, Mein Führer.'

Clenched fists on the table, Hitler leaned forward and looked from side to side at Canaris and Himmler. 'It must improve. Both of you must tell your people that we need to know what is happening to the Bolsheviks' Army. And we must know with accuracy! I will not tolerate reports of what a refugee Czarist general in a Paris café says he has heard from the sister of his cousin's husband in'—he waved a hand at the ripped sheets of Himmler's report—'a town somewhere in the Crimea.' He pounded his fist on the table. 'I want to know what is happening in Moscow!'

At the end of the afternoon, when he left Hitler, Hess thought about it, sitting in the back of the Mercedes, going down the mountain road to Berchtesgaden. He thought about it all the way back to Munich in his private rail car.

Ten days later the Foreign Office gave a reception for the new Soviet ambassador, and on Hess's right at the table was the Soviet military attaché, Colonel Starikov.

Waiters moved around the long tables, pouring wine. One carried a bottle of mineral water, and he came to Hess and filled his glass. He moved to Starikov and filled his.

When the waiter had gone Hess said: 'Are you a teetotaller like myself, Colonel?' They had met for the first time this evening, and Starikov had told him he had been in Berlin for five weeks.

'Yes, Herr Minister.' Starikov had a square face; his black hair was brush-cut.

'There are very few of us. Not so?'

221

'It is true.'

'Your predecessor, General Gusev, was certainly not one of us.' Hess sipped his mineral water, watching Starikov, and thought he was about his own age, about forty-four. He looked unhappy, Hess thought. 'Do you know General Gusev, Colonel?'

'I did, Herr Minister.'

'Did?'

'I regret that he is dead.'

'Dead?' The firing squad, Hess thought. 'But less than two months ago he was here, in Berlin. I spoke with him, and he was in fine health.'

'He was in good health when he died, Herr Minister.' Starikov sounded very bitter. 'Our political leaders decided that it was time for him.' He sipped his mineral water. 'He was a good friend.'

'I'm very sorry to hear it, Colonel. Truly.'

'Thank you.'

'Your Army has lost many fine officers, these past months. And you have lost many friends, no doubt.'

'Both true, Herr Minister. Many fine men have died, and many of them were my good friends. Many.'

It seemed to Hess that the Russian wanted to talk about it, but he decided not to press it now. They finished their meal and listened to a speech by the German foreign minister, Ribbentrop, welcoming the new ambassador, and a speech by the ambassador, assuring the German people of the undying goodwill and friendship of the government and people of the Soviet Union.

When the applause had died, and they were sipping more mineral water, Hess said: 'Of course you will be going to Grafenwöhr next week, Colonel, to observe the demonstration of our tanks.' Military observers had been invited from all the embassies, to watch the 1st Panzer Division stage a battle exercise at their training area.

'Yes, and I look forward to it, Herr Minister.'

'I shall be travelling to Nuremberg in my private railway car. It would give me great pleasure if you would ride with me.'

'That is extremely gracious. Thank you, Herr Minister. I should be delighted.'

Next week, on the ride down to Nuremberg, they sat alone in the lounge of Hess's private car, and Starikov talked of his days as a young cavalry lieutenant in the Imperial Army, fighting against Germany in the Great War.

'It was a tragedy that we had to fight each other,' Hess said. 'More tragic still that in your Civil War you had to fight alone against the Bolsheviks. It was unfortunate that we were in no position, in nineteen-eighteen, to come and help you.'

Starikov looked at him and said nothing, and Hess saw that he was moving too fast.

'Perhaps it was indiscreet of me to say that to you, as you are now, Colonel, an officer of the Red Army—but I was expressing a feeling that was in the hearts of many Germans, I assure you. I say it frankly.'

Starikov glanced at the doors at either end of the lounge and saw they were shut tight. 'Yes, I know it, Herr Minister. If it could have happened as you say, history would be very different. But I am, as you say, an officer of the Red Army.'

Hess nodded and watched him.

From Nuremberg they drove out in Hess's Mercedes. Hess and Starikov in the back, and in the hour's drive, north-east to the armoured-warfare training area at Grafenwöhr, Hess spoke of little but the scenery, and how much he loved the mountains. Starikov was fond of the mountains too, and both of them said how pleasant it was that they were finding they shared so many tastes. They both liked chamber music too. It was incredible, they said, how much they had in common.

They stayed together all through the exercises, and Hess could see how impressed Starikov was, watching the tanks and armoured troops. When the exercises were over the foreign military observers were taken to inspect the weapons and equipment, especially the tanks. They walked up and down the rows of the division's tanks, Panzer I's and Panzer II's, light tanks, their crews at attention in front of them in their black tank troops' uniforms.

'They're very impressive,' Starikov said. 'Beautiful machines.'

'Come with me, Colonel,' Hess said. 'I will show you some very special things.'

They drove away from the other military attachés, to an isolated part of the base, in a forest, and among the trees

223

Hess's car was stopped four times at roadblocks by armed troops, who recognised him but still insisted on seeing his identification and Starikov's.

Just beyond the last roadblock Hess's chauffeur turned the car off into a parking space among the trees, and Hess and Starikov climbed out and walked on down the road. In five minutes they came to where the trees on one side had been cleared to make a neat, square bay, and in there, under a canvas roof, was a tank bigger than the ones the foreign observers had seen in the exercises. Above the canvas roof, hung from trees all around, was a camouflage net covered with leaves.

Starikov looked at Hess.

'We call it the Panzer Three, Colonel.' Hess held out a hand to it. 'Go and look closely, if you wish.'

Together they walked around the tank, and climbed on it and looked down inside, through the turret hatch.

'It has a speed of forty kilometres an hour,' Hess said. 'And a cannon of thirty-seven millimetres.'

'It's beautiful.' Starikov jumped down from the tank and stood looking at it.

'Come this way,' Hess said.

They walked down the road, passing more tanks on each side among the trees, all Panzer III's, hidden under camouflage nets.

'There!' Hess said.

Starikov stood looking at a bigger tank, with a much bigger cannon in the turret.

'What is that gun, Herr Minister—a seventy-five?'

Smiling, Hess nodded. 'Seventy-five millimetres. Come and look, Colonel. This is the Panzer Four. The same speed as the Three, but much more powerful, as you can see.'

They climbed all over the tank, and when they got down again Hess saw how it had affected the Russian officer.

'We have nothing like this,' Starikov said. 'Nothing at all.'

'With these we might do what we were unable to do in nineteen-eighteen,' Hess said. 'We might one day help you against the Bolsheviks.'

Starikov smiled carefully and said nothing.

'It must happen one day, Colonel. You know it, and I know it.'

'Yes, Herr Minister.' Starikov was looking at the tank, not at Hess. 'It must happen.'

'Colonel, I ask you: will you help us?'

'What is it you would want?'

'Information.'

Starikov said nothing.

Hess was afraid he had misjudged the Russian. They had seemed so compatible. He had been certain Starikov would agree. But suddenly there was nothing between them, and he was afraid he had made a mistake.

Starikov turned and looked back down the road. 'Do you object if we go back, Herr Minister?'

'No. Of course not.'

They walked side by side down the road, past the tanks in their bays. Hess wished he had waited to know Starikov longer, to understand him more fully. Then he might have approached him differently, and been successful. He wondered if he might offer money, but no, he knew that would be the worst mistake. Either Starikov would do it from conviction or he would never do it, and nothing would make him.

'We are not children,' Starikov said. 'We both know what you asked. How could you expect me to betray my country?'

'Not your country, Colonel. That maniac Stalin is destroying your country. He is our enemy, yours and mine. He is the enemy of my country and of you and your friends—of all your people. You know it.'

Starikov said nothing, and they walked past the last of the tank bays, back toward where they had left the car and chauffeur.

'What kind of information would you want?' Starikov said.

'Anything, Colonel. Everything. What we are most interested in now is the state of morale of your brother-officers, after all that this lunatic Stalin has done.'

'They must all hate him as I do, Herr Minister. It is impossible to express to you how much I hate him.'

'We would like to know all about them, Colonel. Who have been killed, the attitudes of those who survive, everything.'

Starikov nodded. 'I will do it.'

Hess held out his hand and Starikov gripped it.

In the next few months Starikov passed a quantity of information that came from Moscow to his office in the embassy in Berlin, some in letters from friends, some in official communications.

Early in January, 1939, when they had been working together for almost four months, Starikov sent a message that he must see Hess, and they met in Berlin, in a suite in the Adlon Hotel that they sometimes used for secret meetings.

'I have some news that may be good or bad,' Starikov said. 'I have been ordered back to Moscow.'

'When do you go?'

'At the end of the month.'

'Does it mean trouble?' Hess was concerned. It was not just that he might lose the source of valuable information; he liked Starikov and respected him.

'Who can say? I have been told to report to Army headquarters—but that means nothing. They could tell me that to ensure my return, then stand me against a wall as soon as I crossed the border.'

'Stay here, Igor. You have no family there, no one. There is no reason for you to go back. You would be valuable to us and I can assure you of the recognition you deserve.'

'Thank you, Herr Minister.' Starikov shook his head. 'I must go back. Perhaps there's no reason to be nervous. If they wanted to shoot me, I think they would have ordered me back at once, not allowed me three weeks to prepare for it.'

'Perhaps.' Hess was not confident and he knew Starikov was not.

'Unless they put me against a wall I shall, of course, continue to send you information. If it all goes well, I shall be of much more use to you in Moscow than here.'

'You're risking your life.'

'Many of my friends have lost theirs. Mine has little meaning now, except to do this work for you and your country, the enemies of Stalin and his system.'

'Very well. If this is what you have decided, we must make plans for our communications.'

They arranged their radio frequencies and the time schedules for transmitting and receiving, and agreed on a code. Hess said he would set up his radio in his headquarters at Pullach, and would use an operator whose loyalty would be unquestionable. He himself would encode and decode the messages. He would do everything to ensure Starikov's safety.

Three weeks later Starikov went back to Moscow. He was not executed. By then the purge was finished and there were great gaps in the list of officers, many places to be filled by fast promotions. Starikov was made a major general and appointed to the General Staff of the Red Army.

From a signals regiment Hess took a young lieutenant, Gunther Langkau, on to his personal staff and made him responsible for operating the secret radio in a guarded underground room at Pullach.

On April 10, 1939, Langkau received the first coded message from Moscow. When Hess decoded it, it was signed with the name he and Starikov had agreed: Mikhail. Starikov had chosen it, in the suite at the Adlon, because it had been the first name of his uncle, Marshal Tukhachevsky, one of the eight officers killed by Stalin at the beginning of the purge.

*

'And that was Mikhail—General Starikov?' Strang said.

Hess nodded, looking at his feet on the chair, in the bedroom slippers. 'Igor Starikov, yes.'

'Would he be dead now, Herr Hess?'

'Most likely. If not, he would be very close to it. He was my age.'

'And this is the story that would've been made public if they'd executed you at Nuremberg?'

'Yes.' Hess looked at him, head on one side, his eyes in the shadows under his thick brows. 'You do not approve?'

'I didn't say that.'

'But you do not approve. You wonder what would have happened to Igor in nineteen forty-six.' Hess nodded. 'This is true. Perhaps he was alive then and perhaps not. I did not know. This is true. But remember that I was in a courtroom, being tried for crimes that had not been crimes before in the history of the world. They created the laws after the fact, to fit the cases. Therefore I was a criminal, and I thought I would die—because the Russians wanted it. I had few thoughts but desire for revenge against them, any Russian. I was not without

227

concern for Igor—I thought of it very much—but I think, if he was still alive then, he would have approved of my action, and he would willingly have died if his death would have damaged Stalin and those Communists—and it would have damaged them, made public as my lawyer would have made it public. Igor would have understood that. Now he is almost certainly dead, and that is not a problem for my conscience.'

Strang wondered what Hess would say if he knew Mikhail had still been operating in fifty-two. But that was twenty-five years ago. Now he was, as Hess said, almost certainly dead.

'Did he work alone, Herr Hess?'

'No! You should have seen the quantity of information! No, no. He gathered other officers with him.'

'Did he tell you who they were?'

'Of course! Each new one, he sent me the name and something of his background. That was essential, so that I would know the worth of the information from them. Yes, of course he told me the names.'

'Do you remember any of them?'

'Of course! I remember them all. There were not that many. I remember everything of them. They have never left my mind. I remember their names, the dates when Igor recruited them, and their ranks and units at the time.'

'Tell me, Herr Hess.'

Chapter 37

With a transcript of everything Hess had told him, Strang landed at Washington in the afternoon, and drove out to Langley. Hess had given him six names, including General Starikov's, and he went looking for them in the data banks of biographies of Soviet officers, all the information that went back to the old wartime German intelligence files.

Hess had told him that General Starikov had recruited the other five members of the Mikhail group in less than four months, by the beginning of May, 1939. General Anton Kalinin, Chief of Staff of the Air Forces, was recruited on March 4; Major Alexei Filatov, aide to the commanding officer, Kiev military district, on March 10; Colonel Andrei Grossman, chief of staff, 5th Infantry Army, April 8; Colonel Vladimir Zamyatin, chief of staff, Leningrad military district, May 3. Lieutenant Nicolai Boldin, a signals officer, had been assigned as Starikov's aide on February 10, and he was recruited to the group on March 28, as their radio operator.

Strang looked first for General Starikov, and found he had served on the General Staff until August 10, 1941. Then he was transferred to the Stavka, a supreme planning group that had been created a few days after the German invasion, and was directly under Stalin's control. In the Stavka were between fifteen and twenty senior officers of all the services, and they developed the Soviet war strategy. In 1946, when the Stavka was dissolved, Starikov, by then a marshal, was named Chief of the General Staff. On March 14, 1952, he died of a heart attack in his Moscow apartment.

Air Force General Kalinin served in Moscow until September, 1942, then was transferred north to command the air forces on the Baltic front. He died in an air crash in November, 1944.

Major Filatov served in the Kiev military district until only a few days after June 22, 1941, the opening of the German attack. Then he was sent south and promoted to command a regiment in front of Odessa. After the Germans captured Odessa he fought in the Crimea, in command of a division, and lost a leg there in April, 1942. He was promoted major general on November 21, 1942, and was transferred to the General Staff in Moscow, where he served until the end of the war. Then he was transferred to Berlin and was in the occupation army until December 4, 1948, when he retired, a lieutenant general. He was now living in Odessa.

Colonel Grossman served on the staff of the 5th Infantry Army until April 9, 1943, when he was transferred to the staff of the 6th Guards Army on the Voronezh front. On November 12, 1944, he was transferred to the 8th Guards Army, and was killed in action in April, 1945, on the Russian drive to capture Berlin.

Colonel Zamyatin served in Leningrad all through the German siege, and on January 31, 1944, four days after the city was relieved, he was transferred to garrison duty in the Urals, his health having been broken by more than two years of semi-starvation. He retired from the Army as a major general in August, 1953, and went to live in Vilkovo, on the Black Sea, where he was still living.

The only member of the Mikhail group still on active duty was Lieutenant Boldin, who had served as Starikov's aide until the marshal's death in 1952, when Boldin, by then a major, transferred to the Chief Intelligence Administration of the General Staff, the GRU. Nothing more was known of him until March 11, 1961, when he became head of the GRU's most important department, the First Division, which was responsible for foreign intelligence. In September, 1970, then a full general, he became deputy director of the GRU. On June 30, 1976, Boldin became director.

Chapter 38

In his big office on the seventh floor, the top floor of the CIA headquarters, Holmes, the Director, read Strang's report and the printouts of the biographies of the Mikhail group.

He closed the folder on them, pushed the button on his intercom, and said: 'Send Mr Strang in, please.'

His secretary showed Strang in.

'I've read it all.' Holmes laid a hand flat on the closed file. 'This is the way it happened, you think? It wasn't a Soviet operation, after all. Not really.'

'No, sir. It was Boldin's own. A personal job, to get the names of the Mikhail group, to protect himself. To kill Hess too, just to be sure.'

'It's amazing.' Holmes looked down at the closed file. 'When Marshal Starikov died, Boldin decided to break contact with us and lie low. As simple as that. He must've been sweating it out for years, wondering if there was anything lying around that could incriminate him.'

'I'm sure he was, sir. I imagine the first thing he did when he took command of the GRU was look in their files for a mention of Mikhail, and he saw the report of their interrogation of Hess's adjutant in forty-five. Then he knew Mikhail had been recruited by Hess—and there was a risk that Hess might still be able to remember. Obviously he decided not to take a chance on Hess's amnesia.'

Holmes smiled. 'I'm damn sure I'd've decided the same thing, in his place.'

'So would I.' Christ, but Boldin must've been desperate. 'July is a month when the Soviets are in control at Spandau, but I guess by the time he'd found the Hess connection with Mikhail it was too late to do anything in July, so he had to wait for their next month—November. And that's when he had one of his people bug that visiting room. Everything else went on from there.'

'I'm damned.' Holmes raised his hand from the file and dropped it again. 'Head of the GRU—and once the bastard worked for us.'

'I think he can be persuaded to do it again.'

Holmes sat staring at him.

'We've got the information he was working so damn hard to hide, sir. We've got that—and we've got Boldin. He won't argue with us. He can't.'

Monday
July 4, 1977

Chapter 39

At the United States embassy in Moscow there was a reception to celebrate Independence Day, and invitations had been accepted by members of the Soviet government and the senior bureaucrats, as well as diplomats from the other embassies.

Strang stood at one side of the great ballroom with Scully, the cultural affairs attaché, watching the guests arrive. They both held glasses of champagne, but they had sipped only once, though they had been standing there more than twenty minutes, watching the guests as they entered.

Two Soviet generals walked in with their wives, and behind them a big man in a dark grey suit, whom Scully knew was a senior officer in the KGB. The man smiled and nodded across the room to him, and Scully raised his glass. As Scully knew the senior Soviet intelligence officers, they knew him as chief of the CIA station in Moscow.

'Is that Boldin?' Strang muttered.

'No, that's a KGB man—General Samsonov.'

Watching more guests walk in, Strang said: 'I hope to God he comes.'

'He'll be here,' Scully said softly. 'You'll have him.'

Strang took another sip of his champagne. It was warm and flat, but he was not aware of the champagne. He was watching the wide entrance to the ballroom. He had been waiting two months for this, the time when he would face Boldin. It hadn't been easy to persuade Holmes to let him come. Holmes had wanted Scully to make the approach to Boldin, just because it was simplest. But in the end, because it was Strang's work that had given them Boldin, Holmes had agreed that he should be here for the end of it. Strang had flown to Moscow the day before.

A heavy-looking man walked into the ballroom, in full general's uniform, with braided shoulder boards and three rows of medals.

'Here's Boldin,' Scully muttered.

Boldin stood near the door, looking around the room. He nodded at Scully. He was alone. Scully had seen his wife only twice, but he knew Boldin spent a lot of time with a senior woman officer of the GRU.

Boldin saw the KGB general, Samsonov, in a group of people, and at once looked away. Scully knew he would not go near that part of the room. The antagonism between the two Soviet intelligence organisations was very strong: the military, the GRU, against the political, the KGB. The old rivalry was always there.

'Let's go and do it,' Scully said, and Strang moved with him through the crowd, toward Boldin.

'Good evening, Mr Scully.' Boldin smiled and held out his hand. He was medium height, with grey hair that grew back from a sharp widow's peak.

'Good evening, General.' Scully shook his hand.

'Congratulations on your Independence Day. I hope you have many more in the future.'

'Thank you. I'd like to introduce Mr Strang.'

'How do you do, Mr Strang?' Boldin shook hands. 'You are a new member of Mr Scully's staff?'

'No, I'm just visiting, General. I flew in yesterday, from Berlin.'

'For a holiday?'

'No. I came to talk to you.'

'Yes?' Boldin's eyebrows went up very slightly, but he gave no other sign.

Scully looked around the ballroom, for a corner where they could talk. 'Let's go over this way, General,' he said.

Boldin glanced from Strang to Scully, and he looked curious, but he said only: 'If you wish.'

They walked through the groups of men and women. The ballroom was becoming crowded. A waiter offered a tray filled with glasses of champagne, and Boldin took one.

Scully led them to a corner on the far side of the room, and when they stopped Boldin gulped at the champagne. It was the first sign of nervousness Strang had seen him show.

Boldin finished the glass. 'What is it you wish to speak of, Mr Strang?'

'Mikhail wishes to be remembered to you, General.'

Boldin showed almost nothing. He blinked very quickly, but there was no other sign of shock. He took it very well, Strang thought.

'Mikhail? Mikhail who, Mr Strang?'

'Mikhail who was your chief until nineteen fifty-two.'

'Excuse me, but I'm afraid I don't understand this.'

'We know it all, General. The man in Spandau told us all about Mikhail.'

'I believe you are confused.' Now Boldin was trying to rebuild his confidence.

'No, I'm not confused. Two of your old friends are still living—General Zamyatin and General Filotov. Their names could be passed to the KGB, General. I imagine they'd talk very soon. They'd name you.'

Boldin looked down at his empty glass, then raised it to his lips and tried to drink the last drop. He looked at Strang and took a slow breath. 'I thought it was all finished and I was safe, after so many years.'

'We can never be sure we're safe, General, and the years don't change that. Hess wasn't safe, even in prison.'

'Is this the reward I get? Once I worked for your country, and is this the reward?'

'You weren't working for us. You were working against Stalin. You were working against someone you didn't approve of. That's all. What it really means is, you were working for what you wanted. It's what we all do—Communists, Nazis, or even a liberal Democrat like me. When all the rationalising's been done, we're working for ourselves. No idealism about it.'

'What do you want, Mr Strang?'

'We want you to work for us again—really for us, this time.'

Boldin stood holding his empty glass.

'We'll be very discreet, General, and you'll be safe. You're too valuable for us to allow anything to happen to you.'

'I think I have little choice.'

'No choice at all.'

Tuesday
July 21, 1987

Chapter 40

While the British Airways 737 circled for the landing at Tegel, Strang stared down at the sun flashing and glittering off the windows of the office blocks and off the roofs of the fast lines of cars threaded tightly along the *stadtautobahnen*. There had been a lot of changes. It was nine years since he'd left Berlin, and he couldn't believe all the new buildings. The place never stopped renewing itself.

Not like some of the people he'd known here. Kluger, for instance, whose marriage had fallen apart after a couple of years of that vigorous activity, and who was in Bonn now, deputy director of the Internal Security Office. Kluger's career, at least, was healthy.

When he walked out of passport control and into the reception area, watching the crowd, he saw Sheehan standing near a car-rental counter, looking just like the description he'd given of himself on the phone: tall and slim, with high cheekbones and a black crew cut. Sheehan looked very American. Conspicuously American. Someone should tell him.

Strang moved through the crowd. Sheehan saw him coming and held out his hand.

'Bill Sheehan. Welcome back to Berlin, Mr. Strang. It was good of you to come.'

'Your phone call made me curious,' Strang said. 'And the weather in London is God-awful. I thought it'd be good to get away, even for a few hours.' He nodded at the sunlight outside the big windows. 'I was right. I feel better already.'

'I hope I won't spoil your mood.'

'So do I.'

'Would you like to talk here or out in the car?'

Strang glanced at the people standing at the car-rental counter. 'In the car.'

They walked out and Sheehan led the way among the cars in the parking lot to a white BMW.

'Is there somewhere you want to go?' he said.

'Maybe later. After you tell me what this is all about.' Strang hoped she'd be in her office. That was the risk with surprise visits. It would be good to see her.

They sat in the front of the car. Sheehan was in his early thirties, Strang guessed. Young to be station chief.

'Does the name Mikhail mean anything to you?' Sheehan asked.

Strang sat staring at him. 'Why should it?' What had gone wrong? Thank God Sheehan hadn't mentioned the name on the phone. Even with the secure line, you could never be sure.

'Old Rudolf Hess spoke to one of the civilian guards yesterday, one of the Americans, and told him he'd decided finally to tell all he knew about Mikhail.' Sheehan bounced his right palm lightly on the edge of the steering wheel, watching it. 'And he said he hoped it wouldn't cause Mr. Strang any distress or inconvenience.'

'I'll be damned,' Strang murmured. Why had old Hess decided to do it now, and blow everything?

'How did he know your name?'

'I spoke to him ten years ago. Obviously it was a conversation that left an impression.'

'Who's Mikhail?'

Strang stared at him.

'Sorry,' Sheehan said. 'I don't need to know that.'

In these ten years Boldin must've fed The Company an incredible amount of intelligence, Strang thought. Boldin and the group he'd recruited. Nine years ago, when he'd left Berlin for home, to work at Langley, there were eleven other senior officers in Boldin's group, from every branch of the Soviet forces. He'd been out of touch with it since then, though once at Langley he'd spoken to the officer running Boldin, who'd told him the group had grown considerably. Between five years at Langley, then three in Paris as deputy chief, and then station chief in London since last summer, he'd long forgotten about it. But he knew Boldin was still in place, director of the GRU. By Soviet standards, he was just in his prime, late sixties. They would probably keep him in the job for years — unless Hess got word out. 'It'd cause a lot of damage, if Hess talked about this. Serious damage.'

'Christ,' Sheehan whispered. 'I didn't know whether it meant anything or whether old Hess'd finally flipped. I didn't know if it was worth reporting to Langley.'

'It's worth it. They'll certainly want to know.' It was the need for revenge against the Soviets that still drove old Hess. That was all he had. In the last ten years it must've grown, and now he couldn't wait any longer. Now he was ninety-three, and still locked up because the Soviets hated him. No one could blame him for wanting revenge. 'Why did the jailer tell you about this?'

'I told you: he's American.'

Strang watched him. 'The staff of Spandau never had any contact with us.'

'This one does.' Sheehan's face was blank. 'He's on our payroll. Must've been for a few years. He's one of the assets I inherited when I came here, two years ago. I presume he was recruited after you left.'

Strang nodded. 'You'll have to see that Hess doesn't get a message out of Spandau.'

'As you know, that'll be hard to do. There are a lot of leaks from that place.'

'The holes'll have to be plugged.'

'I'll send a report to Langley. They can decide what to do. May I drive you somewhere now?'

'No. Thanks.' Strang stared at the dashboard. He'd been looking forward to seeing Karin. But he couldn't go now, thinking about Hess again. She'd sense there was trouble. He reached for the door handle. 'I'll get the flight back.'

Monday
August 17, 1987

Chapter 41

In the afternoon, Strang left his office, rode the elevator down to the embassy garage, and drove his car out past the Marine guard on to Upper Brook Street.

As he swung into Grosvenor Square he switched on the radio, for the news, and heard: ' . . . was Hitler's former deputy, died today in the British Military Hospital in West Berlin. He was ninety-three.'

Strang jerked the car around the square and headed back to the embassy. 'There was no immediate report on the cause of death, but Mr. Hess had suffered from lung, heart, and stomach ailments, and in late years was almost blind. He had been confined in Spandau Prison for more than forty years.'

Strang drove back down into the garage, ran for the elevator, and on the fourth floor ran down the hall to his office. He grabbed up one of the phones on his desk, and as he moved around to his chair he told the operator to connect him on the secure line to Sheehan, in West Berlin.

Sheehan came on almost at once.

'How did it happen?' Strang said.

There was a silence. 'It seems he killed himself. There'll be an official statement tomorrow, saying that.'

'How did he do it?'

Quietly Sheehan said: 'He went out in the prison garden with one of the jailers. There's some kind of small outbuilding in the garden, and the jailer let him go in there, to be alone for a while. But when he looked in, a few minutes later, Hess'd wrapped some electrical wire around his neck and strangled himself. They rushed him to the British Military Hospital and tried to revive him, but it was too late.'

Strang sat holding the phone. 'Who was the jailer with him? American?'

'Yes.'

'The one you told me about?'

'Yes,' Sheehan said.

Oh, Jesus! 'Thanks.' Strang put the phone down and sat back. No more problems for old Hess. It had been a long time, but it was all over now. And Boldin was safe. That made it worthwhile, didn't it? There was a time when Hess would've thought so. But what had he thought at the end?